THE BRIAR PATCH

McAnally Flats Press
Alcoa, Tennessee

Library of Congress Control Number: 2023909499
ISBN: 978-0-9819209-8-6
Copyright information available upon request
v. 1.0

First Edition, 2023

To the Greatest Generation

THE BRIAR PATCH

Larry Henry

MCANALLY FLATS PRESS

TABLE OF CONTENTS

PART 1

Lookout Mountain

SNOW WAS COMING DOWN IN HUGE WHITE FLAKES that accumulated on the ground in ever deepening drifts caused by the swirling winds whistling through the pine trees and the white oaks. The breeze suggested a storm was brewing but the sky remained slate gray, filled with the falling snow. No thunder or lightning appeared, only a cold November wind.

A little girl stood at a living room window staring out at the snow. She had never seen snow before. It gave her a feeling of appreciation because it covered all the wreckage and horror that lay down the mountainside. Here and there a hand or a knee protruded above the glistening white mantle, but no bodies could be seen. A mile down the slope abandoned trucks and automobiles littered Interstate 24.

The fighting had been vicious with no quarter asked and none given. Men fought with knives, entrenching tools, clubs, anything they could lay their hands on when their ammunition ran out. Bullets were scarce, serving as currency the same as food and medicine. Anyone with twenty rounds or more was looked upon with envy. Some had sharpened stakes they used as spears while others carried sickles and sharpened axes. Boots were a sought-after luxury. Most had only their street shoes wrapped in rags and twine.

The little girl finally turned from the window to address the men sitting around a kitchen table. There was no electricity. They warmed their hands from a Coleman lantern sitting in the middle of the table. It produced a welcome heat while giving off a hissing sound.

"Do you think they'll come again … in the snow?"

"No, honey, the roads will be snowed in. They'll not bother us again for a while. Come over here and warm yourself."

She walked over and seated herself beside the man they called Captain. "I'm hungry. Is anything left?"

"Yes, we saved a big slice of bread for you and some gravy. The gravy is in that cup beside the lantern. Be careful you don't burn your mouth."

After she had finished her bread and gravy, she turned to Rocky. "I'm glad you found me. I would be dead now, wouldn't I?"

"God led me to you, Nancy. God didn't want you to die."

"But I almost died, didn't I? When that bad man came into the house and Mama and Daddy tried to save me. The bad man killed my mama and daddy. He was going to kill me too."

"I heard you screaming. I wish I had gotten there in time for your mother and father."

Tears ran down Nancy's cheeks. She buried her face in her arms on the tabletop, softly crying.

Captain spoke. "We mustn't talk about that anymore. It just upsets her."

Rocky responded. "I'm sorry, Captain. I spoke out of turn."

Paul joined in. "You done good, Rock. You got her out of that hellhole."

Captain: "Let's turn in for the night. It's cold as hell and we're wasting kerosene."

Roger stood watch while the others got into their makeshift sleeping arrangements. Little Nancy crawled in beside Rocky, placed her arms around him, and fell sound asleep. Rocky smiled to himself before drifting away. *Twenty-nine years old*, he thought, *and never married. Now I got me a daughter.*

Paul dreamed about the men he had killed and the young girl he found in a barn on the other side of the mountain. She was wearing a pretty pink dress with a big bow in front. Her patent leather shoes with silver buckles and her pink panties lay several feet away. She was twelve, maybe thirteen. Her dress was pulled up around her shoulders and there was blood. A lot of blood. It was apparent she had been raped again and again. She was lying on her stomach where they left her to die on the dirt floor.

Paul carried the body outside and buried her down by the creek where they had butchered the horses for their meat. He found a heart-shaped river rock and used that for a headstone. Then he prayed over the girl, asking Jesus to find her a nice place to live in Heaven.

He awoke with a start. There was no sound in the room except for the snoring of the men. Roger came over, so Paul got up and spelled him.

It was cold.

Dire Consequences

Massive nuclear explosions three hundred miles above the surface of the earth over the eastern seaboard knocked out the power grid from the Atlantic Ocean two hundred miles past the Mississippi River. Nothing worked anymore, automobiles, trucks, airplanes, gas pumps, cell phones, nothing. The electromagnetic pulse from the nuclear explosions short-circuited electrical equipment.

China had employed a newly developed masking technology. This allowed ICBMs to rise above mainland China and come down undetected through the American radar screens. Consequently, the U.S. missile defense systems failed to engage the incoming warheads.

Similar nuclear explosions took place above the western seaboard, wrecking the power grid infrastructure from the Pacific Ocean past the Rocky Mountains to Dodge City, Kansas. Southwest Canada was knocked off the Canadian grid. Northwest Mexico suffered the same fate.

As a further threat of what lay in store, New York City was targeted with a nine-megaton ICBM. The city vanished in a horrific fireball as hot as the surface of the sun. Skyscrapers were blasted into mountains of rubble. Devastation lay for miles in every direction. Millions of people were vaporized in seconds. Millions more were injured or dying.

Peking demanded immediate access to the oil fields.

A few cars and trucks did survive, those parked underground or in concrete garages. Some military hardware was still operational, and hundreds of ICBM silos in the Midwestern states, and a portion of Middle America was spared. Red China had gambled that Washington would not retaliate with nuclear weapons for fear of starting World War Three.

But China had miscalculated badly. Peking was now a radioactive wasteland. So was the Port of Shanghai. The Chinese globalists had been after the oil fields in Oklahoma, Texas, and Louisiana. And the rich farmlands in the Midwest for growing corn and wheat. Capturing those thousands of oil wells had been a misguided Chinese fantasy.

Vladimir Putin called for a council meeting the minute he heard the Chinese capital had been destroyed. Every nuclear ICBM in England and France was aimed at Russia and China. Uncle Sam had been badly hurt but still retained enough military assets to annihilate the planet.

Winston Churchill said it during World War Two. Rahm Emanuel repeated it again in 2008: Never let a crisis go to waste.

The newly installed, billion-dollar power grid protector, North American Alliance, overloaded and began arcing bolts of electricity. Maintenance personnel in the control center at Palo Verde, Arizona, ran for their lives. Minutes later, Max, their twelve-ton computer, went ballistic, blasting a twenty-foot hole in the roof. The grid collapsed.

Within weeks, people began to starve for lack of electricity and transportation. So, the Democrats in the nation's capital opted for another grab at the brass ring. Already political outcasts, they marshaled their followers across the nation for a Marxist takeover of the republic. Donald Trump and Ron DeSantis countered immediately. Then Greg Abbott of Texas and the Southern leadership followed suit. Midwest politicians joined in. Armed conflict broke out between the police and ANTIFA, the John Brown Gun Club, Jane's Revenge, and numerous other left-wing organizations.

American submarines cruising beneath the rolling swells of the vast Pacific Ocean kept Red China at bay while American Marxists and American Capitalists fought hammer and tongs for control over their United States. It was December 2024, and blood and tears were flowing in the metropolitan streets, as well as thousands of smaller towns and villages. Suicide became prevalent.

Stolen Glory

The Soviet Union began a slow deterioration in 1989 following Mikhail Gorbachev's decision to allow free elections. That, combined with the crushing military expenditures over Ronald Reagan's Star Wars, political miscalculations, and the Chernobyl nuclear disaster, led to a final collapse in 1991. Satellite nations fled the Soviet bloc, leaving the Russian motherland abandoned.

Nuclear war had been avoided during the Cuban Missile Crisis and again during the Cold War. The Missile Crisis was long since over and so was the Cold War. But the Vietnam War had badly damaged the reputation of the United States. The 2008 housing collapse was created when the Congressional Democrats forced subprime mortgage lending on the banking industry. Barack Obama contributed further unrest and ruin between 2009 and 2017 by promoting racism and his personal contempt for policemen and the American Armed Forces. Donald Trump righted the ship of state during his four years in the oval office and prosperity returned to America. But a second four-year term was stolen from President Trump in 2020 by the corrupt Democrats and their lockstep media, and given to Joe Biden, a career politician with diminished mental capacity who continued with the anti-American policies of Barack Obama. What followed over the next four years was chaos, riots, murder, and treason until full-scale war broke out in March 2025.

Russia

Inside a magnificent baroque banquet hall filled with crystal chandeliers, ancient portraits of Russian generals, a huge marble fireplace, massive oaken doors, and a twelve-foot wall tapestry of the Battle of Stalingrad, Vladimir Putin and twelve of his trusted Communist Central Committee faithful, plus a dozen Army and Naval officers, were mired in political controversy. They were seated around an elegant mahogany table that once belonged to Czar Nicholas. The topic under discussion was the possibility of war with the United States. No consensus had been reached following two hours of deliberation.

Finally Chairman Putin threw his hands in the air. "It's a gamble, yes, but what in hell's name are we going to do? Is this not a time for Russian glory rather than standing down like Russian dogs? "

Alexander responded. "I understand your frustration, dear comrade. But we must tread with great caution. Donald Trump is now in command at the Pentagon. We know what he did to the Chinese. Our economy is still a thing of weakness. We cannot afford to lose our heads. Patience, Comrade Chairman. Please have patience."

"Patience is for weak-minded politicians. Are we not men? This opportunity will not come again in fifty years. It is our honorable duty for the future of Mother Russia. I say tread with caution, but seize this golden opportunity."

Admiral Popov, "Chairman Khrushchev predicted in 1965 that they would destroy themselves, and we would not have to fire a single shot. Just look at what they're doing right now, today. Civil war! The same as we fought in 1917. Perhaps they will destroy themselves without being a nuclear threat against us. I'm afraid of what Trump might do. I believe we should wait and see what develops."

"And if the Capitalists carry the day? We will have lost our greatest opportunity since 1945. I say make a tentative approach. We can pull back if their response becomes ominous. We have our bombers and missiles just as they do. The Chinese were stupid and greedy. We Russians are wise men."

"I agree with Comrade Putin," Admiral Popov continued. "He is right. This opportunity may never come again. If we act quickly and show a determined face, the Imperialists will not risk another attack on their homeland. They will be angry but we will gain valuable territory."

"This is madness. We are risking everything over a damned frozen island," Alexander added.

"Greenland is an island, yes, but this island is the size of South America. It has great strategic potential, plus rare earth minerals, uranium, oil, diamonds, and gold. It would bring great wealth to our nation."

"And great misery if the Americans choose to honor our foolish venture with their ballistic missiles. Our families would be dead, our countrymen. We would cease to exist as a world power."

"We must also be mindful of the British Royal Navy. Their ships are but a few hundred miles away. We would have only minutes to prepare in the event of a missile attack."

"The Americans have five main battle groups with twenty aircraft carriers and sixty-nine submarines. We have one aircraft carrier and fifty-nine submarines, including twelve nuclear-powered subs. Their

Second Fleet is based in Norfolk, Virginia. They patrol the Atlantic from the North Pole down to Antarctica. That is the surface fleet we would be facing. We could station our submarines around the island if we decide to go through with this. We would lose subs, possibly a dozen or more. But if we manage to destroy their Second Fleet, would that lead to war? I believe it most certainly would. Mister Trump is an unpredictable fellow. He might sue for peace or kill us all. So, I ask you, comrades. Is Greenland worth the gamble?"

"I don't like it. I don't like this one damn bit. To risk Mother Russia for Greenland is insane, like something Hitler would try. He was considered a political genius until the Battle of Britain. Afterward, he was just another tin-pot dictator with no concern for anyone but himself."

"Well said, Comrade Grominenski. But we are missing the greatest opportunity of them all. The Americans are engaged in civil war. Yes? Americans killing Americans. Yes? Their transportation system is a shambles and their military assets have been compromised, but they still retain the ability to destroy us. Is that not so, comrades? Yes! Yes! Yes! But we are wasting valuable time talking about Greenland while the opportunity of a lifetime is staring us in the face. Support the American Marxists! Help them win their civil war. With the Chinese leaders all burned to ashes, the world could be ours for the taking!"

The room fell silent for several moments then erupted in wild cheers and clapping and laughter. Everyone was pounding Milokovich on the back. Vladimir Putin came around the table to hand him a golden goblet of vintage wine. Twenty-five loyal disciples of Lenin began singing their favorite song of patriotism, "The Sacred War." Colonel Devin sprang atop the table, performing the squat dance, thrusting out his legs, his arms folded, amid howls of approval and raucous laughter. Many bottles of vodka were consumed that memorable evening, celebrating a new era, a new Russian adventure.

The threat of nuclear war had been resolved. World domination lay at hand, minus the possibility of another bitter campaign of blood and sorrow. And thirty million war dead, fighting for survival against the Nazi hordes on the Eastern Front.

Mexico

Operation Phoenix began May 15 at 0300. Governor Greg Abbott, Ted Cruz, and Daniel Crenshaw had orchestrated a trade deal with President Andrés Obrador of Mexico. The Texas Rangers and the Texas National Guard would work with the special forces of the Mexican military. Generals of the Ejercito Mexicano were handpicked by President Obrador and his Army Intelligence officials to insure there were no compromised individuals in the Mexican-American alliance.

In exchange for the Texans helping the Mexicans clean up the human trafficking and drug cartels along its border, President Obrador promised to supply the Capitalists with trainloads of food and ammunition. The night operation took place along the border from El Paso all the way down to Laredo. The cartel headquarters were caught with their pants down. They had never been confronted before with any kind of organized resistance.

Twenty-one men stood huddled together in the shadows beneath a growth of massive tule trees. The temperature was 69 degrees with a mild breeze wafting out of the southwest. Before them sat an imposing compound surrounded by nine-foot walls of concrete and heavy timbers. This was the home and nerve center of the drug kingpin Delgado Ortega Emanuel. Emanuel was the notorious killer of Mexican policemen and purveyor of tons of illegal substances across the Rio Grande to corrupt drug dealers in America. Armed men patrolled along the top of the compound walls. A brilliant silver moon shone down, illuminating the trees and the white structure.

"I can't get a bead on the bastard. He's back in that dang hole."

Carlos spoke. "I will be for you the decoy duck. When he comes out, you shoot him."

"You're the man, Carlos."

"Don't miss, *gringo*."

Carlos Regondo Bernado Antonio began his leisurely stroll across the rocky soil toward the compound gate. He'd gone maybe seventy-five feet when the guard in the alcove came running out, shouting.

"You! Stop! Stop or I will shoot."

"I need the job, *senior*. My wife, she is sick. My little boy, he is hungry."

"Stop or I will shoot your crazy ass."

The guard's head exploded from Lieutenant Smith's silencer-equipped 7.62 mm M-14.

Carlos ran for the gate. A second guard came running around the top of the wall to see what all the shouting was about. When he spotted Carlos, he raised his AK-47. Lieutenant Smith squeezed the trigger.

The silencer made a *thump* sound.

The second guard toppled over backward into the courtyard.

"The fucking gate, *amigos*. She is metal."

"Hey, Mike, bring up one uh them satchels."

Mike engaged the fuse then everyone flattened themselves against the wall. Shouts were heard coming from inside. The sixty-second fuse seemed to take forever.

A terrific blast blew one of the nine hundred-pound steel doors thirty feet across the courtyard driveway. Twenty-one men charged through the billowing smoke and falling debris and into the pages of history. Evil was being confronted by honest men, which was long since overdue.

Mexican History

Mexico is composed of thirty-one states with a population of one hundred and thirty-one million, and a Texas border that spans one thousand, nine hundred forty-five miles. In 1810, Mexico declared her independence against Spain. The revolution that followed cost the lives of one to two million Mexicans. The Mexican rebels were eventually victorious in 1821.

The Mexican-American War was another bloody conflict from 1844 to 1848 and cost the lives of thousands more. Mexico was defeated by the American forces which cost Mexico all of her territory north of the Rio Grande River. That conquered land became part of Texas, Oklahoma, Kansas, Colorado, Wyoming, Idaho, and all of New Mexico, Arizona, Utah, Nevada, and California.

Another revolution took place between 1910 and 1920, which ended a thirty-year dictatorship. Then, in 1929, a group of army officers seized power which lasted until the year 2000. This seventy-one year reign by a one-party dictatorship finally ended when the Mexican people rose up, demanding democratic elections. But the corrupt politicians, multiple crimes, and endless murders never ended. Drug cartels with their violent gang associates gained control of cities and entire regions, particularly within close proximity to the American border. Bribery, prostitution, drugs, blackmail, kidnapping, and murder remained commonplace. Murders went unpunished. The politicians were on the take, consequently the whole country fell into a bottomless pit of lawless corruption. When Andrés Obrador was elected president in 2018 he endeavored to improve the lives of his fellow citizens. But a vast sea of gangsters and corrupt politicians didn't want change.

Then civil war came to America.

Gulf of Mexico

Monterrey, Mexico, was chosen as one of the collection centers for food, guns, and medical supplies being trucked east a hundred and ninety-five miles to Matamoros then up the coast by cargo ship to the seaport of New Orleans where it was offloaded and hauled inland.

"Can you tell what that is? I can't make it out with these glasses."

"No, Captain, but it's gaining on us. I can tell by the horizon."

"I would guess it about six or seven miles. What is your estimate?"

"About the same, sir. Six or seven miles."

"Helmsman, bring us up to full ahead."

"Aye, Captain. Full Ahead."

"Put on your thinking cap. If that's the enemy, we're in danger."

"If they catch us, what do you think they will do?"

"Do you remember the story about the *Santa Maria*?"

"No, my Captain."

"They were boarded by one of the cartels. One of the crew members hid in a paint locker. Afterward he slipped away when they made port. He told of what the pirates and their MS-13 gang did to the captain and his crew. He couldn't see what was going on but he could hear the screaming and their laughter. I leave the rest to your imagination. Come, we must go below and see what we can find for defending ourselves. Helmsman, tie off the wheel and come with us. Sparks, you come too."

They descended three stairwells into the bowels of the cargo ship.

"Right there. That's a crate of rifles. See about ammunition."

"Sir, I found dynamite. There's dynamite over here."

"Search for fuses and blasting caps. We'll need those too."

They loaded up with what they could carry and went topside. There, he assembled his crew, fifteen men, including himself, Sparks, and the helmsman.

"I served with our naval special forces, the Fuerzas Especiales."

"We know, Captain. They told us. That is why we volunteered."

"Excellent. Now I will show you how we're going to defend this ship. Tape two bundles of dynamite, four sticks to a bundle. Use a pencil for boring a hole for the blasting caps. Insert the blasting caps then cut two pieces of fuse one and a half inches long. That way, the pirates won't have time to throw them overboard.

"Two of you will serve as dynamiters. Four men will serve as riflemen. Switch your weapons to full automatic. You'll hide behind the railing of the ship until I give the signal."

"What will be the signal, my captain?"

"When I take off my cap. Now, let's take another look and see how close they are."

Using the ship's binoculars, the oncoming craft was still four miles behind. So, the captain repeated, "Full ahead," and they sailed on in silence for another hour.

Six men sat huddled against the railing with M-16 rifles and dynamite. The craft that finally approached them was an aging twenty-eight foot speed boat with seven men onboard. Three of the men sported tattoos on their arms and backs.

"Ahoy, there! Stop your engine. I'm coming aboard."

"You're not authorized. Who are you?"

The speaker fired a volley into the pilot house, sending glass flying. "That is my authorization. Do you understand now? Lower your gangplank!"

"Don't shoot, sir. I will do as you ask."

With the gangplank down the pirate leader began his ascent while his crew remained vigilant with weapons at the ready. When he stepped onto the deck of the cargo vessel, the captain removed his cap. Up rose four seamen who opened fire. Over went the first bundle of dynamite which missed and landed in the water. The explosion blew a plume of water ten feet above the deck. The second bundle landed in the back of the boat and blew out the transom. The craft began to settle. The pirate leader screamed his outrage. The captain pulled his .38 revolver and shot him in the face. Over he went, backward, into the sea.

"Well done, lads! Well done! You did it. I couldn't be more proud."

"Captain, look!"

Standing in the back of the pirate boat, thigh deep in water, a young boy had appeared. Surrounded by floating corpses he just stared up at the men above him with sad and frightened eyes. He knew he was about to die. But he didn't utter a sound. The cargo crew was aware of a large shark circling the sinking craft.

"Sir, we can't leave him."

"There's rope in the pilot house. Quickly, man, quickly."

The first toss landed in the water. The second toss, the boy caught it.

"Tie it around your waist. Then sit on the side of the boat and we'll pull you across."

As the boy entered the water the shark sensed a disturbance. It circled the boat at a faster pace.

"Heave, lads. Heave."

"Captain, the fish ... he's coming."

"Pull, lads, pull. Pull."

"Captain, captain, the fish ... "

The great white turned on its side, exposing its white belly, homing in on the feast.

"Haul away, men, pull for all you're worth. Pull, goddammit, pull!"

The boy was yanked from the sea just as the shark passed beneath him, knocking off one of his shoes with its ivory teeth.

He sat in a heap on the wooden deck, trembling and crying, terrified by his ordeal.

"There's brandy in the pilot house. Fetch out the bottle."

"Here, lad. Take a swig of this."

The boy choked. Then he took another swallow. "You ... you saved ... you saved me. Oh, thank you, sir."

"What is your name, boy?"

"Mar ... Marcus."

"Here. Drink some more of this. You're shaking like a leaf."

"My name is Marcus Antonio Napoleon Constantin. I am from Venezuela. "

"Well, Marcus, welcome aboard."

"My father was a white man. He was a great chef in New Orleans."

"Are your parents still alive?"

"The bad men killed everyone in my village. They killed our mayor, the old priest, our doctor. They killed my mama and poppa. They … they …" The boy began to cry again.

"Why did they spare you, Marcus?"

"My poppa, he let me wear his chef hat sometimes. I was wearing it the day the bad men came into my village."

Field Marshal Feng

Field Marshal Feng was addressing the officer cadets at the Naval Academy of Zhanjiang on the South China Sea. Marshal Feng, an older gentleman with many battle decorations on his chest, was much revered by his young colleagues. Age was a thing of respect among the Chinese people. Feng had been invited by the Naval High Command to talk to the young officers who were in a vile mood over the destruction of Beijing and Shanghai.

"Xi Jinping was a damned fool. His vanity cost us two of our greatest cities, plus millions of dead and injured. But Xi Jinping and his Politburo are no longer with us. Their departure is of no great loss. But I too mourn our lost cities. Now the entire Western World has a thousand rockets aimed at China, and that, my fellow warriors, is stupidity beyond the pale.

"Like you, I am angry but we must wait and do nothing. Comrade Putin is supporting the American socialists. If they win their civil war, we may join forces with Mister Putin. Then it could be only a matter of time before the Americans unite with the Russians and the Chinese under one global banner. But if the Capitalists defeat the American Marxists, we'll cross that bridge when we come to it.

"Now, someone asked earlier about Chairman Mao. Another cadet asked about Stalin. Mao Tse-tung, now Mao Zedong, is the father of our country. You know that from your history books. Mao was a complicated man, some good and some not so good. The history books tell you he was responsible for eighty million deaths. A hundred million is closer to the truth.

"His Great Leap Forward in 1958 caused a terrible famine. Millions starved to death. Korea was another mistake and so was his 1966 Cultural Revolution. His Red Guards were communist hooligans who tortured and murdered Chinese civilians. Mao caused more deaths than Hitler and Stalin combined. But he did unite China through his revolt against Chiang Kai-shek in the 1920s. And for that he is remembered as a great statesman.

"Most of our soldiers he sent to Korea to fight against General MacArthur were killed or froze to death because some did not have proper winter clothing. The Americans controlled the skies so our poor soldiers suffered horribly from napalm and fragmentation bombs.

"Life is a fragile and precious thing. Remember that when you're in the field working. Dictators do not recognize these human qualities. Treat people with respect and they will respect you.

"Mao believed communism and a utopian world would unite someday. That was his great dream. But centralized government is not compatible with society. It becomes corrupt and mistreats its citizens. Mao was no exception.

"Joseph Stalin was one of my favorite subjects in military school. We held spirited discussions over how such a wicked individual could rise to become the leader of the Soviet empire. Certainly, he kept his Siberian gulags busy. Life expectancy for a gulag prisoner was only one winter.

"Stalin was a paranoid. He imagined conspiracies behind every door, executing friends and foes alike. In 1937 and 1938, he imprisoned or killed forty thousand officers from his armed forces. Then, when Hitler invaded Russia in 1941, Stalin's armies were in disarray.

"The Russian people hated Stalin. They were afraid of him. So, when the Germans appeared, they welcomed them, but the Germans were just as cruel as Stalin and his NKVD. The Nazis murdered whole villages which led to our Russian partisans ambushing the German supply columns.

"This neurotic man was able to change opinions when the German Wehrmacht stood at the gates of Moscow. Stalin appealed to the people's patriotic spirit to save Mother Russia. The Russian winter had already taken a terrible toll. That and Stalin's appeals stalled the German advance.

"Farther south at Stalingrad, he summoned General Zhukov and his million-man Siberian army. Stalin's spy in Japan had assured him the Japanese were not going to attack eastern Russia through the Sea of Okhotsk. Zhukov counterattacked the 6th Army with his T-34 tanks and the rest is history.

"After Stalin brought the Eastern Bloc countries under his control, he was responsible for the Berlin Wall and the Berlin Airlift. That turned world opinion against Russia. Korea and Berlin infuriated Stalin. It is believed that Beria poisoned Stalin in 1953 to keep him from starting a war with the United States. Beria was the head of the Soviet Secret Police.

"China and the Soviet Union were both involved in the Vietnam War. We supplied North Vietnam with weapons, trucks, military advisers, doctors, nurses, and technicians for those missile batteries. We were friends with Ho Chi Minh.

"The Soviets lost the Afghanistan War after the US supplied the Afghan rebels with Stinger missiles. Congressman Charlie Wilson was responsible for that undertaking. The Soviet Union finally collapsed in 1991 after they went bankrupt trying to keep pace with President Reagan's Star Wars. After that, the Soviet satellites drifted away.

"I didn't come here today to bore you with a political speech, so I'm making my lesson brief. And historical. Now I will tell you about a real *jiangshi*, Adolf Hitler. Hitler could have won the war in Europe but he made blunder after blunder, like those *bai chia* Obama and Biden. He refused to allow his generals to manage the fighting. With the fall of France, Hitler fancied himself a military genius. So, he constantly countermanded sound military advice. He forbade his scientists to work on anything that would take longer than one year to complete. Hitler believed the war was won. That left the Messerschmitt 262 jet fighter and the fearsome Tiger tank on the drawing board until 1942.

"His arrogance cost him Dunkirk and the Battle of Britain. By halting the panzers on the outskirts of Dunkirk, he gave the British enough time to evacuate three hundred and thirty-eight thousand troops that were trapped on the beaches. Then, when his Luftwaffe was finally winning the war of attrition, Hitler switched his bombing campaign from the British airfields to London. That stupidity gave the Royal Air Force time to regroup.

"On December 7, 1941, the Japanese bombed Pearl Harbor. Four days later Hitler declared war against the United States. That was one of his greatest mistakes. Up until then the majority of the American people were against the fighting in Europe. Hitler's blind ambition allowed President Roosevelt to turn America's industrial might against Germany.

"Operation Barbarossa went from victory to defeat because Hitler delayed the invasion for weeks with a sideshow down in the Balkans against the British. This allowed the Russian winter to catch his armies with only summer uniforms. When advancing on Moscow, they were winning. But Hitler split Guderian's forces, sending part of his panzer army south for an engagement of less importance. With their forces weakened, the Wehrmacht bogged down in the freezing snow within sight of Moscow and never recovered.

"At Stalingrad, General Paulus managed to get his 6th Army surrounded. He requested a retreat, which was still possible, but Hitler refused. The 6th Army was annihilated, which cost the Russians one million, one hundred thousand soldiers. Five months later, at the Battle of Kursk, Hitler delayed and delayed until the Russians had constructed defenses fifteen to twenty kilometers deep. The Russians suffered eight hundred and sixty thousand casualties, and the Germans two hundred thousand. But the panzers were beaten. That was the turning point on the Eastern Front.

"Hitler had fifty-six U-boats when he attacked Poland in 1939. As the Battle of the Atlantic progressed, his U-boats almost strangled the lifeline being shipped across the Atlantic Ocean from America to England. What do you suppose might have been the outcome of the conflict if Germany had ninety or a hundred U-boats at the beginning of the war?"

"Sir, are you going to be our next chairman?"

"Not likely, I don't believe in centralized government."

"Couldn't we have a government like Norway or Sweden?"

"We can discuss that on my next visit. I will tell you then about the Imperial Japanese who almost won the war in the Pacific."

"Great one, we shall miss you and pray for you every day."

"Young dragonflies, you are China's future. Learn your lessons well. Get plenty of exercise. And study the tactics of Sun Tzu. I will return again with the appearance of the second full moon."

Boss

A Gypsy leader was discussing a caravan trip with his people. They had worn out their welcome in a small Cajun community where food was scarce and tempers were beginning to flare. Telling fortunes and Gypsy circus were no longer payment enough for rice and beans and cornbread. It was time to move on and Boss knew it.

Esmeralda spoke. "We have no food for the journey. And the children, Boss. What about the children?"

Charity chimed in. "Yes, what can we give the kids when they cry for cabbage rolls or bread and honey?"

"We have our shotguns and rifles. There will be game along the way, and herbs in the fields. It will not be so hard. Have faith, dear ones, and remember your prayers. We will be in God's hands."

"We need more flour and salt for baking and more lard or bacon grease. Anything that will make the cooking easier and taste better."

"I have forty-four dollars in the treasury. I will barter with the Cajun chief for you in the morning."

"Thank you, Boss. Our prayers will be with you when you go to see the French ones."

Carlos spoke up. "We'll be lucky if we find one 'coon for the pot. Too many people are searching for vittles."

"Think positive, Carlos. Don't put those negative vibes out in the universe."

"We must have meat or we will turn to skin and bones."

"Faith, Carlos. God will show us the way."

The next day Boss went to barter with the Cajun chief. He was gone for two hours. When he returned he was carrying a large cardboard box filled with flour and five pounds of salt. He set his box down on the ground and asked for refreshment. Charity brought him a wooden mug of strong cider.

"They had no bacon grease to spare but I got enough flour to last a couple uh weeks. This will feed us 'til we find our new home."

"Was it a good trade, Boss? Did you come out on top?"

"They wouldn't take the paper money. Said it was no good no more. They asked me for my silver cross, so I gave it to them."

"Ohhh, Boss, I'm so sorry. That was your father's cross."

"I did it for you, my people. You are more important to me than a simple piece of silver. My father would have done the same."

"Indeed he would, God rest his soul," Esmeralda declared. "Tonight we shall dine on cider and fresh biscuits. Tomorrow we begin our journey."

The next morning a caravan of thirteen Gypsy souls began their trek along Highway 10 toward New Orleans. It was a warm spring day and excitement was in the air. They were looking forward to a new place to live and a new adventure.

"Up ahead. What is that?"

"Looks like the farmer's cows got loose."

"I see him sitting by the fence. Maybe we can trade for a lame one."

"Hey, mister. You need some help?"

"I shore do. One a them heifers stepped on mah foot."

"Let Esmeralda take a look. She's the doctorin' kind."

"You got mashed pretty bad, mister. I'll mix up a poultice and you'll be up and around in no time."

"I'll tell ya what. You folks get mah cows back in, tote me up to the house yonder, an' I'll put ya up fer a spell. You can work on mah farm, mend the fences, weed mah crops, earn yer keep. I'll have Maw feed youns an' throw in a few dollars ta boot."

Up at the farmer's old Victorian residence, an aging woman with graying hair came out the kitchen door with a wooden spoon in her hand. "Land sakes, Paw. What in tarnation is all this?"

"These here Gypsies done rescued me, Maw. They got the cows in an' tended mah busted foot. The farm needs work. I told 'em they could stay an' work a spell. You alright with that?"

"Why shore, honey. Get 'em ta bring ya inside. I'll mix up a batch uh sweet tea fer ever body. Yer foot ain't broke, is it?"

"No, Maw, jus' mashed good."

"Elmer, you rest now. I'll get some food in 'em then show 'em 'round the place."

Colonel Moran

Colonel Sabastian Moran was a psychopath. He was a rapist and a murderer. He delighted in young women, raping them while slowly choking them to death. He termed this "the dying quiver." Redheads were his favorite, but any female would do between the ages of ten and fifteen. Moran had made his escape up the Florida Keys to Miami where he took a passenger train north to Atlanta, Georgia.

His career with the Cuban Secret Service ended when he tortured and murdered the young daughter of a government official. His uncle had bribed the guards to allow him to escape. That didn't sit too well with the murdered girl's influential father, so the uncle and the two prison guards were forced to take Moran's place. Five days later they were hanged.

Atlanta had become the southern processing center for the One World Government Alliance. Socialists and revolutionaries flocked there from hundreds of miles in every direction. The military arm for those men and women was ninety-seven miles due west out Interstate 20 at the Anniston Army Depot in Bynum, Alabama. Before the war, the Anniston Depot had been responsible for repairing combat vehicles with damaged weapon systems. With the power grid partially restored, dozens of armored personnel carriers and Abrams tanks sat ready to be deployed.

When Colonel Moran reached the front gate at the depot he explained who he was and that he wished to speak with the commandant. A call was put through and Moran was escorted into the inner sanctum of the compound. What he encountered when he entered a mahogany paneled room, with indirect lighting and a picture of Che Guevara on the wall, was not what he expected.

A tall, athletic female with close-cropped blonde hair and wearing battle fatigues rose from behind an antique desk to greet him. She was strangely attractive with perfect breasts, a flat stomach, and cold gray eyes. On her collar was a pair of silver stars indicating her rank as a brigadier general.

Thinking he might score a chance at getting into her pants, Moran complimented the attractive woman. "I never expected to find such a beautiful lady in charge. My name is Colonel Sabastian Moran. I was with the Cuban Secret Service for twelve years. I would like—"

"You would like what? A young girl, perhaps? A little boy to torment? Or would you like to put on your red dress, and parade your silly ass in front of my troops? Atlanta called Havana and checked you out. You're a deviant, Mister Moran. A skinny, cold-blooded deviant."

"All lies, I assure you. I am innocent. I am a good—"

"Shut your mouth. Speak only when you're spoken to."

"But I—"

"Shut the fuck up or I will have you thrown in the stockade."

"You can't do this. I have rights!"

The commandant pressed a red button beside an Italian 9 mm Beretta on top of her desk. Four muscular guards burst into the room. She nodded toward Moran and they commenced beating him with rubber truncheons.

After he was beaten to his knees, she nodded for them to stop. "Can you hear me now, Mister Moran?"

"Ya … Yes …yes, ma'am."

"That's better. I have use for your talents, but you will not be allowed to associate with my people. You will be housed separately. You will not go to the mess hall. Your meals will be delivered to your quarters. You will not leave your quarters until I summon you. Any questions?"

"What do you intend to do with me?"

'You will serve as my new interrogator for special prisoners. Our old interrogator sadly departed us. He enjoyed his work too much, so I had him shot."

"Am I to use any means necessary?"

"Any means short of killing them. If one of them dies, you will be disciplined severely. So, mind your manners, Mister Moran, or you won't live to see our glorious final victory. Guards, take this man to his quarters."

The War

Sporadic fighting had been ongoing for one hundred and thirty-three days. Three major battles had taken place which cost the lives of more than one hundred and ninety thousand American citizens. Thousands more were injured or unaccounted for. Neither the Capitalists nor the Marxists had gained an upper hand. Hospitals were filled to overflowing. Doctors' buildings were full, dental offices, even animal shelters. Gangrene had become a nightmare. Food remained in short supply. A large percentage of the population were desperate for something to eat. But the truck drivers were afraid to drive into enemy territory for fear of being hijacked and killed. Russia maintained a fleet of cargo ships loaded with food and ammunition for the Marxists. China remained neutral. Canada and Mexico were helping the Capitalists with everything they could spare.

NATO had gotten into a shooting war with Iran. Japan and Australia were fighting in the Persian Gulf. Israel was attacking from the northwest. The Book of Revelation was upon the land. And the multitudes did take a sup of the bitter vintage.

A Bitter Lesson

Captain had drawn up a legal document naming Rocky as Nancy's adoptive father. The men had been scavenging abandoned houses for food, weapons, and anything of value. In a springhouse they discovered a trove of canned goods and a bag of silver coins. Two five-gallon cans of coal oil were also there. Two skeletons in the backyard were all that remained of the property owners. A grave was dug and they were buried. The empty farmhouse was larger than their present accommodations and it had a fireplace. So, Captain had the men move their belongings to the new location.

Rocky and Nancy were having a picnic. A jar of canned peaches and a small pail of blackberries they had picked sat in the middle of their blanket. Wild rabbits were munching clover on the other side of their picnic clearing. It was a pleasant morning with no clouds in the sky. The war seemed far away and the two of them were at peace with their surroundings.

"I love the rabbits. They're such sweet little things."

Suddenly, a hawk swooped down and flew away with a small rabbit in its talons. Nancy screamed and burst into tears.

Rocky placed his arms around his daughter. "Don't cry, baby. You'll learn soon enough that life is not fair. Bad people take advantage of the good people. The same thing happens in the animal kingdom. Big ones eat the little ones. We eat pigs and chickens. I don't reckon they care much for that, do they?"

"But the little rabbit. It was awful."

"Some creatures go into shock when they're about to die. I'll bet the little rabbit was like that."

"I want the little rabbit to go to Heaven where my mama and daddy live."

"We'll all be in Heaven someday. Maybe you'll see the little rabbit then."

"I wish the fighting would stop. I hate seeing all those dead people."

"We'll be moving on soon. Captain is taking us to a base camp near Franklin, Tennessee. One of our armies is there. "It's too dangerous to stay here because of Atlanta. I'll find a place for you to stay when we go off to fight."

"I don't want to stay by myself. I want to be with you and the others."

"What if we get killed, like the little rabbit?"

"Then I'll die too, and we'll all be together in Heaven."

"You're something special, Nancy. My something special, beautiful little daughter."

"Yes, I am. I'm your daughter and I can carry ammunition for the men."

"I'll speak to Captain. I don't want to leave you behind. I love you too much."

"I love you too, and I want us to be together forever and ever."

"You'll be ten years old in two weeks. What do you want for your birthday?"

"Can I have a doggy?'"

"If I can find one. I'll ask Captain to help."

"Captain is my friend. He tells me things girls are supposed to know."

"Captain is smart. He was a philosophy professor in a big college before the war."

"What is philosophy?"

"I asked Captain that same question once. He replied, 'What does it all mean?' I've heard of philosophers like Aristotle and Plato, but you'll have to ask Captain. I'm not educated enough to give you a straight answer."

"You're smart enough. You just ain't read it yet."

"Speaking of reading, how are you coming with that math book we found?"

"It's really hard, but Freddie helps me. He can do math stuff in his head."

"Fred was a math teacher. We have some smart men in our squad."

In the distance they heard muffled reports of enemy artillery. Another skirmish was underway.

The barrage continued for twenty minutes then silence. The rabbits across the field had returned from hiding and were eating the clover again.

"What did you do before, Rocky? You never told me."

"I was a powder monkey."

"What's that?"

"I worked for a company that built roads and bridges. When they ran into rock, they brought in mechanical drills for drilling holes in the rock. My job was to load those holes with dynamite. Then I'd blast the rock so it could be moved and leveled with bulldozers."

"That sounds scary."

"Actually, I enjoyed my work. I can bring down a mountainside with enough dynamite."

"Maybe you can do that to the bad people."

"If we get the chance, you can push the plunger."

"These peaches are awfully good."

"Yes, we're lucky to have found such good things to eat."

"Do you think we'll have good things to eat at the new place?"

"Captain said a truck convoy delivers food there from New Orleans. They'll have food."

"Do you think we'll win?"

"I believe so. I don't think God will let the bad people win."

"Have you ever met God?"

"No, Nancy. Jesus was crucified on the cross to take the punishment for man's sins. I'll find a bible for you. All of your answers are in the bible. It's called the Good Book. It took forty authors fifteen hundred years to write the bible."

"Is Heaven in the Good Book?"

"Everything about Christianity is in the Good Book. Great stories are in the bible, David and Goliath, Abraham, Samson and Delilah. You'll learn about Jesus and his twelve disciples."

"I hope when I get to Heaven I can see the little rabbit."

"When I'm with you, I can see the good in people. There for quite a spell all I ever saw was the dark side of man. All this fighting and killing. That's why I believe God led me to you, Nancy. You saved me. You're the future and I intend to see that you get there in one piece."

"I love you, Rocky. You saved me too."

Henry

Colonel Mosrie was in the war room with his noncommissioned officers. Mosrie's war room consisted of one 14 x 20 army tent, two sawhorses, a piece of 5/8-inch 4 x 8 plywood, a dozen maps, ten cloth folding chairs, an army cot, a footlocker, seven crates of ammunition, two kerosene lanterns, and a dirt floor.

"That bitch has one of our guys, Sergeant Paul. She's an evil fuck. She'll squeeze him 'til he pukes out ever thing he knows. Paul is a good soldier, so I won't blame him none if he rats us out. No man can stand having his bare feet stuck in hot coals or bein' skinned with a potato peeler. We found some of her handiwork when we overran her compound up in Kentucky. But the bitch got away. I almost caught her but one of her guards shot out my damn radiator. I'd give up my front seat in Hell to get my hands on Miss Delores Finch."

Sawbucks spoke up. "What I don't get is how she became commandant of that corps. She lost four thousand men in Kentucky and most of their equipment. Hell, it was '68 Tet in reverse."

"Politics, Sawbucks, politics. With liberal assholes it's always politics."

The Legionnaire, Frenchie, added his two cents. "We'll never get inside that depot. Too many soldiers. We're gonna have ta snuff 'im. I hate sayin' that but there ain't no other way to shut him up."

Colonel Mosrie. "You're readin' my mind, Frenchie. Who's the best shot in the outfit?"

"That would be Private Henry, sir. He can shoot the balls off a gnat at five hundred yards."

"Go get 'im. Let's see how he feels about this?"

"I can't do that, sir. He's in the stockade."

"What's he in for this time?"

"Drunk, fightin', the usual shit."

"Go tell the brig sergeant I said ta let him out an' bring 'im here."

"Yes, sir."

Twenty minutes later Private Henry walked in with a black eye, a busted lower lip, and all the buttons missing from the front of his white dress shirt. The right sleeve of his sport coat hung precariously by a few threads. Henry saluted and was told to take a seat. The Legionnaire took the chair beside Henry. The stockade sergeant saluted Colonel Mosrie and left. Mosrie laid out the proposed assignment then asked Henry a question.

"How do you feel about killing one of our men?"

"Is that a trick question?"

"Take this asshole back to the brig!"

"I meant no disrespect, sir. I thought you was joshin' me."

"Sergeant Paul knows our troop strength, our battle maneuvers. The whole nine yards. They'll torture him 'til he can't stand it any longer. We can't get in ta save the poor man, so the next best thing is to put him out of his misery. That's what I'd want. Wouldn't you?"

"I know Sergeant Paul. Him an' me got sideways a time 'r two. What's the layout uh that place?"

"They's a few hills and some swamp. And we know where she keeps her interrogator. A shot from the northwest corner is about seventeen hundred yards. There's a better shot due south of maybe fifteen hundred, but your cover down there is pretty sparse."

"I don't fret none 'bout cover long as I can fix me up a camo outfit. I'd look like a bunch uh weeds."

"Then you'll go?"

"If'n I make it back alive, will you give me a week off ta go see Sweet Thang?"

"God deliver me! Okay, you got five days!"

Johnson and the Legionnaire were assigned to go with Private Henry for his protection. It took the better part of four days driving at night with no lights then hiding back in the trees in the daytime. West of Birmingham they were confronted by two Marxist police officers in an electric government Humvee. Johnson stepped out to show his papers, dropping his wallet in the middle of the road as a distraction. The Legionnaire slid open his door and shot them both. They loaded their bodies in the Humvee and drove it off into a swamp of cattails and quicksand. Forty minutes later there was nothing left but bubbles.

After Private Henry got himself acclimated with the terrain of the depot and the interrogator's hut, he spotted a stand of bushes he liked, grown over with vines and honeysuckle. That afforded him and his accomplices perfect cover. Johnson cleared out the interior of their hiding place with his trench knife while the Legionnaire peered through the foliage with a range finder to judge the distance.

"I got fourteen hundred and forty-two yards, give or take a yard or two."

Henry stuck a forefinger in his mouth then held it up above his head. "About three knots, ya' reckon?"

"Closer to four, I'd say, right to left. There's a nice breeze today."

Henry took out his notebook and studied the numbers for a couple of minutes. Next he pulled a bolt-action rifle out of a leather carrying pouch.

"What the hell is that thing?"

"This here is Miss Whoop-Ass. She's uh 1942 8 mm Czech Mauser I found at a garage sale. I bought my scope at a policeman's auction fer six hundred bucks. Brand-new they cost over three thousand. My cousin made this here silencer, quiet as a little ol' church mouse. The bore ain't got no pits an' my effective range is over one thousand meters with uh maximum range of three thousand meters."

"Well shut my mouth! I'll go getcha somethin' solid to rest your stock on."

Johnson crawled out. A few minutes later he crawled back in dragging a six foot section of dead cypress tree. They pushed the log up against the honeysuckle and settled down to wait. Henry fell asleep while the others kept watch.

"Wake up. We got company."

"We can't kill 'im. He'll be missed. Stay real quiet. Maybe he'll go on by."

A young sentry was walking up the slope carrying an AK-47. He paused before their hiding place, unzipped his pants, and relieved himself on the bushes. He smoked a government-issue Lucky Strike and moseyed on.

"We been pissed on again. Them government bozos is all alike."

"He looked pretty cool ta me. I'm glad we didn't kill 'im."

A silvery moon rose in a star-spangled panorama of faraway mystery. The moon cast its silver splendor across the hills and the parade grounds down below. An owl hooted in the top of the sycamore tree beside their hiding place. In the distance a dog howled at the moon. The Legionnaire crawled out and stood gazing up into the heavens. Henry and Johnson joined him.

"I ain't never seen nothin' like this before," Henry said in an awed voice.

The Legionnaire's voice was hushed. "There's no pollution out here like you have in a city. It was like this when my battalion fought in the desert. We would attack the Arabs at night when they were sleeping. I love the night. You can move around in the shadows and never be seen."

"Where all did ya go?"

"Morocco, Western Sahara, Algeria, Tunisia. We went all over."

Johnson spoke up, "You ever get hurt?"

"I was lucky. But they captured one uh my friends in a firefight down in the Sahara. We found Theodore two days later, trussed up like a pig and sliced to ribbons. We waited five days then crept into their camp at night. We used our knives. They never heard us coming. The next day those that were still alive packed up their tents and left. We never saw 'em again after that."

"Do you miss the Legion?"

"I like it better here. You Americans are interesting individuals."

They turned in, surrounded by a cocoon of greenery and sweet-smelling honeysuckle. Next morning they were awakened by a commotion down on the parade ground. A bugler had sounded revelry and the soldiers were lining up single file. A pickup truck pulled up in front of the assembly and a man was dumped out on the ground. The truck drove away.

"That's him. That's Sergeant Paul." Henry checked the wind again and made a correction. The man on the ground was too weak to stand. "And there comes that son-of-a-bitch, the Colonel. Should I take 'im out now or wait?"

"Go ahead. Do it now."

"Sight for me if'n I miss. Tell me where the bullet strikes."

"Go on. I gotcha covered."

Henry placed the crosshairs on the front of the Colonel's jacket to compensate for his forward momentum. He took a deep breath, let it half out, and slowly squeezed the trigger. The silencer made a little *thunk*.

"You just missed 'im. It hit right in front, off to his right. I'm guessing you're off maybe four or five inches left."

The Colonel started to run. Henry took his time making another adjustment.

"Hurry up. The fucker's gettin' away."

Henry placed the crosshairs on his target and fired. The target spun sideways, sprawling on the asphalt.

"Shazam! You nailed the bastard. He's still alive though. Hit 'im again."

This time the crosshairs were on the target's head. He was trying to crawl away.

Thunk.

"That did it. You blew his head clean off."

"You sure as hell did. Great shot, Henry."

The soldiers all fled. Sergeant Paul struggled to his feet and turned to face the hill. He spread his arms out wide, as if he were Christ on the cross. He knew they had come to end his suffering.

Henry could see the smile on his bloody and broken face.

Thunk.

Private Henry lay his head down in the honeysuckle and wept.

Delores Finch

Delores Finch was beside herself with anger. Both her prize prisoner and her chief interrogator, that Cuban fuck, had been shot and killed that very morning. The woman was furious that she had been beaten again by that backwoods buffoon, the one called Mosrie up in Tennessee. She knew it was him. No one else had the *cojones* to infiltrate this deep into her territory.

But deep down inside she admired his daring. He was a cunning individual, smart and quite capable.

What might she do to repay his foul trespass? Two of her pursuers had been killed when they blundered into an ambush twenty miles east of Birmingham. This was personal. She would devise a plan of equal intrigue and rub his face in it!

Mister Peabody

Nancy often played make-believe in the backyard of the old farmhouse. There was a creek back there that meandered across the rear of the property and down beside the springhouse, with frogs and little black salamanders and the occasional turtle. Dozens of beautiful flowers cultivated by the old couple were in bloom. Nancy wondered sometimes what they had been like before they were murdered.

Fred and Rocky had built a treehouse for Nancy with a circular wooden landing three feet off the ground. That led up to the main structure with two windows four feet above the landing with a trapdoor that opened and latched. Nancy kept her dolls in the treehouse. Captain found the dolls in the home where the young girl had been raped and left to die in the barn. Marxists had ruled Middle and West Tennessee until the Capitalists drove them out following the Battle of Chattanooga. Those that weren't killed or captured retreated down Interstate 75 to Atlanta.

Captain knocked on Nancy's wooden platform. "Nancy?"

"Captain! You're back."

"Come down. I have something I want to show you."

Nancy climbed down and stood looking at a small cardboard box Captain set down gently on the deck. "What is it?"

"Look inside and see."

"Oh, look," she cried. "

"Be careful picking him up. He's still a wee one."

Nancy picked up the little fox, tenderly holding him against her chest with both hands. He made little *chittering* sounds, snuggling himself against the warmth of her throat.

"Oh, Captain. I love him. He's just perfect."

"I'll find things for him to eat. We have to be careful until he grows some more."

"I'm going to name him Mister Peabody, after that show I like so much."

"Mister Peabody is a proper name for this youngster."

Captain signaled the squad by raising his arm and pumping his fist. The men filed out the back door singing Happy Birthday. A cake magically appeared and was placed beside the birthday girl sitting on her wooden platform. Rocky came out last with a silver urn of lemonade and a bucket of ice. Summer had arrived and Mister Peabody was christened their mascot for the squad.

Marxist Mischief

Boss and the work crew had just returned from the fields for lunch. Gathered at the kitchen door, they were discussing what they had seen in the fields on both sides of the highway from their vantage point up on the ridge.

"Hit's them danged cominists. They been haulin' up from Alabamy. I seen 'em two nights in a row. They got uh war goin' on agin them Christians. Boys down at Lowe's tole me 'fore I hurt mah foot. I tole Maw all about it. They's tryin' ta take over the whole country. Gonna kill off a bunch uh folks cause uh somethin' 'bout the climate. Sounds plum crazy if'n ya ast me."

"I heard the same story when we was livin' with that Cajun tribe," Boss said. "They was all stirred up about it. I never told my people. Didn't want 'em frettin' over things we got no control over."

Maw said, "Theys uh Christian army up 'round Franklin, Tennessee. Maud tole me when she come thru here las' time. I reckon them nogoods is gettin' ready to go up there an' do mischief."

"By jingies, Maw, that's hit! They ain't no good reason fer 'em ta be over here. They's goin' up thru the backdoor."

"Somebody better warn 'em. I'd drive up there but my eyes is poorly," Long Tom said.

"Maw's right. They're gettin' ready to do mischief. Long Tom, you wanna ride up with me?"

"I'd be proud to, Boss. If we can warn 'em in time that might help out the whole country."

Esmeralda spoke up. "We Gypsies been looked down on for a

thousand years. That's just the way it is. But if we can help out, I'm with Boss and Long Tom. It's our country too. Leastways, we can hold our heads up no matter what some people say about us."

Boss patted a pocket. "I got forty-four dollars for gas. Anybody got a buck or two to chip in?"

"Me an' Maw got sum dough. How much ya think ya need?"

"Thirty more dollars oughta put us on the safe side," Long Tom said.

Maw made off for the bedroom. A minute later she was back. "Here's a hundred dollars, Tom. You fellers get on up there an' be careful. Me an' Paw likes havin' ya around. We been talkin' 'bout raisin' a mess uh crops. Taters, corn, beans, 'maters. An' sellin' 'em down on the highway. Folks is hungry. We can do some good and make a little money ta boot. All pullin' together, Christian-like. Tell 'em the way, Paw."

"Drive west 'til ya see I-65 North. That'll take ya up thru Montgomery. Jes keep on a-goin'. I-65 runs acrost Highway 96 rite below Nashville. Go left. That's Murfreesboro Road. That 96 goes straight ta Franklin. I drove uh rig back in the day. Hits about four hundred an' fifty miles. I'll draw ya a map."

Melissa stepped up. "Tom, take my .32-20 revolver. It's only got three shells but it might come in handy."

"You want a shotgun?" Maw asked.

Boss considered the offer. "We better not. A shotgun would be hard to hide if we get stopped."

Two hours later they were packed, gassed up with gas siphoned from the farm tractor, a picnic basket packed with sandwiches, and a thermos of hot coffee on the front seat. Paw insisted they drive his 2021 Ford pickup. Thirty minutes later they were headed up I-65. Boss drove until dusk then pulled off into a field behind a grove of pine trees, so they couldn't be seen from the highway.

"Has the world gone off its rocker, Boss, or is it just us?"

"I never cared much for politics. Too many hands in the till. They sure have screwed things up though, ain't they?"

"Time will tell, Boss. If Franklin can whip that bunch behind us, it oughta help."

"You're right, Tom. Do you think those no-goods have started yet?'"

"Can't be sure. Might be waitin' for foul weather so they can try an' sneak in."

"I never thought uh that. You learn that in the Army?"

"They sent us to school a lot. School was interesting."

They each ate a BLT and turned in for the night. Next morning they were awakened by a raging thunderstorm. Lightning spider-webbed across an ominous black sky. Rain was coming down in sheets.

"They might be movin' now, Boss. We better pick up the pace."

"We got about two hundred and seventy-five miles to go. Tank's a little over half full. With that five-gallon gas can in back we don't have to stop, but if I see a station open we oughta pull over and gas up.

"You still got Melissa's gun?"

"Right here in my pocket."

Ninety minutes later they saw an Esso station up ahead. The rain had slacked off to a drizzle.

Boss went inside to pay while Tom stood beside the pump. Tom saw something inside he didn't like. So, he ambled slowly toward the station's front entrance. The door opened.

"Get in here you half-breed son of a bitch."

"No speaka da English, suh."

There were two of them inside. A skinny, tall man with long, stringy hair was holding a revolver on Boss. A fat man was motioning Long Tom with a wrench in his hand. Long Tom walked in, pretending to be dumb and friendly. Fat Man raised his wrench to strike. Tom shot him in the crotch. He turned quickly and fired his last two rounds into Gun Man who stumbled sideways against a cinder block wall and collapsed, dead. Then Tom smashed Wrench Man in the face with his empty .32-20. He went down and Tom kicked him hard in his private parts. Fat Man screamed.

"My God! You learned that in the Army?"

"Yeah, Boss. I was in Special Forces. Get Slim's .38 and see if there's any shells in that old desk."

Boss picked up the revolver off the trash-littered floor, handed it to Tom, then pulled open the drawer. He froze, staring down at the contents inside the wooden desk. "Tom, you better come over here."

Long Tom cursed. "These sorry bastards been busy. I'll lay odds the backyard is fulla bodies. There must be fifty thousand here, not counting the watches and diamond rings. See that packet of hundred-dollar bills? That's probably ten thousand. And that silver Rolex could be another ten thousand. Those diamond rings, I don't know about. We'll take all of it with us. Our womenfolk will love the jewelry. The money we can use on Paw's farm. We can make Maw's dream of a produce stand come true."

"There's a box of shells in there too. Fat Man's still alive. He can identify us."

"Get one uh them paper sacks an' take this stuff out to the truck. Fill the tank. I'll turn the pump on, then shut it down when you're done."

When the tank was full, Boss waved to Tom behind the plate glass window. Moments later he heard a gunshot. Long Tom walked out and got into the truck. Boss looked over at Tom.

"There won't be a problem about anyone identifying us. I took care uh that. Don't mention this to anyone at the farm. Women can't keep a secret to save their lives."

"You have my word, Tom. I'm glad we're together. You're the bravest man I ever saw."

The Warning

Three hours later they were on Highway 96 driving into Franklin, Tennessee. Up ahead an armored personnel carrier blocked the left side of the road. Two uniformed men stood beside the machine. A third man was visible up top behind a .50 caliber machine gun.

"What are you two doin' in these parts?"

"Are you part of the Christian Army?" Boss asked.

"Christians. Capitalists. It's all the same. Why are you here?"

"We came to warn you about Atlanta."

"What about Atlanta?"

"They're headed this way."

"You jackin' me 'round, mister?

"No, it's true. We think they're not far behind us."

"Step outta the truck, sir."

"Cut the bullshit, son," Long Tom advised. "While you're doin' your Dudley Do-Right number, there's an enemy column a day or two down I-65."

"Who are you?"

"Special Forces, 1995 to 2003, Middle East."

"Show me some ID."

Long Tom obliged the young soldier.

"Charlie, go with these men and take them to see Captain."

Twenty minutes later they were standing before a middle-aged man with captain bars on his collar. He was seated behind a long table with folding metal legs. A little blonde girl was sitting next to him. There was an open bible on the table. The middle-aged man asked Boss and Long Tom to have a seat.

"The corporal tells me you have information about Atlanta. Whaddya got?"

Long Tom glanced at Boss, who nodded. "Sir, we saw a dozen fields full of trucks and flatbeds just east of Mobile on Interstate-10. They had tanks and artillery, all kinds of military equipment. We live on a farm close by, so we drove up here to warn you. We think they're comin' up Interstate-65."

"Damnation! That confirms it! We got another report from a truck driver fifteen minutes ago. Nancy, go find your father an' bring him back here pronto. You guys want some coffee? We got doughnuts an' there's some chocolate cake beside the coffee machine."

Boss smiled. "Sounds like we got here at the right time."

Rocky returned with Nancy and Mister Peabody. An alert went out over the PA system, requesting all officers and enlisted personnel to report to the auditorium building immediately.

Captain stood at the front of the auditorium behind a wooden podium before an audience of uniformed men and women.

"We believe an army of communist sons a bitches are headed this way. Two reports have come in that confirms this. Colonel Mosrie left two days ago with most of our troops and equipment, so we're short-handed. It's your duty, I repeat, it's your duty to look after your people and keep their spirits up. Things are about to get hairy around here and real soon. So, I'm counting on each one of you. When the going gets tough and you think you ain't gonna make it, that's when you reach down deep inside and pull out your primal self. A creature called the Id lives inside every human being. Fear will leave you. You will no longer be afraid of death. You will become a killing machine and you will kill your enemy."

Rocky whispered to Nancy. "I never heard Captain talk that way before. And he's a Christian. You got a place to hide Mister Peabody?"

"I'll keep him with me in my backpack. He likes it in there. "

Captain continued. "Junior, take the backhoe and dig two pits out front two hundred yards apart for the tanks. Then dig a zigzag trench five feet deep between the tanks. Dig another trench up on the ridge. A long zigzag one. Dig another zigzag down in front of the tree line. "Torello, have your crews move those 105s to the camouflaged gun pits then pull that 155 up on the ridge. Take all the shells we got left. You're gonna need 'em.

"Judy, you an' Leroy an' Hollis get all of our shoulder-fired missiles out of the armory. Carlos, you and Franko spread ammo boxes along the trenches. When the shootin' starts we may not be able to get back to the armory.

"Pilots, get your choppers armed and gassed up.

"Drivers, pull your trucks around back up in the trees and space some personnel carriers out front twenty yards apart. Medics, load up on morphine and bandages. Machine-gunners, take all our belted ammunition. Cover our tanks and that front trench with camouflage netting. Stake it down good. And put some over those personnel carriers. Stake them down too.

"We're gonna kick Miss Finch's communist ass up between her damn shoulders!"

The Legionnaire looked over at Henry and Johnson. "Boys, the bad news is, we're outnumbered fifteen or twenty to one. The good news is, they ain't been trained worth dog shit. Progressives an' guns don't mix, so I'd say our odds are about even. Henry, set your sights for a thousand yards. That'll get their attention. Johnson, you bring a Stinger and I'll get one uh them Javelins."

Johnson, "They got good troops too. This ain't gonna be no cake walk."

"I want to see assholes and elbows, people," Captain addressed them with compassion. "Our survival depends on each one of you. Now, get out there and make things happen."

Henry looked doubtful. "Looks like we're gonna get the bejesus blowed outta us."

"Get you a Stinger and meet us up on the ridge," the Legionnaire instructed. "That might be the safest place."

Night fell and everyone was still busy preparing for the battle. The compound lights were switched off to confuse General Finch and her officers. Over at the mess hall the soldiers were being fed in shifts, steak and potatoes which was standard fare for soldiers going into harm's way.

Nancy was sitting on a mound of fresh earth up on the ridge overlooking the valley with her dad Rocky.

"Do you think we're going to Heaven to be with the little rabbit?"

"No, Nancy. You're gonna live to be an old granny lady."

"I want to stay with you tonight. I'm scared."

"Sure you can. Is Mister Peabody in your backpack?"

"Yes. I gave him an apple."

"When the shelling starts, we'll hunker down in this ditch. We'll be okay here. Let's go down to that gray building and find us a bunk bed. You climb up top. What about Mister Peabody?"

"He can stay on the floor. He won't run away."

"I'll get our little mascot some water."

At 0200 hours they were awakened by helicopters overhead, flying out. Forty-five minutes later they were awakened again by helicopters overhead, flying back in. They didn't hear what had taken place fifty miles down Interstate-65. To the mess hall personnel and those pulling guard duty, it sounded like distant thunder.

Desperate Hours

Long Tom and Boss were sitting on a mound of fresh earth beside one of the compound's tanks. They were down in front of the forward trench. Colonel Mosrie had taken the rest of the tanks with him.

Boss was asking Long Tom about combat and what it was like. "I don't mind telling you, I'm scared. I'm not brave like you, Tom."

"Everybody's afraid their first time. That's normal. To be honest, I'm a little nervous myself."

"You're one brave *hombre*, Tom. I'm just a scared ol' gray-haired Gypsy man."

"You're like a virgin, Boss. You're about to lose your cherry."

"Yes, but I like being a virgin."

Long Tom laughed and patted his friend on the shoulder. The two of them sat quietly for a few minutes, watching the soldiers scurrying about with last-minute preparations. Word had come down that contact had been made during the night. A few tanks and trucks had been blown up and set on fire.

Overhead a trio of gunships flew out for another engagement. Long Tom and Boss watched until they disappeared in the distance. A rumble of explosions soon followed. The enemy was not far away.

Nancy picked up Mister Peabody and placed him on the bottom tier of the bunk bed. Rocky had gone to the mess hall and brought back a steaming tray of biscuits and gravy and two cups of coffee. Nancy used a small plastic plate she kept in her pack to feed Mister Peabody. He gobbled his biscuit and white gravy.

"He's such a sweet little thing. How can I protect him when the fighting starts?"

"Seal the top of your backpack real good so he can't get out. I'll dig a place in the side of the trench and place him in there. We can take two of these blankets to shelter us from the falling rocks and dirt. Put on your helmet and buckle your chin strap. We better get on up there."

Rocky slung his rifle on his shoulder and they departed the building. Up on the ridge they found six hundred men and women armed and ready. A tall, muscular man next to them in the trench had a javelin laid out on the front of the parapet with a rifle and a pile of bandoliers. A brown-haired youth to his right had a strange looking bolt action rifle with a big telescopic sight. An African American man farther over had a Stinger missile, an M-16, and another pile of bandoliers.

"People call me Frenchie. This here is Henry and Johnson. Looks like we're gonna be together today."

"I'm glad to meet you fellas. My name is Rocky and this is my daughter, Nancy. She has a little fox in the backpack that's the mascot for our squad. Are you from France?"

"Yes, I am, but I'm a naturalized citizen now. Henry is a crack shot. Johnson over there ain't good fer nothin'."

"I heard that. Don't make me come over there, frog-eater."

"Rocky … I … help me …"

Nancy zoned out. Conversations faded, drifting away. The dugout, Rocky and the men, the soldiers in the background, their weapons, everything took on a strange luminous glow. The world went into slow motion. Nancy could hear the beating of her heart. And the coursing of the blood through the veins in her neck. Fear took hold, dragging her down into a terrible dark underground where evil dwelt.

She saw the man with the knife stabbing her mother again and again. Her father was on the floor, trying to get up, but he was dying. And the blood. An ocean of blood. It was on Nancy's legs and on her shoes.

She screamed and screamed again.

People rushed over to help.

"What's wrong with her?"

"It's okay, everybody. She's having a flashback. PTSD. She saw her parents murdered. Nancy! Come back. Nancy! NANCY!"

Through her tears, Nancy looked up at Rocky. "I went away again, didn't I? The bad man with the knife, I saw him stabbing Mama. Then he was after me."

"That will go away in time. Here, take your Zoloft."

The Legionnaire handed Nancy a can of grape soda. "Little lady, you'll be safe here with me and my pals. Rocky, we'll watch over you two when it starts."

"I'm not bad sick. I want to help."

Johnson made his way through the trench and sat down beside Nancy. Underneath his fatigue jacket he wore a bulletproof vest. He was a muscular man, like the Legionnaire, with short black hair turning gray above his ears. A machete dangled from his web belt. Henry stood up and joined them.

Henry was slender but physically toned. A cheerful youth with blue eyes and tousled brown hair and a tooth missing in front.

"You say you got a fox in there?"

"Yes. His name is Mister Peabody."

"Can we see Mister Peabody?"

Nancy undid the top of her backpack, lifted the fox out, and set him on top of the ditch. Johnson lay his big hand down beside the little animal. Mister Peabody sniffed the black man's hand and started licking it.

Henry was astonished. "That's the dad-dangdest thing I ever seen. A fox lickin' a feller's hand."

"You want to hold him?"

"Golly be, I shore would."

Henry held him against his midsection with both hands while Johnson stroked his head. Mister Peabody made contented *chittering* sounds. Nancy was delighted with her new friends. So was Rocky. He knew these men were professional killers, but he sensed that somehow they were going to play a role in Nancy's life.

In the distance they heard the *wop wop wop* of the gunships returning. As the helicopters passed overhead, they could see bullet holes in the fuselages.

"Them ol' boys been in a fight."

"Yeah. Looks like we're next."

"What about the fox? You better put 'im someplace safe."

"Rocky is going to dig a place in the side of our trench."

Henry handed Mister Peabody back to Nancy, took out a trench knife, and gouged out a place for the backpack. Nancy secured Mister Peabody, and slid her pack inside the hole. It fit perfectly with an inch to spare. Minutes later they heard the booming of artillery.

The first shell landed short. The next round whistled in much closer, making a muffled *crump* sound.

There was a spotter somewhere across the valley. A third salvo landed behind them back where the trucks were parked. Word came down. Hold your fire. Shells began blasting shrapnel all over the hillside.

The bombardment went on for forty minutes. Then stopped.

The barracks had been hit. One building was burning. The mess hall had its entrance blown off.

A number of people were injured, keeping the medics busy. The two camouflaged tanks remained silent.

The Legionnaire was pointing a finger, speaking softly with his comrades and Rocky. "That brick house with the metal roof, see it?"

"Uh-huh."

"Come left about fifty yards then straight back in the tree line. Can you see anything?"

"Is that a tank?"

"That's a Type 99 Chinese main battle tank. It takes a three-man crew, has a 1500-horsepower engine, and a 125 mm gun. I recognized the sloping turret. That's one serious gun platform."

"You think the Chinese have thrown in with the Russians?"

"You got me, but there's another one over to the right behind that hay baler back in the trees. You can see his turret above the bushes. How far is that, Henry?"

Henry looked through his rangefinder "She's about … two thousand and thirty yards."

"Think you could hit that bad man if he sticks his head out again, Mister Henry?" Nancy asked.

"This young lady is a danged warrior."

Rocky laughed. "She's that all right. Nancy has seen and done things most people never dream about.

She's a sweet child, but there's a quality about her that none of us have ever seen in a young person.

Captain talks about it. He thinks she's gifted."

"Well, she done give me a notion." Henry got out his equations booklet and started reading. He picked up the Czech Mauser and made adjustments on his telescopic sight. "Nancy, if that feller pokes his noggin up again, you let me know."

Intermittent harassment fire continued through the night. A sergeant came by at 0300, warning everyone to hold their fire. Dawn arrived. With the morning light came the arrival of enemy columns moving across the open plain. Word swept through the ranks: Wait for Captain. Do not fire until Captain fires. Twenty tanks were leading the enemy formation. Behind the tanks were dozens of armored personnel carriers and mechanized artillery. Behind all of that came a sea of infantry.

Captain was standing beside the Legionnaire. Henry was busy spreading a blanket on the loose earth in front of his position. He had just finished resetting his telescopic sight when Captain climbed down into the trench beside Henry.

"You see that middle tank with the white flag on the radio antenna?"

"Yes, sir."

"That's the commander of their armored column. He's standing out of his hatch. Think you can hit 'im?"

"If'n I hit ol' doodlebug might'n we throw a shindig fer Nancy an' Mister Peabody?"

"You nail that bastard, and I'll buy the beer."

Henry looked up and grinned. "Better start savin' yer pennies, Captain."

Henry rolled over onto his stomach, made one last adjustment, and sighted in on the tank commander.

At eight hundred yards the silencer made a quiet little *thunk*. The tank commander was knocked backward then collapsed into the tank turret.

Captain had forgotten about Henry's silencer. He ran down the back of the trench shouting, "Open fire! Open fire!"

The 105 mm howitzers belched high-explosive rage. Javelins soared into the sky, searching for prey. Machine guns chattered angrily. Hundreds of rifles opened fire, adding to the deafening racket. The tanks fired simultaneously, kicking up huge clouds of dust. Incoming shells raked the defenders. Soldiers were struck and blown to bits. Others fell wounded. Henry was methodically killing one enemy soldier after another while geysers of dirt danced merrily across the battle scene.

Nancy lay in the bottom of the trench with a blanket pulled over her head. Johnson got hit and spun around, falling on top of the little girl.

Johnson looked up and smiled. "Sorry, Nancy."

A bullet had struck him in the shoulder. His bulletproof vest saved him from serious injury but he was bleeding.

"You're hurt. Let me fix it."

Nancy opened their First Aid kit and got out the disinfectant. Johnson opened his vest and Nancy dabbed the damaged flesh with a damp square of white gauze.

"Damn! That stuff burns."

"Don't fret, Mister Johnson. You'll be good as new in a jiffy."

They ducked as another shell landed nearby. Then a shell exploded behind the trench, showering everybody with dirt.

"Get back under your blanket, Nancy."

Another shell crashed down in front, raining down more dirt and gravel.

Henry sang out. "Hit's that dang tank out yonder on the fur end."

Their Javelins were expended, so Frenchie ran down the back of the trench looking for an extra. He found one in between two dead men. Dozens were wounded, some dying, but the living stood their ground. Every gun was now crucial.

The Legionnaire jumped up in front of their position, pointed his weapon in the direction of the Abrams and squeezed the trigger. A missile popped out. The propulsion system ignited and it shot skyward. They watched the trailing fire as it soared across the valley and started down.

There was a flash-bang, and black smoke began pouring through the blown hatch. Something was burning. A forward hatch flew open and a man scrambled out. A second man came out right behind him and started running. A third man was making his exit when the tank exploded, hurling its twenty-seven-ton turret forty feet in the air.

Cries of "Medic" rang out among the shell craters. Cursing and yelling, and tears of sorrow. Ammunition was a growing problem. Dead soldiers lay in the trenches where they had fallen. The thousand-yard stare had arrived. Captain and his lieutenants were in the forward trench discussing what more might be done.

"Thank God she's a political appointee. She must have five thousand dead down there. They should have flanked us or come in the back through the damn trees. The Colonel radioed he'll be here in four hours. Part of his gunships were lost but what's left will be here in about ninety minutes. Get maintenance ready. They'll be running on fumes. Pass the word. Go easy on the ammunition. We've got to make do until the Colonel gets back."

A 125 mm burst nearby, showering more dirt. Six 105s landed in succession, marching up the hillside. Four more 105s came down in the trees. A 155 exploded up on the ridge. One of the tanks fired a grapeshot round, mowing down half a platoon. The Marxists were two hundred yards and closing.

Brothers

Field Marshal Feng was talking on a secure line with his brother General Hu in Djibouti, Africa.

They were discussing a rogue group of Chinese officials General Hu had stumbled upon inside the People's Liberation Army. Type 99 tanks and tons of munitions were secretly being shipped to sea ports at Fort Bragg and San Diego. The confidant Marshal Feng had assigned to investigate the matter had been found murdered in his home. His tongue had been cut out as a warning.

"We must proceed with extreme caution, General Hu. Our Army is as crooked as a dog's hind leg. Corruption is rampant throughout the ranks. We don't know who we can trust. Colonel Ming was a loyal and trusted comrade. These stupid men could get us into a world war with the Western powers."

"I'm surprised they haven't moved against Putin's Russia. Sadly, every country has its share of liberal utopians. You and I are among a growing minority. More of our citizens are seeing the handwriting on the wall. Centralized government is an abomination against its citizens. But what can be done about those fools sending weapons to America?"

"I've given this much consideration. Colonel Ming made several clandestine inquiries before he was murdered. The one place that raised his suspicions was Gwadar, our naval port on the Arabian Sea. The commander there was rude and condescending. He even questioned Ming's patriotism. All Ming asked the man: Was he aware of any unusual military activity?"

"That certainly does raise a red flag. They're probably part of it, but this has to be more involved than just one seaport. Do you know of some way to infiltrate that base? We need proof before we act."

"I've been teaching a group of cadets in Zhanjiang. They're receptive to new ideas. That is gratifying to me personally because of all the brainwashing instilled by Chairman Mao. There is one boy there I will approach."

"Be careful, my brother. We don't want your young cadet being led like a lamb to the slaughter. These men we are dealing with are evil."

"Indeed they are. I have several friends with our Naval Marines in Hong Kong. The commander there thinks as we do. He will be a valuable asset when the time comes. The sacrifice of Colonel Ming may prove to be their poison pawn."

"I shall pray to the Dragon Tortoise and burn incense for our success, and for your continued health, Marshal Feng. Our cause is a just cause. The fate of China hangs in the balance."

"Yes, General Hu. Even if we lose our lives, we will be remembered by our comrades as men of destiny who sought freedom for our countrymen. Remain vigilant, my dear brother."

Alina

Vladimir Putin had just concluded a telephone conversation with his beloved mistress, Alina Kabaeva.

Alina was unhappy. She complained to Vladimir about having to remain in hiding, protected by four bodyguards. Even their phone calls had to be secured from enemy ears. She wasn't allowed to go out in public, to shop at the supermarket, or even to attend the opera with armed escorts. Alina missed the limelight of her past gymnastic career, the adoration of the crowds, and her happier days of visiting with Vladimir in Moscow. Enemies of President Putin sought to kidnap Alina and the children, and perhaps do them harm. She cried over the telephone, making Vladimir feel helpless and miserable.

He missed their two sons and his twin girls. Alina and their children were the only things dear to the most powerful man in Russia.

His sixteen years with the KGB taught him to trust no one inside the political arena, especially the military. Two attempts on his life had been made following the Ukraine War. Those responsible were hunted down and sent to gulags in Siberia where they would be worked to death or freeze from the insidious cold.

Lyudmila Snkrebneva, his divorced wife and their two daughters, were also given protection, but they posed a lesser emotion than Alina and her four youngsters. He felt concern for their safety too, but not to the extent over the woman he loved.

Alina was forty-one and in her sexual prime. Vladimir was seventy-three, her senior by thirty-two years. His days of sexual prowess were gradually fading. This troubled Vladimir, causing him to fret about their age difference. He wanted his beautiful Alina to be happy.

His Marxist counterparts in America were a strange lot. No matter how much he tried to help with armaments and medical supplies, they never stopped complaining. He had just overseen the shipment of four more cargo ships loaded with enough arms and food to equip a hundred thousand men for a month. Yet the complaints and asking for more, always more, never ceased. He was sick of dealing with Adam Schiff and Jerry Nadler. Vladimir was well aware of the privations suffered by the Russian soldiers during the Second World War. Men like Nadler and Schiff wouldn't last a week under such conditions on the Eastern Front. Still, he had to keep the pipeline flowing if communism was going to become the permanent force at the United Nations.

He was busy drafting a request to Nicholas Maduro in Venezuela for more fuel oil. The American Marxists were cut off from the oil fields in the middle of the United States, and needed imports for their land vehicles and aircraft. Putin thought to himself, *What a pack of nincompoops. They should have secured some of those oil fields before the war.* But no, progressives reminded him of foolish children.

A knock came at his chamber door.

"Enter."

"Sir, I have a dispatch from the captain of those ships that just left port."

"Read it."

"'Under attack by unknown surface ships … many dead … on fire and sinking. Bering Sea 58 …' It broke off there, sir."

Putin sat silent for a full minute, thinking. Then he remembered the young soldier standing before his ironwood desk.

"There was nothing more? No coordinates given?"

"No, sir. The machine stopped printing after the number 58."

"Send out a squadron of float planes. I don't think they will find anything, but we must try."

"Yes, sir. Very good, sir."

The young soldier left the room and closed the door. *Who can it be,* Vladimir wondered? *This is impossible! Another thorn in my side! The Brits, the French, it could be any one of a dozen countries.*

This will create shortages in the States. Schiff and Nadler will be on the rag. Well, fuck those sob sisters!

Souls Freighting Starward

Boss was unconscious, lying on his back on a loose pile of dirt dug up by the backhoe. He opened his eyes. Long Tom was placing a bandage on his forehead.

"What happened?"

"Air burst. A chunk hit your helmet. You're damn lucky. Your helmet's stove in like it was hit by a sledgehammer. You scared the daylights outta me."

"Does this mean I lost my cherry?"

Long Tom burst out laughing. "And then some! Come on. We gotta go up the hill a ways."

They ran through the smoke and shell craters until they came to a mortar pit. One man was manning the weapon by himself. His gun mate lay dead in the bottom of the dugout. Enemy shells were bursting all around.

"You need a hand, mister?"

"I'd be much obliged. Say, what happened to you?"

"My helmet got hit by shrapnel. Tom here fixed me up. Ever body calls me Boss. What's your name?"

"My name is Sergeant Loveday. My buddy there is Corporal Norris. He was a good soldier."

Tom lifted the limp body out of the dugout so there would be enough room. He was young, nineteen maybe, with a bullet hole above his right ear. Boss said a quick prayer, and they began stacking the four-pound projectiles scattered around the dugout floor.

"You ain't got but eleven. That ain't gonna last long. I'll run over to armory and see if they got any more." Tom took off.

A 105 mm shell came whistling down, striking the base plate of the mortar, blasting Boss and Sergeant Loveday into eternity. Tom turned and ran back. He sat down in the bottom of the pit, holding the bloody hand of his dead friend, and wept brokenly.

The air grew thick with shot and shell. Another attack was forming up down below.

Deliverance

Colonel Mosrie stopped his convoy a mile from the battlefield and began unloading his machines of war.

A low ridge up ahead shielded him and his army from view. General Finch and her Marxist soldiers were completely unaware of his presence. True to form, she had neglected to post sentries on her outer flanks. Mosrie instructed his men to fan out and attack.

When they burst out of the trees into the rear echelon of the Marxists, panic spread like wildfire.

Dolores Finch was caught between the advancing Capitalists and her own terrified soldiers. A hundred men fell with the first volley.

Mosrie's soldiers smashed into the ranks of the Marxists, scattering them like tenpins. Another hundred went down. Those able-bodied souls remaining on the hillside rose up and attacked. Finch was desperately seeking a way out, any avenue of escape. Her staff car had taken a shell in the transmission. Dolores Finch was on foot.

Facedown in a shallow depression, covered with dirt and sweat, she cursed her rotten luck. She had almost destroyed Mosrie's base of operations, only to be denied success at the last damn minute.

What irony, she thought. *I had that son-of-a-bitch in my grasp. Now I'm hiding in a filthy ditch while my men are being shot to hell.* A dead man lying beside her had a Russian tommy gun. She took the weapon and crawled to the end of her hiding place. A Jeep came bouncing her way. She rose up and killed the driver. Once she was behind the wheel, she drove for the open highway. A 155 mm exploded behind the Jeep, flipping the vehicle end over end. It crashed upside down, breaking her left arm. She crawled out and ran. She ran until she was exhausted. Dolores fell to her knees in a patch of brown grass.

Behind her the fighting rages on. Men are blown to pieces by artillery shells. Others are run down and crushed beneath the tracks of tanks and armored personnel carriers. Small arms fire plows the bloody landscape.

The pain in her arm became excruciating. Exhausted, she contemplated capture. Capture was unthinkable. Would they give her truth serum, forcing out secrets and confessions? Would she be tortured with electricity or stripped naked and whipped?

Rape? The thought of men thrusting into her body made her convulse. She vomited. Then she cried. She had been beaten again by Colonel Mosrie.

Her dreams in ruins, her command in tatters, Dolores vows she will not be taken alive. Better to end it now than suffer like this any longer. Removing a Beretta from a holster on her web belt, she cocks the pistol. Slowly, with a trembling right hand, she raises the weapon toward her open mouth.

An escaping truck driver spotted her kneeling on the ground and stopped. "General! What the hell? Are you alright?"

"No. I'm not alright—and you are a blessing I don't deserve. Let's get the hell out of here."

The burly truck driver helped her into his cab and they sped away toward Interstate 65.

Rainbow Bridge

Colonel Mosrie and Captain were walking the compound grounds with Rocky and Nancy. Damage was extensive, but some areas hidden behind the trees had escaped destruction. They stopped while Nancy adjusted Rocky's arm sling. A piece of shrapnel the size of a dime had been removed from his shoulder.

"It looks worse than it is, sir. They missed the fuel depot and the armory. It's just about empty anyway but more stuff is on the way. What concerns me the most are the wounded, three hundred forty-nine. Thank God you got here when you did. Another hour or two and we were dead ducks.

"Well, two hundred and seventy-two dead ain't nothin' to write home about."

"They fought gallantly, Colonel. I was in the trenches with them. I saw men shot time and again, but they fought on until they collapsed or just died. It humbles me to talk about it."

"We were taking names and kicking asses when you called. I disengaged as fast as we could. The men managed to recover most of our dead. Some just weren't retrievable. Are most of our wounded over in Nashville?"

"Yes, sir. The hospitals sent twenty-four ambulances. We took the rest in trucks. Those with minor injuries stayed here. Our doctors and nurses are looking after them."

"There's a big difference between men fighting for their country and men fighting for some goofy religion or another lost cause. The North Vietnamese were like that. They fought on against impossible odds, against China, against France, and finally against us. They died by the millions but they never quit. George Washington is another example. He lost damn near every battle, but he hung in there against the mighty British Empire and won our independence.

"All those crackpot ideas the Left believes in became like a religion. Most don't believe in God, so big brother and climate change swallowed their asses whole. Common sense was thrown out the damn door and they regressed into hive think. Hell, I believe honey bees are smarter than the average liberal."

Nancy asked Rocky a question. "Do all those dead people go where the little rabbit lives?"

"I believe so. But there's another place where pets go that's called Rainbow Bridge. Mister Peabody might go there when his time comes."

"I don't want Mister Peabody going anywhere without me."

"Foxes have relatively short lives, Nancy. So, when he dies, it's off to Rainbow Bridge. The story goes that when pets go there they become young again, with no pain or broken bones, and they're very happy, and they play together. And there's lots of good things to eat. Then, when you die, you'll go there to find Mister Peabody and the two of you will go on up to Heaven together."

"Are you making this up?"

"Well, I did read it someplace a long time ago."

"It's a pretty story, but I want Mister Peabody to go to Heaven and wait there for me with my mama and daddy. And you'll be there and Captain and all of our friends, and Colonel Mosrie too."

"I'm glad you included me, Nancy. I don't wanna get stuck in that other place."

"Frenchie says Hell is right here on earth."

"Who is this Frenchie person?"

Rocky replied, "He's a former member of the French Foreign Legion. We met him in our trench. He had two sidekicks with him straight out of a Hemingway novel. The young one is a sniper. The black man carries a machete. Bad *hombres* but super patriots."

"I want to meet them an' right away. I need replacements for the troops we lost."

"I know the Legionnaire and those other two, Henry and Johnson," Captain said. "I'll vouch for all three. The Frenchman is a hardcore professional with street smarts."

Later that afternoon Rocky and Nancy were able to locate the trio. They brought them back to the mess hall which was serving peach pie and coffee. Captain and the Colonel were over by the windows, enjoying their dessert. Colonel Mosrie laid out what he had in mind to the Frenchman. Then Henry and Johnson huddled with Frenchie at the next table, discussing the proposition.

Frenchie returned and addressed his superior. "Sir, I'm very flattered … we're all flattered … but we have to decline your offer. We're a team and that's just how it is. These men are my brothers. If we go into battle, we go together. If we get waxed, that's the breaks. I don't want a platoon or a promotion and they don't either."

Mosrie studied the Frenchman for several moments without saying a word. Then he whispered in Captain's ear. His second in command smiled and nodded in agreement.

"I know quality when I see it. I can tell by a man's eyes. Captain tells me you're one of a kind. So, I'll tell you what. I'll put you in charge of training our troops and your two friends can be your subordinates. Teach the soldiers the things you learned in Africa. Make my army a force to be feared. Train 'em like your Legionnaires."

"I'll have to ask, sir."

A new discussion ensued at the next table that lasted two minutes. The Legionnaire returned a second time to address Captain and the Colonel.

"They like your idea, sir. I consider it an honor. But they have a couple of requests. Johnson wants a 12-gauge shotgun. And Henry wants a few days off to go see his Sweet Thang."

Captain and the Colonel burst out laughing.

"Tell Henry to have his girlfriend move here. I don't want him getting waylaid on the highway. I'll find his lady a nice bungalow. Tell Johnson I'll get him a 12-gauge pump over in Nashville."

So began the training. Some took to their classes like ducks to water. Physical training was more demanding. The rifle range delivered a number of black eyes from the recoil with their thumbs resting on the receivers. Communication using code, map-reading, battle tactics, mortars, machine guns, night maneuvers, tanks and artillery, mines and booby traps. It was hard beyond anything they had experienced before. Everyone got their share of blisters and calluses. A few bones were broken. The more they bitched and bellyached, the harder Henry and Johnson drove them. Frenchie was relentless.

The women loathed crawling under barbed wire through mud puddles. Six-mile marches with full field packs were murder. Some collapsed. Others fell out along the trail. After mess hall they fell asleep the minute their heads touched the pillow.

Four weeks passed. The bitching slacked off and things began to take shape. Some of the women could outperform the men. That made for friendly competition. Frenchie trained them to work in teams of five and ten and platoon strength. They didn't know it then, but they were becoming just as good as the Marine Corps or the Special Forces.

Anastasia

Following the battle, Long Tom had gathered up several rifles and two cases of ammunition to take back to the farm. Captain had given Tom permission to take the weapons. Boss was given a proper send-off in the camp cemetery. Colonel Mosrie and Captain thanked Tom for the warning. In parting, they gave him blankets and pillows for his friends on the farm.

The glaucoma eye drops he got at the camp dispensary helped, but he stopped every seventy miles or so to rest his eyes. With two hundred miles to go, he decided to spend the night in an open field beside a dilapidated barn. He was almost asleep when he heard someone open the barn door. Creeping around to the front with a loaded M-16, he peered through the cracks. A pretty young girl was sitting on the earth floor in the middle of the open space, crying.

Tom eased open the door. "Ma'am, is there something I can do to help?"

The girl screamed and fled to the rear of the structure. There was no backdoor. She screamed again.

"Lady, I'm not going to hurt you. Tell me what's wrong."

She collapsed into a miserable pile of arms and legs and long brown hair, sobbing uncontrollably.

Tom approached within ten feet and sat down on the dirt, facing her. "Tell me what I can do to help you. Would you like something to drink?"

Between sobs and tears, she blurted out, "Wa … Wa … Water."

Tom went out to the truck and brought back a cold bottle of spring water. She turned it up and drank the whole thing. It was then he noticed the bruises on her face and arms.

"Who did this to you?"

"Those men."

"What men? Where are they?"

Just then he heard laughter. Tom stepped back into the shadows with the rifle. The door swung open and in walked three less than average-looking male specimens.

"Time fer another round, honeypot. We ain't done with you jus yet."

Tom recognized the enemy uniforms. The men were drunk. They started for the girl.

Long Tom stepped out of the shadows. "I wouldn't do that if I were you."

"Who the fuck are you?"

"I'm the Angel of Death. I've come to harvest your souls."

"Sic 'im, boys."

All three began fumbling for their revolvers. Tom pressed the trigger. Three Marxist rapists tumbled ass end over teakettle, straight into oblivion. Tom took their weapons and boots.

"God, mister, you really are the Angel of Death. You saved me. You saved my life."

Tom brushed her hair out of her eyes to get a better look at his damsel in distress. She was about twenty-two, very pretty, with a battered and bloody face.

"Come out to the truck and I'll clean you up some. You can sleep in the cab. I'll bunk in the truck bed."

Tom was asleep when he felt the girl snuggling in beside him.

"I'm cold. Do you mind?"

"Not at all."

He pulled the blanket over the two of them and she fell asleep almost immediately. Tom gazed up into a star-studded sky, thinking about Boss and how he might interpret this encounter. Boss would take the girl back to the farm for her protection. Out here by herself she wouldn't last long. He smiled at the way she wolfed down the sandwich he gave her. Those men had raped her and never given her anything to drink or eat. He drifted away, thinking about Boss and how much he missed his friend.

Tom opened his eyes. It was morning.

She was beside the truck, holding a bouquet of daisies. "I picked these for you, Mister Angel of Death. There's a creek behind that old house. Can we go down there so I can take a bath?"

"Sure thing. Hop in and I'll drive you."

"You're an unusual person, Mister Angel of Death. I never met anyone like you before."

"Maybe you weren't looking hard enough."

She smiled and kissed him on the cheek. Then she ran down to the creek and stripped off her clothing.

Tom saw the bruises on her back and legs where they had beaten her. They probably would have killed the pretty young thing. Fifteen minutes later she was back, still damp and all smiles.

"I could fall for a man like you."

"Young lady, I'm old enough to be your father."

"That doesn't matter. I've dreamed about a man like you all my life. I didn't know they existed. Then you walked into that barn and found me ... and saved me!"

"You're funny. Maybe we can be friends."

"I want more than friendship. I want to be your woman."

"You're rushing things, aren't you? I could be an escaped convict or some kinda crazy ..."

She grabbed Tom and kissed him.

"Now hold on a minute. We need time to get to know one another."

She kissed him again. Tom pushed her away.

"I don't even know your name. Now cut the sex act and behave yourself. What's your name? What are you doing out here?"

"My name is Anastasia Sofia Romanov. I am Russian. Anastasia was my great-great-grandmother. She survived the 1918 murders. My adoptive mother and father are communists. I hate communism. They're friends with that awful woman in Alabama. Mama and Poppa came up here to observe the fighting.

That's when I slipped away to go over to the American side, but I got lost and those dreadful men caught me. Then the Angel of Death swooped down and rescued me." She giggled, touching his cheek softly with her fingertips.

"You're the great-great-granddaughter … Good Lord! You are something special. My name is Thomas Toulouse Oriel. My friends call me Long Tom. I was with Special Forces for eight years in Africa and the Middle East. Now I live on a farm two hundred miles south of here. You'll be safe there."

"Thomas, I want with all my heart to be your woman. I'll cook and clean for you. You can have me any time you want me. I want to take care of you."

"I'm a commoner and you're a royal bloodline. How do you think that would work out?"

"Nobody would ever know but you and me and Mama and Poppa. I'll let them know I'm safe and all, but I will never tell them where I am. They would send the secret police to take me back to Russia. I hate it there."

"Anastasia, take your time. Find your footing. Expand your horizons. America is at war with itself. If the Marxists win, this place could become as bad as Russia."

"As long as I'm with you, my star will shine in the heavens. You are my soulmate."

"You're a hopeless romantic, young lady. Are all Russian women like you?"

"No, many are bitter and sad because of our evil government. The Russian people are gay and carefree, but always the communists take away their happiness. People disappear and you never see them again. Communism is a big lie. You must obey or they will come for you or your family."

"I'm glad you got away from all that."

"You are my champion, Thomas. You are brave and kind and a

gentleman. But there's something about you I've never seen before. You're a different breed."

"You shared a great secret with me. Some people would pay a fortune to get their hands on you. So, I guess maybe I should share my secret with you. You should know this about me. When I was in Saudi Arabia, the women there were treated like possessions, like cattle or donkeys. I worked with an Arab captain in charge of the local prison. He was a cruel man who tormented his prisoners. Foreigners were not allowed to get involved with local matters.

"One morning at the village well, I saw him beating his wife with a riding crop. He whipped her until she fell down. That didn't stop him. He kept on beating the poor woman. I heard later that she died. I swore then I would get him someday. So, one night I slipped into town and killed the sorry bastard. Then I stuck that riding crop down his throat."

"You are an avenging angel like Michael the Archangel in the bible. The judge and executioner of sorry bastards. That's just one of the reasons I care about you so much."

"Ya know, Anastasia, I like you too. You sure are a lotta woman. "

"Now we're getting someplace!"

Chickens Coming Home to Roost

Dolores Finch was in her usual "It's not my fault" mindset. Gazing into the crystal ball of life at her recent misfortune was not her forte. She did not believe the defeat in Franklin had anything to do with her. The men were well armed, given adequate transportation, but they failed. Her broken arm had been set and she wore a black sling. *How could I lose so many troops and not overrun that damned dug in hillside? Why does this shit happen to me?*

She summoned her five surviving captains, and the truck driver who saved her life, into her office for some Q and A. She addressed the truck driver first. "When we were in the truck, you mentioned that you served once before. Where were you stationed?"

"Afghanistan. I was there three and a half years with the U.S. Army."

"I have a personal question to ask. You may be frank and speak your mind. Did my men do anything wrong in Franklin? Was something not right about the battle plan?"

"Best I can tell, General, we walked into a killing ground. Their guns were registered and they shot our asses off. My whole squad was wiped out. That's when I jumped in the truck and found you."

"What could we have done differently?"

"I ain't that smart, sir. You better ask the brass over there."

She nodded toward Snyder, the eldest of the five. "Can you clarify what happened out there, Captain Snyder?"

"Yes, ma'am, I can … but you won't like it."

"Go on, tell us."

"Major Lowery met with us before we shoved off for Franklin. He told us a frontal assault on that position would be suicide. We should try and flank the enemy, maybe come in behind them. He told us that he warned you about the danger, but you ordered a frontal attack to conserve fuel. Now the major is dead and so are a lot of our people."

General Finch sat still for several moments, stunned. What a horrible thing to say. Snyder was insinuating that she was at fault. The audacity of the man. The sheer balls-out audacity!

Controlling her temper, she asked Captain McCollum, standing next to Captain Snyder, "Did you hear Major Lowery say that?"

"He said it, ma'am. We tried to flank, but by then the road ahead was blocked with burning tanks and personnel carriers. The ground was marshy where we were, so we were stuck on the road. We were backing out to go around when the main enemy force showed up. I'm one of the lucky ones that got out."

She called on Captain Higgins. "What was your experience in the fight, Captain?"

"I was with one of our self-propelled 155s, General. We got about halfway across that open plain when the whole hillside opened up. I remember counting our rounds. We got off four shots before something blew off our right track. Then all hell broke loose. I could hear the small arms fire peppering our armor when the lights went out. When I came to, we were over on our side. Our driver was on top of me. He was dead. I crawled out an open hatch and ran."

Delores pondered more discussion then decided against it. "Thank you for your cooperation, gentlemen. That will be all for today. You may return to your duty stations."

The door closed. Her arm hurt. It was time for another pill. She was angry with Snyder about what he said. But deep down inside she felt pangs of uncertainty. This job was not what she had been promised.

Nancy Pelosi and that herd of Capitol Hill sycophants told her all she had to do was issue a few orders now and then. And blame any mistakes on underlings. Typical fare for political appointees, they said. But counting the losses in Kentucky and now in Tennessee, she was being blamed for thousands of dead men.

Dolores reached down into a drawer and brought out a bottle of Bulleit bourbon. She poured herself a stiff one and drank it down in two swallows. Her job at the White House had been fun and easy. This job was a pain in the ass.

"FUCK!" she screamed, hurling her glass across the room, shattering it against the far wall. "What I need is another Georgy Zhukov."

Johnny Poe

"Did you enjoy your tomato pudding, Master Poe?"

"Very much, Great One. It was delicious. The best I ever ate."

"You flatter my humble kitchen. My mother made this for us kids. Would you like some more? The wok has plenty. You need to put some meat on those bones."

"If I asked for another serving, it might appear I am an ungracious guest. But it is so good. Yes, please. May I have another helping?"

Field Marshal Feng chuckled to himself as he ladled out another serving for his guest of honor. The young cadet worshiped the old Field Marshal. Everyone in school knew about his exploits.

In 1950, he led a force of Chinese against the Americans at the Battle of Unsan in North Korea where the American soldiers were soundly defeated by the Chinese and North Korean troops. Marshal Feng was part of the uprising in 1967 against Mao's Cultural Revolution and his Red Guards. Thousands of Chinese citizens were tortured and murdered by the Red Guards. Feng was involved in 1969 with the Sino-Soviet border conflict near the Zhenbao Island on the Ussuri River. He was shot in the back by a Russian fanatic while negotiating a truce.

In 1973, the Field Marshal assisted Henry Kissinger with the Paris Peace Accords which helped end the Vietnam War.

In 1984, he was arrested and sentenced to hard labor by a corrupt and jealous politician. A month later the politician met with a mysterious death. Feng was released amid much bowing and words of apology.

Field Marshal Feng is 92 years old and has many powerful friends and associates. And dozens of political enemies.

"Your teachers tell me you are most proficient in History and Warfare. Tell me, Master Poe, what is your assessment regarding the Peking attack against the United States and the American response?"

"Great One, you have accomplished so much, and I have only my school books. My knowledge is a small thing compared with your global insight."

"Knowledge is the key to winning battles. Know your enemy and you will find his weakness. Master your emotions and the facts will reveal themselves."

"Then I will share with you what my schoolmates say and I, too, believe. May I speak candidly, sir?"

"Speak as if I am an old man thirsting for knowledge. Look upon me as your trusted friend."

"Xi Jinping was drunk with power. He and his followers ventured beyond their sphere of understanding. They rolled the dice in an atmosphere of arrogance and greed. When Japan bombed Pearl Harbor in 1941, it turned a peaceful nation into the world's mightiest war machine. It is small wonder the powerful Americans did not destroy China after what we did to New York City."

"Spoken like a true sage. There is a problem inside our country that I and a few others are working to resolve. Being in the top five percent of your class, you will have your choice of assignments after graduation. One of those assignments is Gunboat Training at our naval port in Djibouti on the Gulf of Aden. Would you consent to working with me on a secret mission?

"This assignment is fraught with danger. If found out, you would be killed. If you are not so inclined, that will not detract from my affection for you. You are a fine young man, Master Poe. I would not ask you to go into harm's way if our country were not in jeopardy. Go home and think this over. Then you can give me your answer in a day or two.

"Now would you like a glass of Dragon's Tooth wine? It is an inexpensive little wine but it soothes the palate."

"Great One, I am honored to tears by your faith in me. Excuse, please, while I dab my eyes. I will do whatever you ask."

For the next two hours the Field Marshal explained everything he knew about the weapons and supplies being shipped to the Marxists in the United States. He told Johnny Poe of the understanding between their countries that China would stand down with no further interference in American affairs. He and several others had given their word to Donald Trump and his generals at the Pentagon. Marshal Feng explained that a breach of their promise could lead to war. He went on to inform Master Poe how he might infiltrate the smuggling ring.

Johnny Poe took written notes, memorized them, then burned the papers. Three weeks later he was onboard a Type 055 Renhai-class cruiser with his own private stateroom.

Nobody suspected Poe was connected with the Field Marshal. He was seen as an up-and-coming cadet from the Naval Academy. Thus began his education on navigation, battle tactics, radar, missiles and gunnery, fire control, and a hundred other things a Chinese sea captain must know.

Great Britain

Commander Fitzsimmons was in communication with his Prime Minister at 10 Downing Street. The topic under discussion was a top secret naval operation just concluded.

"We got within fifteen thousand yards without being detected. I elected then to engage. Our missiles reached their targets in less than a minute. Two lead ships blew up. The third and fourth ships caught fire and went down in about two minutes. I felt sorry for those Russian sailors. They did get off a partial SOS but sank before he could give his location. We turned tail and headed for base."

"You did well, Commander. We can't afford for those damned Bolsheviks to take over the United States. That would be the end of us and all of Western Europe. You may have to do this again in a week or two. Are your men capable of keeping this under their hat? We don't want a war with Russia."

"They understand that if the United States goes down it's only a matter of time until it's our turn. They know to keep a cork in it, sir. They know the fate of our country is at stake."

"I rely on you, Commander. I recall Sir Winston speaking about the New World coming to the rescue of the Old World during the Blitz. It's our job now to repay that debt."

"I expect next time they'll have a naval escort. How do you propose we deal with that, sir?"

"We may need a tight-lipped submarine skipper. See if you can round one up."

"I can think of a couple, sir. Give me a day or two. I'll be in touch."

"Thank you, Commander. Good luck."

"Thank you, sir. God bless you and God bless England."

God and Jesus

Nancy was hosting a tea party with her dolls in the backyard of the house where she and Rocky and Captain lived. The owner of the property was killed in the big battle two weeks ago. The dolls are discussing God and Jesus. Matilda is the grandmother doll. Moxie is the daughter and Missy is her little-girl doll. Nancy uses her deep voice for Matilda and her baby voice for Missy. She uses her normal voice for Moxie.

Missy: "I don't think God loves us anymore."

Matilda: "You shouldn't say things like that. Captain says it's naughty."

Missy: "I don't care. God should do something about all this killing and stuff."

Moxie: "Missy, you stop that right now, and be nice to your grandmother. She loves you and cooks for you and does the laundry."

Missy: "I'm sorry, Grammie. But I want somebody to do something. Dead people stink."

Matilda: "They're doing all they can, baby girl. Those big machines are down there right now burying the bodies. They came over from Nashville. Wasn't that nice?"

Missy: "I guess so. Why can't Jesus make it stop?"

Moxie: "Jesus is busy looking after the poor people. He doesn't have time to fool around with dead ones."

Missy: "Well, it's not right."

Matilda: "Don't blaspheme the Lord. You'll die and go to Hell."

Missy: "No I won't. I'll go to Rainbow Bridge and the little rabbit will be there."

Matilda: "Someday, we'll all go to Rainbow Bridge and the little kitties and doggies will be there too."

Missy: "I want to go now, so I can pet them."

Moxie: "You have to be dead to go there. It's not your turn yet."

Missy: "Will I stink when I'm dead?"

Matilda: "No, baby girl. You'll smell like a pretty little flower and Jesus will love you."

A Jeep pulls up in the driveway. Captain has come to fetch Nancy. She puts her dolls away in a cardboard container she keeps in her bedroom. Nancy climbs into the Jeep with Captain.

"Where's Rocky?"

"He's at the Vanderbilt Stadium in Nashville helping set up the sound equipment. The Colonel is going to give a talk on how we got into this mess and how we might get out of it. Rocky asked me to come pick you up. This will be an education for both of us."

History Lesson

They drove the twenty-four miles and parked in a lot marked STAFF ONLY. A long line of people wound through Security. No weapons were allowed inside and no alcohol. One man started an argument. Nancy recognized the Legionnaire. He was with Security. The Frenchman relieved the man of his pistol then allowed the man inside.

"Hi, Frenchie. It's me, Nancy."

"Hey, you! Come on over. You and Captain can go in here."

Once inside they were amazed at the thousands of people. Military personnel were there, Grand Ole Opry entertainers, police and firemen, doctors and nurses, and thousands more from Nashville and surrounding counties. Senators Marsha Blackburn and Bill Hagerty were seated on a front row, two of Tennessee's best-ever politicians sent to Washington. A few minutes later the stadium was packed, with hundreds more waiting outside. It was decided to let those people in to sit on the football field.

A hush fell over the stadium when Colonel Mosrie stepped up to the microphone.

"Good afternoon, ladies and gentlemen, and honored guests. I invited you here today to give you a rundown on events in Franklin and Illinois, and the progress we've made. We had a setback two weeks ago over in Franklin, so I'll give you the bad news first. That battle was a close one. We lost two hundred and seventy-two killed and three hundred and forty-nine wounded. Parents and loved ones have been notified. The enemy from Georgia and Alabama surprised us. They attacked right after we left for Chicago. I should have anticipated something of that nature, so I blame myself for our losses. Chicago was my decision. We did fairly well up there before pulling out to come back. But you can be proud of the men and women who defended our Franklin base. They held off an army almost twenty times their size for six hours. They fought like tigers. I can't say enough about those magnificent men and women.

"When we got word that Franklin was under attack, we loaded our dead and wounded and headed home. When we got here, we came in behind the enemy on his left flank. Their commander is not very experienced, so we caught them flat-footed and they panicked. We lost thirty-four soldiers in that skirmish. Our losses in Illinois were five hundred and twelve. All together our dead total seven hundred and eighty-four. Enemy losses are estimated at ten thousand, eighty-five hundred of which took place right here in Franklin.

"War is a filthy business. You always lose friends and loved ones. But this war is different from past wars with the exception of our American Revolution. We're fighting for our way of life and our freedom. Any loss is for the sacred preservation of our Constitution and our United States.

"I'm going to give you a brief history on how socialism got started in America and the presidents in office during those time periods. I'll start with Franklin Delano Roosevelt. President Roosevelt was a great man in many respects and not so great in other ways. He held the country together with determination and his fireside chats when unemployment reached twenty-five percent during the Great Depression. It was even worse in some parts of the country. Folks were losing their homes and farms left and right. It was a time of terrible suffering and loss. To his credit he allowed his generals to run the war. Hitler did the exact opposite and lost crucial battles he should have won. But FDR kept the blacks and whites segregated in the military because the Democrats demanded it. And he tried to expand the Supreme Court to fifteen to float his New Deal. That failed, but he did initiate a number of socialist programs, including the expansion of labor unions and the size of our Federal Government. The country was financially on the ropes, so I believe he did a good job, considering. Yalta was a terrible mistake, but the man was dying, so I can't hold that against him. He passed away during the Okinawa campaign. The Roosevelt years were when socialism took root in America.

"Harry Truman dropped two atomic bombs on Japan. That has been a topic of controversy ever since. I believe he was justified. It saved a million allied dead and wounded, and as many as ten million Japanese lives. Many of the Japanese soldiers were trained fanatics who committed untold atrocities across China and throughout the Pacific Theater. Germany and Japan both surrendered in 1945.

"In 1950, North Korea attacked South Korea and our guys stationed there were getting their tails kicked. Truman sent in General MacArthur. MacArthur is not one of my favorite generals, but he did request permission to use the atomic bomb on Chinese military targets. Truman refused, fearing war with China. The general was eventually fired for insubordination. I suspect we should have used the bomb. It might have changed the course of history. In 1953, the Korean War ended in stalemate. However, General MacArthur did an excellent job getting Japan back on her feet.

"The Eisenhower years ushered in an era of peace and prosperity. Dealing with Congress, Ike soon realized, he was dealing with self-serving politicians, so he said to hell with it and spent his spare time on the golf course. He was more of a diplomat than a general. He sponsored the Interstate Highway System. And Ike balanced the budget three times.

"John F. Kennedy had the potential to become a great president. It's believed our CIA was involved in his assassination. Kennedy blew it big time at the Bay of Pigs, but he stood toe to toe with Nikita Khrushchev for thirteen days during the Cuban Missile Crisis when the world stood on the brink of nuclear war. Khrushchev finally backed down and the crisis ended.

"JFK wanted to pull our troops out of Vietnam. But certain powers in Washington had other plans. The Warren Commission lied about the investigation, so we may never know who actually pulled the trigger. Then Bobby Kennedy was murdered, followed by Martin Luther King Jr. Riots swept the nation over Martin Luther King's death. His passing was a tragedy. Hundreds were killed and entire city blocks were burned to the ground.

"During those turbulent years, socialism was spreading its tentacles throughout our Capitol Hill bureaucracy and the mainstream media.

"Lyndon Baines Johnson made a terrible president. He lied about the Gulf of Tonkin torpedo boat attacks and he lied repeatedly about the Vietnam War. It's believed Johnson never intended to win the Vietnam War. He saw Vietnam as a big chess game between himself and Ho Chi Minh. He believed Ho would come to the bargaining table someday, but LBJ was dealing with an individual who viewed history in the long term, plus Ho had the American press on his side.

"LBJ's Great Society was a failure, but he did manage to get his Civil Rights Act passed in 1964 with help from Senator Dirksen and the Senate Republicans. Forty percent of the Senate Democrats voted against the Civil Rights Act. During this period, Democratic meddling destroyed the nuclear structure of the black family and lost the Vietnam War. That's why so many African American youngsters today have no father.

"Meanwhile, the major media took permanent roost with the Democrats against anything Republican.

"Richard Milhous Nixon was our most beloved president. He believed in America. Nixon ended the Vietnam War and he recognized Red China as a world power. He fought against racism and Nixon established the Environmental Protection Agency. He was familiar with all the corruption in Washington and he intended to do something about it. The Democrats were having none of that. They already hated Nixon for exposing their Alger Hiss as a communist. So, they set up Nixon over Watergate.

"Four of the five plumbers were CIA operatives. One of the reporters on the Watergate story was not an actual reporter. He was brought in from the Navy to do a hatchet job on the president. Deep Throat was a member of the FBI. They impeached Nixon and destroyed his presidency. The Washington Swamp was learning to flex its political muscle.

"Gerald Ford became our thirty-eighth president following Nixon's resignation. President Ford tried to save South Vietnam from the Hanoi communists, but a Democrat-controlled Congress refused to release our B-52 bombers when the invasion began and South Vietnam went down to defeat in 1975.

"Jimmy Carter was a presidential disaster. He claimed to be a Christian while making friends with American enemies around the world. His naivety and political ignorance led to the overthrow of the Shah of Iran in January 1979. That February, a fanatical Muslim cleric took control of Iran.

"Ayatollah Khomeini initiated torture and murder on millions of Iranians. November 1979, Iranian students seized the American Embassy and held it hostage four hundred and forty-four days. In December 1979, the Soviet Union, viewing Carter as weak, invaded Afghanistan which lasted nine bloody years. November 1980, war broke out between Iran and Saddam Hussein's Iraq. When Carter finally agreed to a rescue attempt for our embassy hostages, that too ended in failure and death. Carter's liberal policies and crippling regulations led to record inflation, high unemployment, and a severe gasoline shortage.

"Ronald Reagan made an outstanding president. He reversed Jimmy Carter's failed policies and brought stability back to America. He ended the hostage crisis and gave the world renewed hope. With the aid of Margaret Thatcher he drove the Soviet Union into bankruptcy with Star Wars. The Berlin Wall came down in 1989 and the Soviet Union collapsed in 1991. Ronald Reagan had a hand in all of this. Reaganomics worked but the Democrats lied, insisting it didn't. Democrats and the liberal media hated Ronald Reagan, but the public loved him.

"Let's take a thirty-minute break, everybody. The ushers will tell you where the restrooms are located. We have hot dogs and soft drinks at the concession stands. I'll see you back here in half an hour."

Rocky turned to Nancy and asked a question. "What did you learn from the Colonel's speech?"

"Some Republicans were good and some Democrats were bad."

"That's right. We discovered that pattern when we were at the library helping the Colonel research his speech. The library lady knew where all the presidents were located. She made it easy for us."

"I wish we still had the Internet. I'm too young to drive and I don't even know where the library is."

"There's a small one over in Franklin. I could drive you. If you have to use the bathroom, go now. I'll get us a hot dog. What do you want to drink?"

"I'd like a Pepsi, please." Fifteen minutes later they were back in their seats enjoying their soft drinks and hot dogs. The Colonel mounted the stage and held up a hand for quiet.

"Those hot dogs were good. I had one myself. We have the kitchen staff here at the University to thank for the food and beverages. Let's give 'em a big hand of appreciation."

When the applause ended, Colonel Mosrie continued with his address.

"I'm going to skip over most of Bush One and Bush Two and the Clintons. A lot of important events took place during those years, but discussing them at length would prove redundant.

"In 1991, Bush One initiated the Persian Gulf War against Saddam Hussein which the Coalition quickly won. But Coalition Director Paul Bremer undermined our victory by disbanding the Iraqi Army against sound military advice. His stupidity and arrogance turned three hundred and seventy-five thousand armed and unemployed Iraqi soldiers against the occupying American armies.

"Bush Two was president during the Housing Crash and 9/11, both of which were caused by the Democrats. The Housing collapse resulted in 2008 after the Democrats forced our Banking Industry into subprime mortgage lending, and 9/11 happened in part because the Democratic majority in Congress refused to allow the sharing of information between our Intelligence agencies.

"Bill Clinton did a pretty decent job as president. He cut deficit spending and raised taxes on the wealthy. But Hillary Clinton was a corrupt lawyer all the way back to the Nixon Hearings. President Clinton reduced our Armed Forces by a third and he gave the Russians our submarine technology for silent running. Clinton is credited with balancing the budget but that was actually his Republican Congress.

"Barack Hussein Obama was the Manchurian Candidate. He was

raised a Muslim, hated Great Britain and France as colonial powers, and viewed the United States as much the same thing. George Soros and four of his billionaire colleagues gained financial control over the Democratic Party in 2004. Their influence and money secured the oval office for Barack Obama in 2009. Obama and his White House progressives resurrected racism. He turned citizens against the police and he turned us against one another. His rules of engagement in the Middle East got American servicemen killed. He hated fossil fuels and restricted oil and gas well drilling. His GNP never rose above 1.6% and his Affordable Care Act was not affordable. His 2011 withdrawal from Iraq, against the advice of his generals, resulted in chaos and death. President Obama never took seriously the rise of ISIS and al-Qaeda which were his fault. Unemployment was 7.8% his first term but that improved during his second term.

"Another foreign policy debacle was his Iranian Nuclear Deal. Tennessee Senator Bob Corker ushered that monstrosity through the Senate to the horror of Israel and the Middle East. Michelle and Barak Obama were corrupt Washington elites who looked down their noses at white folks.

"Donald Trump was a godsend. Trump turned the ship of state around and the Left lost their marbles. The Swamp's globalist agenda was unmasked. Years of habitual lies and corruption were out in the open for all to see. The Democrats and the RINOs panicked. Their gravy train was going off the rails, so they tried to impeach President Trump his entire four years in office. Employment for men and women and every race and color was the best ever recorded. He solved problems which is not what most politicians do in Washington, DC. Bad guys were afraid of him. He made America energy independent for the first time since Eisenhower. And Trump convinced NATO to pay their fair share for defense. He accomplished all of this and more while the Democrats accused him 24/7 of treason and behaving like Hitler. Trump was elected by a respectable majority his second term, but the

Swamp, including the FBI and our CIA, rigged the election and gave the presidency to a mentally impaired political hack, Joseph Biden.

"Joe Biden was a mixture of Jimmy Carter and Alfred E. Neuman on steroids. He was corrupt to the core, a chronic liar, and dumb as a post. Robert Gates, the Democratic Secretary of Defense under Obama, once said, 'Biden has been wrong on nearly every major foreign policy and national security issue for the past four decades.' He was little more than a sock puppet for Bernie Sanders, Obama, and Susan Rice. His Marxist handlers tried stuffing Climate Change and Green Energy down the throats of the American public. And damn near bankrupted the country. Big Brother was supposed to step in and take control and it almost worked. Obama and Biden are both responsible for our civil war.

"My parents were Democrats. So were my grandparents. That was a long time ago, before Vietnam or George Soros or Critical Race Theory or climate change. People got along back in the day. Everybody knew their neighbors. They respected the police and our military. Folks went to church on Sunday. There was no Black Lives Matter or school shootings. Martin Luther King Jr. was a wonderful example for all Americans. So was John F. Kennedy, Ronald Reagan, and Richard Nixon.

"Liberals or Progressives or whatever they call themselves these days remind me of psychopaths. You can't reason with a psychopath. You can't live and let live with one. They must have control. They feel no remorse or compassion for others. It's never their fault, no matter the harm or damage they cause. And they will try and destroy you if they consider you a threat.

"There are three armies besides ours in the Eastern United States. Four more out West. I've been in touch with their commanders this past week. Big doings are in the works. I'll give you a heads up when I know more. In the meantime, we're receiving ample supplies from New Orleans, and a trickle is still coming down from Canada. They have their own problems, so that's understandable. If you need food or if you have an ailing family member, come out to Franklin. The hospitals here are full, but they still deliver babies and perform most operations. We have an excellent trauma unit with seven doctors and over two dozen nurses.

"You're welcome anytime. That wraps it up for today. Be careful going home. And remember. If you see something that doesn't look right, or if someone is acting suspicious, call the base. We can be here in thirty minutes or less. There are still a few leftovers roaming around from our battle two weeks ago.

"Good luck and God speed."

Snow White

Dolores Finch was having a good morning. Her request to her contacts in Moscow had been granted.

The man seated before her was a fearsome-looking individual with snow-white hair and rugged features. He wasn't big and muscular, but he had height and muscular definition. When he entered, he reminded her of a big cat, or a white wolf of the steppes, entering a strange new place, poised and menacing. She waited for him to speak but he sat quietly, saying nothing.

"Yakov, I can't pronounce your last name. What shall I call you?"

"My superiors call me Snow White."

"What made your hair white?"

"Compliments of the Arabs in the Afghan War."

"What did they do to you?"

"They enjoyed hooking me up to truck batteries then turning on their engines."

"But you're alive. How did you escape?"

"One of my guards was an opium eater. He was stoned one evening and forgot to lock my cage. I found a kitchen knife and went to work. Afterward, I stole a truck and got away."

"What do you think of my men, those you interviewed?"

"Comrade Stalin would call them useful idiots."

"I don't understand. What do you mean?"

"They lack purpose and initiative. Some didn't even know how to fieldstrip their weapons."

"That's not my fault. They were like that when I got here."

"It's every bit your fault. You're a general in name only."

She sprang from her chair, arms flailing, lips quivering, eyes smarting with anger, cursing the man who had offended her. He sat passively watching the woman. He knew then that he owned this pompous political appointee.

Her rage exhausted, she strode around her desk to stand beside his chair. "How dare you speak to me in such a disrespectful manner? I could have you arrested."

"I noticed your bully boys when I came in. If you value their well-being, do not call them."

"I'm your superior. I can—"

"You can do as you are told. I was sent here to solve a problem. Now sit down and shut up!"

"Didn't you hear me? I can have—"

He bolted from his chair, slapped her hard back and forth across her face. She stumbled to her chair, seeing stars, utterly shaken, holding her burning cheeks with both hands.

"Hear me, woman. Your superiors in Chicago gave me carte blanche. You doubt me, call them. Call them right now. You and this base are under my command, temporarily. My superiors in Moscow are in full agreement with your Marxists. Obey me or I will have you sacked and shipped back to where you came from."

"Alright. Yes. I will obey."

"Excellent! Come over here."

She did as she was told.

Yakov peeled off her jacket then unbuttoned her shirt, laying the shirt and her jacket over on the desktop. He reached around behind her, unhooking her bra. It fell silently to the floor, revealing Delores's proud breasts. Her breath came in little gasps. She was light-headed, and her knees threatened to give way. She had never felt this way before.

He cupped her left breast.

"Oh my. Oh. Yes."

She devoured Comrade Yakov's mouth, pressing her naked breasts against him, clutching him tightly as he unbuckled the belt in her fatigue trousers.

Thus began a torrid relationship between General Finch and her Russian Commander, Yakov Medvedev.

Stalemate

Four months had elapsed. It's February 3, 2026, and snow has fallen across much of the United States.

The armies of the Capitalists and the Marxists have gone to ground for the winter. Food remains in short supply in the northern states and parts of the interior. The Marxists are experiencing fuel shortages. Half of their supplies are being sunk by the British Royal Navy.

War clouds loom over Western Europe. England, France, and Germany have joined forces with the smaller NATO countries. All are aligned against Russia if another convoy of ships sets sail for the United States. Vladimir Putin has threatened nuclear war. The Prime Minister at 10 Downing Street responds with a cryptic message: You Have Sown the Wind.

Opportunity Lost

Field Marshal Feng was concluding a lecture on Indochina and the Vietnam War when one of the cadets reminded him of his promise to deliver a briefing on Imperial Japan. Preoccupied with Johnny Poe,

World War Two had slipped his mind. He gave them a ten-minute recess then began his lecture.

"World War Two actually started in 1937 when Japan invaded China. History books cite 1941 as the beginning of hostilities but that is incorrect. China suffered terribly under the Japanese occupation. A novel entitled *The Rape of Nanking* gives one insight into the Imperial Japanese mindset. Chinese women were raped by the thousands. Chinese men were used for bayonet practice. The occupying Japanese even held a beheading contest. Three hundred thousand Nanking civilians were slaughtered.

"December 7, 1941, Japan bombed Pearl Harbor. Yamamoto attacked with sixty-seven ships, including six aircraft carriers. The Americans had eight battleships stationed at Pearl, four were sunk and four heavily damaged. Two of those sunk were total losses. The three aircraft carriers stationed there were away at sea. The attack was a success with two successive raids by the Japanese war planes.

"But Admiral Yamamoto erred badly by not sending in a third wave to finish off the battleships. And a fourth wave to set the fuel dumps ablaze and to bomb the dry dock. Hawaii was theirs for the taking but they sailed away for home. Hitler made a similar mistake at Dunkirk. Had he sent in his panzers, the Germans would have captured the entire British Army. Hitler could then have turned an intact Luftwaffe against Russia. The Battle of Britain cost Germany over seventeen hundred aircraft and more than two thousand six hundred air crews and pilots. By not following through, Germany and Japan both lost their best opportunities for winning the war.

"Midway was another classic miscalculation. Admiral Nagumo wasted precious time changing munitions intended for Midway Island over to torpedoes and armor-piercing bombs after the American carriers had been detected. He should have sent his planes right then with whatever bombs they carried. American dive bombers soon appeared, surprising Nagumo and setting three of his four carriers on fire within five minutes. His fourth aircraft carrier was sunk that evening. The Americans lost the Yorktown which was the turning point for Japan in the Pacific War.

"World War Two lasted three more years. Japan was on the defensive from 1942 until the *Enola Gay* dropped the atomic bomb on Hiroshima in 1945. *Bockscar* dropped Fat Man, a second atomic bomb, on Nagasaki three days later."

Johnny Poe and the Field Marshal found themselves a quiet corner in the cafeteria, so they could talk without being overheard.

"You look well, sir. I'm so happy to see you again."

"So do you, Master Poe. Shipboard duty agrees with you."

"I followed your advice and it worked like a charm. I have been accepted into the lower echelon of their rebel movement. Once they believe they can trust me, I'll be moved up. Then I'll have names for you."

"Always be discreet. Trust no one. They will be testing you."

"I know, sir. They've tried already, but I saw through it immediately. I know the commander of that port is part of it. He doesn't hide his contempt for you or any of our new leaders. He is a fanatic and a mean person."

"I suggest you find a safe place to hide in Djibouti in case you are found out. Your distress call to me will be 'Climb Mount Niitaka.' I will come as quickly as possible with help."

"Very good, sir. I do enjoy learning about ship command. It's very interesting."

"You must go now. We do not want to arouse suspicion with your absence. Goodbye and good hunting."

"Goodbye, sir."

The Field Marshal watches his young protégé exit the room. The responsibility for China's well-being weighs heavily on the old man's shoulders. He fears for his young friend, just as he fears for his country.

Tonight, he will burn incense and pray to the Dragon Gods for Johnny Poe and China.

Tomorrow, he will attend an important leadership council. Only a handful of Chinese patriots know that he and his brother possess the codes for China's intercontinental ballistic missiles.

Grand Alliance

"Maw, I don't rightly know how ta tell ya this. Hit's somethin' I been a-rasslin' with an' I jus' can't do it no more. I jus' can't."

"Well, what is it, Paw? Somethin' ailin' ya?"

"I just can't kill no heifers no more. I ain't got the heart. They look atcha with them big ole brown eyes. I can't do it!"

"Land sakes, Sweet Thang. That ain't nuthin' bad. You done become uh godly man."

"You ain't mad at me?"

"Shucks, no. I'll ast Tom to do the butcherin' when we need meat."

"Tom changed didn't 'e?"

"Yes, that little filly shore turned Tom around."

"I like 'er, don't you, Maw?"

"She's as sweet as ho-made fudge, Elmer. An' a smart li'l gal ta boot."

"I'm glad you like 'er. She treats the cows an' horses real nice. An' our danged ole hound dog jus' loves 'er."

"I been a-thinkin', Paw. You an' me is gettin' on in years. We ain't got no youngins. Lord knows we tried hard enough when we was young. You like ta wore we slap out but I loved ever minute! We ain't got no kin to leave this place to. Why don't we leave it all to them?"

"Maw, you make uh man proud. That's the bestest dadgum thang we could do. Give 'em a home an' make 'em all family."

"We don't say this often enough, honey, but I love you, Elmer."

"I love you, Christine. We had a good life in spite uh all the hard times an' troubles. I wouldn't change nothin' 'ceptin' us not havin' no kids."

"I think I'll surprise 'em tonight with apple pie. Six pies oughta be enough. I'll hot up the collard greens an' fix maybe thirty roastin' ears. Them field hands eats three apiece."

"Don't fergit sliced 'maters, Maw. We got 'bout two hundred on the vine right now. I'll git most of 'em sold tomorrie down at the stand. Tom's down there now sellin' corn an' okri. We got Irish taters comin' out our ears. Them Gypsies shore is good farmers."

"Hit's uh shame Boss got killed. I wisht he could see how his people turned out. They wuz right poorly when they come here. They's all settled now an' happy as pigs in mud."

"Maybe nobody never give 'em no chance before."

"Why don't you go find Tom an' tell 'im our plans?"

Elmer found Long Tom down at the produce stand serving customers. There were two pickup trucks parked out front and five passenger cars. Esmeralda and Charity were busy unloading Elmer's pickup while Anastasia bustled about sacking orders in paper grocery bags. Elmer hung back and just watched.

For a few moments he imagined those were the children him and Maw never had. He decided to wait until after supper when they were fed and rested. Elmer turned and walked back up the driveway to the house. He wanted to spend the rest of the evening alone in the kitchen with his wife of fifty-three years.

Command Decision

The Pentagon was strangely quiet following the departure of its Progressives and Republicans in name only. Thirty-nine percent of the Pentagon personnel had been fired. It was almost like the massive building was finally at peace following the 9/11 attack.

Donald Trump was holding court with his inner circle out in the courtyard. It was a crisp spring day. The sky was clear blue with no rain in the forecast. Trump's personal bodyguards sat at a nearby table enjoying a lunch of potato salad, pork barbecue, and pink lemonade. That was a real treat, considering the rationing in effect. Outside three hundred and fifty Marines surrounded the building as a further precaution. Stationed a few miles northwest was the Army of the Potomac, nineteen thousand nine hundred loyal Capitalists protecting Washington and the Pentagon. Trump was seeking an answer to a military question but no solution had been reached.

"Sinking Russian cargo ships was vital to our cause a year ago. We owe the British Navy for the risks they undertook. Today we're much stronger. We've replaced the electrical circuitry in twenty-six of our capital ships. We can intercept enemy convoys now, and requisition those supplies."

"What about Putin and the Russian Navy?"

"The Russian Army was defeated by the Afghans in 1989. Thirty-three years later the Russians made the same dumbass mistakes fighting the Ukrainians. I don't believe Putin would risk his navy against our fleet carriers and submarines. He must know he would be defeated."

"He keeps threatening NATO and Japan with nuclear war."

"All Putin really cares about is the Russian image and his place in the history books."

"Don't sell the man short," General Black warned. "He reminds me of a wounded animal. His behavior has become erratic in recent years. He's a narcissist and probably a paranoid. So, his decision-making is suspect. He's an angry man because of the Soviet collapse, Cuba, Afghanistan, and whatever else he perceives as personal. Putin is the type of individual who could start World War Three."

Admiral Wingate agreed. "Putin may not be off his rocker, but he certainly is unpredictable. So, the question we face, gentlemen, is: Is he crazy enough to use nuclear weapons? And if so, what should we do about it?"

"A preemptive strike would settle the issue," Colonel Clark suggested.

Donald Trump: "Gentlemen, we're getting ahead of ourselves. I don't want to go down in history as the man who started World War Three. Are you in favor of boarding Putin's ships? If not, what do you suggest we do?"

Admiral Jones: "Any ship coming here with contraband for our enemies is fair game. We can't afford to sit back and do nothing. That would compromise our troops in the field."

General Black: "I agree. We should board those ships and confiscate their supplies."

Donald Trump: "What about armed escorts?"

Colonel Rodriguez: "We could intercept them in international waters. But I doubt they would stand down unless confronted with overwhelming force. If they sail within our twelve-mile limit, that would give us strategic authority."

The discussion continued.

"There is no middle class in totalitarian societies, just the proletariat and elites. China changed a few years back, experimenting with capitalism. Now they have new leaders, so we don't know what we're dealing with. Russian leaders are the same herd of assholes they were following their 1917 revolution. There are three types of Ivans, true believers, professionals, and ordinary citizens. True believers are hardcore like the Imperial Japanese or the Nazis. If his warships are manned by true believers, we may have a fight on our hands."

"Wouldn't that provoke Putin?"

"We can't base our decisions on what Putin thinks, or anyone else for that matter. Putin likes to throw his weight around with smaller nations. With us he would be risking his life and his empire. Even if he's a Section Eight, I don't believe he's that crazy."

"You can never tell about a narcissist. They will do crazy things trying to prove themselves right. They don't care about other people. It's all about them. Putin might risk a nuclear strike if he imagines he's threatened or somehow justified."

"Our Air Force has six squadrons of B-52s back online. Do you think we should revise a limited fail-safe program?"

"Definitely. And we should increase our missile defenses in Alaska and station another sub in the Arctic Ocean. With our response time cut down to minutes, we could destroy most of Putin's control centers before they could get their rockets off the ground."

"It's settled then. Place our forces on DEFCON ONE. I intend to board or sink every enemy vessel that comes inside our twelve-mile limit. Gentlemen, enjoy your lunch."

Death Toll

With the coming of summer, the Armed Forces of the United States were experiencing a rebirth. Electronic repairs had been underway ever since the Chinese attack in 2024. ICBM silos had not been affected. They were safe underground from the atmospheric blasts. Most of the electrical grid for the nation was back online. Dams were generating electricity again. People were able to drive their trucks and automobiles. Finding food was no longer a life-or-death experience.

Five states in the Eastern United States were under the influence of the Marxist Democrats: Georgia, North and South Carolina, Alabama, and Illinois. Five states in the Western US were controlled by the Marxists: Washington, Idaho, Oregon, Nevada, and California. The rest of the country remained neutral or sided with the Capitalists.

Thirty-three million Americans were dead. The majority had starved to death. Suicide claimed tens of thousands. Many more were killed in the fighting. It was a time of upheaval and war. Foreign enemies kept their distance. They feared what happened to Peking and Shanghai.

Another pressing situation was Iran. The fighting with Australia, Israel, and Japan had taken on a grisly aspect. The mullahs kept sending young men up the line to fight and die for Ali Khamenei. Their bloated corpses and bleaching bones littered the Iranian deserts. Iran's youth were being sacrificed by its Muslim fanatics.

Cutting down Iranian boys like summer wheat was causing allied pilots to seek council with their priests and rabbis. Some quit, refusing to fly anymore. Killing children was more than they could stomach.

Israeli pilots were returning to base with full loads of ordnance. They refused to bomb Iranian boys playing soccer in open fields.

PART II

THE MORNING WAS SUNNY AND BRIGHT. Flowers were in full bloom and the birds were chirping in the trees. Beautiful white clouds filled a blue sky due south above the Gulf of Mexico. A warm summer breeze stirred the honeysuckle vines along the fence line behind the produce stand. Long Tom had opened early. He wanted to catch folks on their way to w ork.

He didn't know death was approaching from down Highway 10.

The last passenger car had just pulled away when an olive drab 6 x 6 pulled up and stopped. Six men got out. Tom recognized their uniforms. One of the men had tattoos on his face and neck.

"Old man, what you got in there?"

"Produce. Beans, taters, onions, okra. What would you like, sir?"

Tom slid his 1911 .45 automatic away from the cash box under the counter.

"What would I like? I would like your money, you fucking redneck."

The tattooed man pulled a revolver from his holster. Tom shot him between the eyes. Men on either side of Mister Tattoo reached for their sidearms. Tom killed them both. The remaining three had retrieved their automatic rifles and opened fire. A bullet tore through Tom's forearm. Another bullet grazed his neck. Tom dove for cover behind the bushel baskets filled with potatoes, but it was too late. A 7.62 mm struck him in the head.

Boom! Boom!

Boom! Boom!

Charity and Esmeralda were coming down the driveway, firing shotguns on the run. One of the men sprayed the women with automatic rifle fire. Bullets tore between Esmeralda's legs and one round went through the frill on her blouse. Charity was not so lucky.

Boom!

Firing point-blank, Esmeralda blasted the shooter into the middle of the highway. A second man was taking aim when she blew the top of his head off. The last man ran behind the truck. Esmeralda bent down, viewing his feet and ankles.

Boom!

The man screamed. She tore around the end of the truck, blasting him across the asphalt pavement into a ditch. She ran back up the driveway to see about Charity. Charity had taken two bullets in the chest. She opened her eyes, looked up at Esmeralda, and whispered goodbye.

The field hands came running. So did Paw and Maw. Charity was dead so they hurried down to see about Long Tom. They found him lying on the floor with his head in Anastasia's lap. She was soaked with Tom's blood, crying hysterically. A bullet had furrowed the side of his head, slicing open the flesh and chipping the bone. Tom was unconscious. Maw took command.

"Get 'im up ta the house an' put 'im on the kitchen table. One uh youns drive thet pickup down ta Lowe's an' bring us uh bag uh ice. Elmer, fetch out mah rag box. Anastasia, hush yer cryin' an' get 'im another shirt. This'ns uh bloody fright. Les git crackin', people. Tom's hurt bad."

With her patient on the kitchen table, Maw cut off his shirt with a pair of scissors. Then she undid his shoes and pulled off his pants. She used rags to mop the blood. Next, she washed Tom's body and his head wound with soap and water. Anastasia stood by holding a first aid kit, tears running down her cheeks. Maw bandaged the arm, and placed a patch over the neck injury. Then she stitched the head wound. She held a rag with disinfectant against Tom's stitches while the Gypsies carried him to his bed. She fixed a pillow beside Tom's head to support ice wrapped in a clean towel to take down the swelling and coagulate the blood.

The bedroom was full. The rest stood out in the hallway. Maw got down on her knees, clasping her hands together while resting her elbows on the bed, and prayed.

"Lord, I don't call on ya often, but I got uh favor ta ast. This here's uh good man. He feeds poor folks an' sells our stuff cheap ta folks what has money. He made us a family an' showed us ways ta rotate crops an' make uh nice livin'. Please don't take Tommy from us. If'n you need another soul up yonder, take mine, Lord. I'll stand 'is place. Anastasia here's uh good un' too. She needs Tom just as much as we do. We love Tommy an' we need 'im down here ta protect us an' show us the way. A-men, Lord."

Two uncertain days pass.

Tom opened his eyes. Anastasia was asleep in a chair beside the bed. He reached over and touched her hand.

"Tommy! Thank God! I was frightened you might not wake up. How do you feel?"

"My head hurts." Tom reached up, touching his stitches. "Do we have anything for it?"

"I'll ask Christine." She hurried from the room.

Maw and Elmer came back with Anastasia. Maw handed Tom two aspirin and a glass of orange juice. She and Elmer pulled up chairs and sat down beside a very relieved young lady.

"We lost Charity. Esmeralda saved yer life. She killed three men. We kept their boots an' guns an' nearly seventeen thousand dollars they had in the truck. Lightnin' an' Stringbean took 'em to the swamp.

The truck we got out back in the trees. We ain't figured out what ta do with it. I'm glad yer comin' along, Tommy. Ever body prayed up a storm over you."

"I'm much obliged to everyone. I'm sorry about Charity. I liked her. She was a swell lady. How long have I been out?"

Anastasia brushed back his hair. "You've been unconscious for two and a half days. The doctor said you have to take it easy for two weeks. You have a bad concussion. He gave you a penicillin shot and a tetanus shot. You have a reputation around these parts, Mister Big Shot. The doctor told us the people call you Mister Tom. We gave him a sack of tomatoes. That's all he wanted. He's really a nice man."

Elmer spoke up. "I best git on down ta the stand. Stringbean's down thar an' he ain't real good with countin'. I'm real happy yer better, Tommy."

Maw touched Tom's cheek, smiling down at him, then went out to the kitchen to start supper.

Anastasia leaned over and very tenderly kissed the man she loved. "I have a surprise for you."

"Is it a good surprise?"

"Yes, it's something quite special."

"Well, what is it?"

"I'm pregnant. We're going to have a child."

Thomas swung his feet out and sat up on the side of the bed. "One kiss did all that?"

She shrieked with laughter and hugged him.

"With a child comin' there's something we oughta do."

"What's that, my love?"

"We oughta git married."

Anastasia sat down beside him on the bed and placed her arms around Tom. Tears ran down her nose. Anastasia was too emotional to speak. Silently, she thanked the Lord for sending her this magnificent champion, destroyer of evil, her very own Angel of Death.

Georgia

Colonel Mosrie was with Captain, the Legionnaire, Johnson, and Henry at Gray's Cocktail Lounge in downtown Franklin. The atmosphere was festive. Local residents were having a good time. Mosrie took them there to get away from the base. Something was going on and he didn't want any eavesdropping.

"I think we have a spy and I think I know who it is. She arrived a month ago from Memphis. Last week one of our convoys was ambushed an' the drivers killed. All our shit was stolen. She works in communications. I don't want to embarrass this woman if she's innocent."

"How does she communicate with the outside?" Frenchie asked.

"Through our base telephone exchange." Captain answered.

"Do we keep telephone records?"

The Colonel shook his head. "No, they're scrubbed clean every hour."

"Get me a bug. I'll do 'er telephone at night."

"The president called yesterday. He's going to start hitting enemy bases with B-52s in three weeks," the Colonel said. "It'll be another seven or eight days before he gets to the Anniston Depot. Russian supply ships are bein' boarded by our Navy which means the Marxists are getting desperate. Dolores Finch and that herd uh misfits are raiding surrounding towns for food. People are going hungry again. Some may even starve.

"Their main fuel depot is just north of Marietta, Georgia, near that airbase. It consists of seven big tanks. If we could slip in an' set those suckers on fire that would cut their raids down to uh bare-ass minimum. It's dangerous as Hell, so I'll ask for volunteers. I don't want ta risk our gunships to ground fire surrounding those tanks."

"If Finch has more than one spy on base, they'll know we're coming. I suggest you leave it to us, Colonel," Johnson said.

Henry looked at him. "Does this mean I gotta git shot at sum more?"

"Maybe they'll shoot off your pie hole an button you up."

Frenchie sighed. "Pay the children no mind, Colonel. They're both boocoo dinky dau."

Three days drift by.

They were eating breakfast in the mess hall. Frenchie and the other two were wearing bib overalls, brogan shoes, and long-sleeved cotton shirts.

"You look like sodbusters."

"Henry's girlfriend suggested we should blend in with the local gentry," Frenchie said. "She's pretty smart. This getup should get us through any checkpoints."

"Did you remember your night goggles?" Captain asked.

"Yes, sir. We got enough hardware ta punch a permanent hole in Miss Finch's gas tank. That old Dodge has a false bed. Our stuff is underneath. We loaded bushel baskets in the backend ta make us look like farmers."

"Is your cell phone fully charged?"

"Yes, sir. I plugged it in last night."

"What about roads? Did you get that mapped out?"

"When we hit Chattanooga, we take Highway 27 down to Rome. Highway 27 is a secondary road that shouldn't have many checkpoints. From Rome we pick up Highway 411 that leads over to I-75. From there it's about twenty-five miles to our objective. Those tanks are right off the highway."

"Drive the speed limit. We'll have a Huey on standby in Cartersville. That's twentysomething miles. He can be there in ten minutes."

0900. They drove out the front gate. Two hours and fifteen minutes later they were on the outskirts of Chattanooga.

Chattanooga used to be an attractive city on the banks of the Tennessee River. A major battle took place there in the spring of 2025 which destroyed most of the buildings downtown. Wrecked tanks and field pieces sat scattered among the bones of thousands of dead men.

The citizens who still lived there had attempted to clear the wreckage and bury the bodies. But tons of ordnance and unexploded shells were everywhere. Two machine operators were killed trying to clear away the explosives, so the townspeople gave up and moved away. Chattanooga became a ghost town.

"Dang! Look at all them bones."

"This is where the Colonel won a big battle last spring."

"This place gives me the creeps."

"Careful, there's uh big-ass bomb in the middle uh the road."

"Lookie yonder! Uh growed skeleton holdin' uh baby skeleton."

"Keep your eyes peeled for that Highway 27 sign."

"Hell couldn't be no worse than this shit."

"Did'ja git the feelin' them skulls was a-starin' atcha?"

"Keep a-pointin' at them damn things an' one of 'em might take a fancy to ya."

"There's the sign up ahead."

The next fifty miles was open country. They saw a few cattle. Finch and her men hadn't been that far north. They ran into their first checkpoint ten miles north of Rome, Georgia.

Two policemen stopped them in a Georgia patrol car. "Where you boys headed?"

"Peachtree City. We took some produce up to our kinfolks."

"You live in Peachtree City?"

"No, sir, just this side. We got us uh little farm there."

"Well, be careful. We hear tell theys saboteurs lurkin' about."

"We will. So long, sir."

They encountered their next checkpoint in downtown Rome. A lone policeman was checking IDs at a decommissioned traffic signal. They were last in line.

"I recognize that guy. We let him go four or five months ago. He's uh climate change freak."

"Gimme your revolver with the silencer."

When it came their turn, Frenchie opened his cab door and stepped out. The policeman reached for his weapon. Frenchie pumped three slugs into the man. Into the truck bed he went with the bushel baskets.

Twelve miles down Highway 411 they came to a large open field. Frenchie drove to the back side of the property and hid the body among a growth of saplings. Then he drove out behind a stand of pine trees to figure out their next move.

"You think our best bet is daylight or dark?"

"Theys bound ta have floodlights on them tanks."

"Henry's right. They'll be lit up like Christmas.

"What about sundown when it's just startin' ta get dark?"

"That oughta work if'n we kin beat them ole floodlights."

"Okay then, we got forty miles ta go. It's four hours 'til dark. Let's kill some time an' get some shut-eye."

Two and a half hours later they put on their bulletproof vests beneath their cotton shirts and started on 411 over to I-75. Halfway down I-75 they encountered a roadblock on both sides of the highway. An M-1 Abrams tank sat in the middle of the median. Finally, their turn came. Dusk was beginning to settle. Frenchie lied like a politician selling a used manure spreader and they were allowed through. Once out of sight he floored the old Dodge. They were running out of time.

"There's the service road. Pull down back an' maybe they won't see us."

Johnson pulled out their rifles and a bolt cutter. Henry dug out the magnetic explosives and the detonator. It took two minutes to cut through the chain link fence. They ran to the tanks and began attaching the TNT. Floodlights switched on.

"You done?"

"I got one more."

Henry attached the last explosive and they ran for the fence. Shots rang out. Henry went down. Johnson slung his rifle on his shoulder and ran back for his friend.

"Come on, ole son. You can make it."

"They got me in mah dang leg. Git me up, hoss."

They were almost to the hole in the wire when Johnson took a round in his hip. Bullets were flying everywhere. Henry grabbed him by his belt, hoisted him onto his shoulders and staggered on. Seconds later, Frenchie came through the hole and pulled them both through. An army of men was running toward them along the outer fence. Frenchie got them loaded in the truck bed then gunned the engine. Bullets began striking the truck and kicking up dirt. Frenchie burned rubber pulling out.

Up the highway three-quarters of a mile he slammed on the brakes and jumped out.

"Here goes nothing, fellas."

He depressed the button on the detonator.

Four hundred and fifty-eight thousand gallons of gasoline, diesel fuel, and aviation kerosene rocked the landscape with a cataclysmic explosion, followed by an undulating mushroom of orange fire the size of a city block. Everything was on fire. The men running beside the outer fence were consumed. Frame structures were blown to pieces. Metal stairwells, pumping stations, and gun platforms plunged into the flames. Fields were set ablaze four hundred yards out. Birds and forest creatures two miles away were screaming in terror. The deafening roar and billowing inferno suggested to Johnson the image of a demon climbing out of Hell.

With a roadblock ahead and pissed-off soldiers behind, Frenchie searched frantically for a place to hide. A narrow, weed-infested driveway appeared. He drove up an incline and into a thick stand of maple bushes. There he gave his injured comrades a shot of morphine.

"You're uh hotrod man, Frenchie. A danged hotrod man!"

"Damn straight! How we gonna get outta here?"

Captain answered Frenchie's cell phone call with a stricken voice. "One of our rotor blades hit a power line and we crashed. The chopper is inoperable. I've called for backup but that's two hours away. I'm sorry, old friend. I wish it were me there instead of you. Find a place to hole up until they get there."

"You heard Captain. Any suggestions?"

"Uh … Look behind you."

Frenchie turned around. An old woman in a faded housedress was holding a double-barrel shotgun pointed at him. He studied the old woman. High cheekbones suggested a former beauty, but the lines in her face revealed something else. Life had not been good to her. The dress she wore was in tatters, old and faded from long ago when she was young and pretty. Washington had done that to her and millions like her. She had become a stranger in her own country.

"You the ones set them tanks on far?"

In the distance the sky was red and the fields were burning.

Frenchie thought for a moment then decided she deserved the truth. "Yes, ma'am. We sure did."

She smiled and lowered her weapon. "I'm glad ya did. Them bastards is mean ta ever body. Pull yer truck around back behind thet big magnolia tree. They'll have drones out in the mornin'. They always do."

Once inside, they got Johnson and Henry settled on a comforter on the floor. Hattie cleaned their wounds and bandaged them as best she could. Moonshine from the springhouse brought welcome relief. Frenchie brought in their rifles and ammunition. Hattie didn't object. She hated the Marxists as badly as they did.

"Hattie, if we get outta this alive, we'll see to it you get whatever ya need. Medicine, food, shotgun shells, anything at all. Just name it."

"I was uh purty little gal forty year ago. Let's see now, I'd like ta have me uh new hairbrush. My ole hairbrush give out two year ago. An' some lipstick an' perfume maybe … an' uh pair uh loafer shoes … some nice underthings … oh, an' uh new dress."

The three men were astounded by Hattie's humble requests. She asked for so little after risking her life helping them.

Henry spoke up. "We'll getcha them things an' uh passel more. I'll ast my lady friend ta help. She's 'bout yer size."

"Right on! Ladies on the base can help with underthings an' dresses an' such," Johnson added.

"I'd be plum tickled. Theys uh doctor lives back in these hills sum place. My neighbor acrost the road knows 'im. I'll run over when the ruckus dies down an' ast 'im ta go fetch Doc. Thet bullet needs ta come out."

Hattie was gone thirty minutes. When she returned, she brought good news.

"Malden is trustable so I told 'im about youns. Said the doctor's place is about seven miles up the holler road. He took off ta go git 'im when I started back."

It wasn't long before a knock came at the front door. Frenchie opened the door with a .45 in his hand. In walked a tall individual wearing a top hat and a formal dinner jacket with tails, black jeans, purple shirt, and polished black knee-high boots. He carried a black doctor's bag, and a large revolver in a black leather holster was strapped around his middle. Silver hair down over his collar, and his eyes sparkled with merriment. He addressed them with a scholarly eloquence.

"Don't mind the gun. I'm a wanted man. The Democrats hereabouts have a bounty on my head. Seems I'm only worth fifteen thousand dollars. I thought they should at least double that reward."

Henry and Johnson both snickered.

"Thank God you're here, Doc. What's your name?"

"My friends call me Professor. My given name is Jack Tyman. I taught medicine at Emory University before the world went crazy. I see youns been in a scrape. Take down those trousers and let me have a look at that leg. Bring a lantern, Hattie."

Henry had a flesh wound. The Professor cleaned off the blood and gave kim a penicillin shot. Then he applied a sterile bandage.

"Now it's your turn, young man. Climb up on the table." The

Professor examined Johnson's swollen hip. "I'm gonna put you to sleep to do this. Then I'll fish out that bullet with a probe. Don't be afraid, my boy, you won't feel a thing."

With his patient anesthetized, he began his probe. "Oh my … this is interesting!" He pulled out an inch-long .50 caliber slug. "He's lucky this didn't break his hip. That would have laid him up for quite a spell. When he wakes up, have him stay off his feet for a couple uh days."

"How much do we owe you, Professor?"

"You've already paid me tenfold with them tanks you blew up. I could use some supplies after you make it back to your base. Anything relating to operations or setting broken bones. Ask your medical staff. They'll know what I need."

"How do we find you?"

"I'll give you my address. A cell phone might give me away. The back of my place is a level field. A helicopter or a small plane could set down back there."

"You can always come back with us, Professor."

"These country people need me. I won't leave them even if I am a hunted so-and-so."

Frenchie's cell phone rang. "Frenchie! You there?"

"Right here, Captain."

"Your Huey will be there in thirty or forty minutes. There'll be three gunships escorting him. It looks like we're done for. Our crash drew too much attention. There must be fifty assholes surrounding this place. Me and Sawbucks are all that's left. The rest are dead."

"Shit! Is there no way out?"

"Afraid not, old friend. I have a box of C-4 with me. I'll touch it off when they bust down the door."

"Captain, I wish we could help. Is there anything we can do?"

"Donate my clothes to the poor farm. The Colonel has my money. Give that to the orphanage. There's a nice bolt action 30-06 in my closet. Give that to Henry. Tell my friend Johnson he is what little black boys should aspire to be. There goes the door. Goodbye, Frenchie. I'll see you on the other side."

The connection went dead.

"Captain just blew himself away. Sawbucks too!" Frenchie had tears in his eyes.

"Your friend sounded like uh brave man, sir. A lot like youns."

"Buck up, ole man. You woulda done the same thing. So would every person in this room. Your job is to kill the sons a bitches. My job is to keep you healthy enough to keep at it. Your friends died heroes. So, on we go to our final rewards. I hope you and your comrades find peace someday."

"Thank you for saying that. You would have liked Captain. He was a lot like you, Professor."

Frenchie's cell phone buzzed. "This is Captain Carroll. Is that you, French Man?"

"You bet your ass it is! Where are you?"

"I'm about twenty miles out, coming down I-75. Make a fire so I can find you."

"Gimme a couple uh minutes." He turned to Hattie. "Hattie, gather up stuff you want to keep. You're coming with us. Professor, can you and Henry get Johnson down to the highway?"

"Sure we can. Pull your truck down there and set it alight. I'll drive my Lincoln around back."

Frenchie drove the shot-up Dodge down into the center of the median and set it on fire. "Ever body get up the road uh piece. The damn thing's liable to blow." A minute later he heard the helicopters.

Four hundred yards down the road an enemy tank pulled out of the trees. He drove into the middle of the highway, swung his long gun barrel around and fired. A 120 mm shell whistled past them inches away, exploding back in the trees. A Hellfire missile struck the tank, blasting the turret into the opposite drainage ditch. A gunship settled down low, strafing down the highway with his Vulcan Gatling gun.

Johnson was loaded onboard. Henry hobbled on. Then Hattie climbed in. Enemy trucks were spotted coming their way.

"Professor, you better come with us. This place is too hot. We can get you home another time."

"Under the circumstances, I bow to your superior assessment of the situation."

Bullets began churning the ground as they scrambled onboard. A Hellfire missile was launched at the leading truck. The truck exploded in an orange fireball.

They soared up and away.

Nancy

When thc helicopter landed back at base they were greeted with cheering and laughter. Everyone wanted to shake their hands. It was a time of jubilation. The troops were weary from all the fighting and a success of this magnitude was a welcome tonic for morale. But there was sadness too over the loss of Captain and his fire team. Nancy took it especially hard.

After the celebration died down, Johnson and Henry were taken to sick bay. Hattie was shown a special bungalow prepared just for her. And Professor was lodging with Frenchie, so he'd have a familiar face to talk to. Frenchie welcomed the company. He missed his friend Captain.

Colonel Morsie made the rounds with his new guests. Then he asked Professor if he would call on Nancy. The young girl had slipped into a depression. Professor held a doctorate in psychology so the Colonel thought he might be able to help.

"I know where you are, Nancy. I was there myself not long ago."

Nancy didn't respond. Professor said nothing for thirty seconds.

"It's a terrible place. A lonely underworld filled with sadness and phantoms of guilt. God doesn't care anymore and you feel abandoned."

Nancy just stared at the floor, saying nothing. He talked to her gently for the better part of an hour. Finally, he shared his own sad experience.

"I felt that way when they killed my wife, Katy, and our little daughter, Clara Jo."

Nancy looked up. "They killed my mama and daddy."

"I know, Nancy. The Colonel told me. He said Captain was your special friend. And he brought you a baby fox you named Mister Peabody."

Nancy jumped up. "I forgot to feed him. He's locked in my bedroom."

She ran out of the living room and down the hallway. When she opened her door, the fox jumped into her arms. She brought him out to show Professor. Professor scratched Mister Peabody's back while Nancy ran out to the kitchen for a bowl of water and a plate of strawberries.

Rocky pulled up in the driveway. He was in Nashville when the Huey landed. Mosrie had called Rocky on his cell phone and briefed him on the situation.

"I'm glad you're here, Professor. How is she?"

"She's over the initial shock. She'll experience sad periods, but time heals most of our tragedies."

"Would you like to stay for dinner?"

"Thank you, Rocky, but I have a dinner date tonight with a very special lady. Her name is Miss Hattie Gibson."

"The Colonel told me. She saved our famous trio down in Georgia."

"Indeed, she did. She brought me into the fray to treat your friends. Hattie is one brave woman."

"How long you gonna be with us?"

"Frenchie said we can leave anytime. The Colonel is getting some things together for my practice. I'll be here another three or four days. I must say I enjoy your mess hall. That's the best food I've had in ages."

"I'll see you again before you leave. Thank you, Professor. Thank you for helping my daughter."

Hattie

Hattie had dinner brought over from the mess hall. She wanted the Professor to have a nice selection because he'd been eating his own fare out in the boondocks. He was delighted when he saw what she had done.

"You know you're a celebrity now, don't you."

"I don't feel no different 'cepin' all them nice things they give me. Do you like my new dress, Professor? Henry's lady friend brung it over this mornin'. She's uh purty little thang."

"It's a lovely dress. Who did your hair? It's quite fetching."

"Ya know sumthin', Professor? I plum fergot what hit's like ta live civilized. I ain't been civilized in uh coon's age. I reckon I know what them Okies felt like. My great granpappy died on the road goin' out west in 1934. Hit's uh sorry thing when the gov'ment turns on its own people."

"You're quite the philosopher, Hattie. I couldn't have said it better myself. Those three young men nearly died fighting for our republic. If it hadn't been for you they might have perished out there on the highway. It's people like us that have to step into the breach when they need us. You risked your life protecting 'em. That makes you special, young lady."

"If'n I was twenty year younger, I'd jump yer bones. You're uh silver tongue devil, ya ole rascal."

Revenge

Yakov Medvedev was furious. Guards posted to protect the fuel depot in Marietta had allowed the enemy to slip through. The fuel depot was destroyed and nearly one hundred of his soldiers killed or burned to death. All nonessential vehicles had been ordered to stand down. Moscow was demanding answers. Nadler and Schiff were raising the specter of his dismissal. Yakov had no one to blame but himself. His affair with Delores Finch was over. She had been relieved of command and sent to Atlanta. He sat at her former desk, contemplating his fate.

A knock came at the chamber door. "Come in. What is it?"

"Sir, a report just came in from our base in Washington State. It's addressed to All Commanders. "

"Well, read it!"

"Bomber attack. Origin unknown. Base destroyed. Many dead. Thousands injured. Request blood plasma. General Endicott."

Yakov bowed his head in disbelief. The tide was turning. He had to do something or face defeat and possibly a firing squad back home.

"You may go now. Turn off the lights on your way out."

Alone in the dark, he recalled his experiences at the hands of the Arabs. Relentless torture and water deprivation had released him from any fear of death. In various situations, death was an old friend. Death takes away one's agony and the terrible dread of next time.

Revenge was another old friend he remembered well.

Someone once wrote, "Revenge is a dish best served cold." He did not equate revenge with vichyssoise. To Snow White, it was best served hot by an AK-47 or a Molotov cocktail.

He pressed the button on the desktop, summoning the guard outside.

"Go out to Building C and round up Sergeant Gustav and his men."

Within the hour another knock came at his door. "Sergeant Gustav reporting, comrade."

"Pull up chairs. Use that sofa over there. Get comfortable. I want to talk to you."

Sixteen men assembled around the desk.

"You men were handpicked. I chose you because you are faithful to the cause and you have no families. Several of you are proficient with helicopters and tanks. We had a serious setback in Marietta last week. The man responsible is two hundred sixty five miles northwest of here. That's the enemy camp up in Franklin, Tennessee. I plan to go in at night and kill as many personnel as possible. We'll use helicopters. If anyone doesn't want to participate, leave the room now.

No one moved.

Sergeant Gustav asked, "What are our objectives, comrade?"

"We'll carry barrels of napalm with thermite grenades attached. We fly in at 0300, dropping our little presents on their largest structures. The armory, the hospital, and the motor pool are primary targets. I have a map of the compound for you to study. Those barrels weigh around four hundred pounds, so don't attach the thermite until you get them onboard. They'll rupture when they hit the deck. We'll form up in front of the Post Office. They'll be caught off guard, so the majority will not be armed. I repeat, the majority will not be armed. Women and children are fair game. Kill them all."

Two days of preparation elapse. Six barrels of napalm were man-handled onboard six helicopters. When 0100 came, they lifted off. They flew west just above the roadways to avoid radar. When their position was directly south of Franklin they swung due north. The landscape passing by down below was quiet and peaceful. The world was asleep.

Two miles out they rose up to three thousand feet. The base was well lit. An alarm sounded but it was too late to shoot them down. The first helicopter released his payload over a large building which was the administration center. Explosion and fire consumed the structure. Next came the hospital. Flaming napalm flashed through the hallways and among the sleeping patients. There was no escape.

Nancy was knocked partway out of bed by concussion from a terrific blast next door. Part of the ceiling fell down. Nancy gathered up Mister Peabody and stuffed him inside her backpack. Then she ran to see about Rocky. Rocky had been struck on the head by a falling ceiling joist. He was unconscious on the bedroom floor.

Professor and Frenchie ran outside to see what was happening. Burning buildings were everywhere. Frenchie recognized the smell of napalm. Gunfire came from the direction of the Post Office.

"We're under attack, Professor. I have weapons in the house."

"Give me one. I'll come with you."

Henry jumped out of bed and ran to the window. The hospital was in flames. Johnson was in there. He yanked on his pants, grabbed Captain's 30-06, and ran for the hospital. Henry found Johnson lying on the front steps. He'd found his way out through that burning Hell only to die from burns over most of his body. Henry screamed in rage.

Hattie was terrified. It sounded like the end of the world. There was gunfire right outside her door. A building down the block was shooting flames a hundred feet into the night sky. She retrieved the .38 caliber revolver given to her by the Colonel and started making coffee.

Colonel Mosrie knew immediately what it was. *How in the hell did they get through our radar?* His people were dying and he felt responsible. *What the fuck could I have done different? It has to be choppers hugging the deck.* He cocked his Thompson submachine gun and opened the front door. An enemy soldier was standing on the sidewalk, firing his weapon into the wooden barracks across the street. The Colonel blew the man into the middle of the roadway.

A few of Mosrie's men had located rifles and shotguns. A battle royal was taking place. Snow White's commandos had the upper hand. Surprise was on their side, plus they had hand grenades and automatic rifles. Dead and wounded littered the streets. One of the enemy helicopters was burning.

"Professor, when I get around behind that white car I want you to open up on that pair of assholes behind the dumpster. That will attract their attention. Then get down behind this truck wheel, so they can't hit you. I'll do the rest."

"Good luck, my friend."

Frenchie made his way around a barracks building coming up behind the white Chevrolet. He waved and Professor opened fire. Two
men stood up, firing back at him. Frenchie came barreling across the
street firing on the run. One man went down. The second man hit
Frenchie before he was shot dead.

"Come on, Professor. I ain't hurt bad. There's another asshole down
this street."

They made it within a hundred feet before he spotted them.
Frenchie got pinned down behind a pickup truck. Professor ran into
the trees. While the commando was trying to shoot Frenchie, Professor
got in behind him.

"I say old chap, is it true your mother is a loose woman?"

The man whirled around and Professor blasted him backwards
onto the asphalt.

Frenchie was laughing in spite of his painful leg. "You're one amaz-
ing person, Doc. You'd make a good Legionnaire."

"I take that as a great compliment coming from you, my friend.
Come on, there's business to attend to around the corner."

Nancy was dragging Rocky toward the back door. The end of the
house was burning. Mister Peabody was squealing inside the backpack. Nancy was almost to the door when she had to stop and catch
her breath. Outside there was yelling and explosions. The door swung
open. It was a commando with an AK-47. Nancy screamed as he raised
the weapon, aiming it at her.

A shot rang out. A red blossom appeared across his chest. He
dropped his rifle, falling backward in the doorway. Henry grabbed his
collar, dragging him down the sidewalk. Then he stepped inside and
knelt before the little girl.

"Don't cry, baby. I'll get Rocky. Is Mister Peabody okay?"

With tears streaming down her cheeks, she clung to Henry.

Colonel Mosrie was moving cautiously behind a row of barracks buildings. Sporadic gunfire came from the far end. He peeked around the corner. Someone was there. He took careful aim at a figure wearing a top hat.

"Professor! What the hell?"

"Come on, Colonel. We got 'em on the run."

Frenchie stepped out from behind a power transformer. "Yeah, Colonel. It's payback time!"

The three of them went running toward the gunfire behind the burning administration building.

Johnny Poe

"Climb Mount Niitaka."

The dreaded message came in on his cell phone while he was asleep. Johnny Poe was in trouble. Field Marshal Feng contacted his naval ally in Hong Kong. Then he telephoned General Hu. The three lines were interconnected.

"Gentlemen, what naval assets do we have in the Arabian Sea? My cadet friend has been found out."

Admiral Ju Han in Hong Kong, "We have a squadron of cruisers patrolling in that region. Plus, a nuclear submarine. I'm not sure about our new destroyers, but we have an old battleship out there for training cadets."

"How far is our battleship from the Port of Gwadar?" Field Marshal Feng asked.

"About one hundred miles, maybe a hundred and twenty."

"Is she armed?"

"Yes, including her fourteen-inch guns."

"General Hu, can you get a seaplane to pick me up?"

"Most certainly. You will need transportation to the airport."

"One of my guards can manage that. Admiral, is there any problem with my taking command of our battleship?"

"No, that captain is one of us. I will tell him to obey your instructions."

"Get me a bearing on that battleship. I will leave for the airport as soon as I have that information. Stay in touch, gentleman, I may need your help. Johnny Poe is worth saving."

An hour later Marshal Feng was in the air above the Arabian Sea. "Master Poe, are you in a secure place?"

"Yes, but they are searching everywhere. So far my luck has held."

"When I am nearby I will call again. Remain silent."

When Marshal Feng boarded the big ship he was informed they were one hundred eight miles from Gwadar. *CNS Fuji* was capable of twenty-five knots, so they had four hours and ten minutes of sailing.

"Full ahead, Captain. A man's life hangs in the balance."

Three and a half hours drag by while the Field Marshal paces a steel deck. Then his cell phone rings.

"Great One, they have found my hiding place. They're breaking down my door."

"Tell that fool commander to call me once they have you."

"I will do as you ask. If you never hear from me again, thank you for everything. The commander of this port is in league with General Wufong at Central Command. There are approximately one hundred men and women involved. They're coming now. Goodbye, sir."

Forty minutes later the great battleship is anchored one thousand yards off shore. Marshal Feng's cell phone rings again.

"Your little friend asked me to call you. How could I deny such an honorable request?"

"It is good to hear your voice, commander. I hope your day has gone well."

"Better than expected. I caught your spy and the penalty for spying … well, I think you know, dear Field Marshal. He will be beheaded on my balcony for your viewing pleasure."

"That would be most unwise. My friends would be most unhappy."

"Oh, but I too have friends, Marshal Feng. You are stale noodles as the Chinese say. My friends will take control of China once we conclude our affairs with the American Marxists winning their civil war."

"One moment please, I'm getting another call."

"Take your time. I'm in no hurry."

"Captain, do you see that prayer shrine on top of the hill above the castle?"

"Yes, Great One."

"Train one of your big guns on that shrine."

Ninety seconds later one of the fourteen-inch main batteries is loaded.

"Sorry about that, commander. It was important. As I was saying, you should return my friend and we'll work out a compromise for your illegal activities."

"You're bluffing. I hold the high cards here."

"Now, Captain."

The fourteen-inch battery produced an ear splitting roar, sending a one-ton shell toward the sacred shrine. A ground-quaking explosion rained dirt and rock across the castle roof. Where the shrine once stood, a smoldering hole the size of a swimming pool appeared.

"You son of a malignant sow. Now you will pay. Watch my balcony, Field Marshal. Watch my balcony!"

"Captain, come halfway down the hill, please. Target that statue of Mao Zedong."

"Yes, Honored One."

The battery roared again. This time the explosion rained hundreds of pounds of debris upon the castle roof. Windows were blown out

"How dare you! How dare you! I will kill him myself!"

"Captain, that warehouse at the lower front of the castle. That's where he keeps his collection of antique automobiles. Can you put one in there?"

"Sir, my regular crew are manning the guns. The cadets are observing. We can put one up his ass, if you so desire."

"Be my guest, Captain."

"My pleasure, Marshal Feng."

Sun bleached boards and antique cars flew in every direction. A Duesenberg was seen tumbling end over end high in the sky. Two miles away they could hear screaming coming from the castle. The commander dearly loved his automobiles. Several excited figures appeared, waving white towels from the balcony.

Next day, in sick bay far out at sea.

"Are you feeling better, Master Poe?"

"I do indeed, sir. That shot they gave me was marvelous. Thank you for saving me. I thought I was a goner for sure."

"That big gun was rather convincing, don't you agree?"

"The first shell scared everybody silly. Looking back, it was really funny how they all panicked when you blew up those automobiles."

"I wish I could tell our people about your bravery, but that would place you in jeopardy. Our country is not out of the woods yet. General Hu has ordered the arrest of those wrongdoers. But there will be others still to come."

"Great One, why do people do such things to harm others?"

"Greed, power, ignorance. Sun Tzu wrote, the greatest victory requires no battle. He also wrote of knowing one's enemy as well as knowing oneself. I studied the commander of Gwadar while I waited to hear from you. I discovered a weakness, vanity. So, I attacked his vanity, which saved your life."

"You are wise beyond words, sir. How might I further serve you?"

"I've given this considerable thought. Mister Trump does not trust us. I want you to travel to America and visit with the president as my secret ambassador. Only General Hu will know about this. There are enemies here and in Russia who covet war with the United States. If another incident arises on our soil I want you to be my go-between to tell the president the truth. If I am killed, or simply die, General Hu will take my place. You may trust him with your life."

"Great One, you make my head swim. Others are more capable than I. Why me?"

"You are a total unknown. In the language of espionage, you are a covert operative. Through you, General Hu and I shall become President Trump's Shangri la. He will know his enemy but his enemy will not know him."

"Then I will go to America whenever you decide."

"You are like the son I never had, Johnny Poe. I will ask the president to accept you as my personal representative. I will explain the need for secrecy. Donald Trump is one of only four presidents who honestly loved America and its people since the Vietnam War. Kennedy, Nixon, and Reagan were the other three. Democrats hate Trump because he stands in the way of globalism. Globalization is just another word for dictatorship. The Left wants to rule the world."

The Frenchman

Hattie had regained her composure following two cups of black coffee. Gunfire, explosions, and burning buildings had turned her evening upside down. She opened the door a crack and peeked out. The fires cast flickering monsters over the pavement. There were bodies in the street. Those people might need help. She gathered up an armload of towels, a bottle of alcohol, and a roll of bandages. The first and second bodies she came across were both dead. A third man was alive but unconscious. She pulled him out of the street onto the sidewalk. Hattie folded a towel and placed it under his head.

He opened his eyes. "Are you an angel?"

"Yes. I'm uh Hattie angel."

"What's a Hattie angel?"

"Hattie angels come outta Georgia."

"Am I gonna die?"

"No. You're gonna live ta be an ole coot."

"My insides hurt."

She opened his shirt, placed a towel over his bloody wound, then rebuttoned the shirt. "That's 'cause you been shot in yer tummy."

"Is that bad?"

"It ain't good. I'll go fetch sum help."

"Don't forget about me, Hattie angel."

Hattie smiled to herself, remembering what her mama told her when she was little. Always be playful and kid around with sick people. It takes their minds off their ailments. She wondered where all the doctors and nurses were. So, she headed for the hospital. She passed another dead man. Then she came upon a woman with badly sprained wrists. She'd been blown through a window when a barrel of napalm crashed through the roof and exploded.

"I'm here, honey. What kin I do fer ya."

"I'm a nurse. There's morphine in my kit. My wrists are jammed up. I can't make my hands work right."

Hattie prepared an ampoule, injecting the lady in both forearms.

"Oh, yes, that's better. I can move my fingers now."

"They's uh man down the street a ways shot bad. I put 'im over on the sidewalk. Can you help 'im?"

"I'll go see what I can do. Thank you so much for helping me, ma'am."

Hattie walked on toward the hospital. The sight that greeted her was something out of a nightmare. Charred timbers protruded toward the night sky and charred bodies lay side by side on a sidewalk. Firemen had hosed down the embers and were bringing out the dead. She forced herself to go closer to ask about a doctor.

"Some got burnt up. The rest are out helpin' people. We got casualties all over the place. Good luck, lady. You're on your own."

"You got any spare morphine?"

"We got extry in that truck yonder. Help yourself. I gotta go back in an' help the guys."

She wandered on, searching for survivors. She administered to a young man sitting on a curb. He'd been shot in both legs. Dead people were all over. Hattie rounded a corner when she spied a figure wearing a top hat.

"Professor!"

"Hattie! You sweet thing. Come over here."

Frenchie was sitting on the steps of a frame building with his head hung down. His left pants leg was soaked with blood. Colonel Mosrie was down at the end of the building searching for enemy stragglers. It appeared the fighting was over.

"Glory be, you been shot like yer friends. Let's git them pants off, so me an' Doc can have uh look."

"Yes'um."

"I'll do the boots, Hattie. Then we'll pull off his trousers."

The exit wound on the back side of his thigh was the size of a fifty cent piece. Blood continued leaking out.

"Back in the day they cauterized places like thet."

"That's right, my dear. That's what we're gonna do. All my stuff is back in the hills and the hospital is gone. I'll go fetch the Colonel. He'll find us a ride. We'll take our patient back to the house and take care of this."

Frenchie lay silent on his stomach. He had passed out.

"Doc, 'es cold. 'E feels like 'es goin' in shock."

Professor was too far away to hear. As a farm girl, Hattie knew about shock. It was a killer. She stood up, pulled her dress over her head, and lay down on Frenchie's back to share her body heat. Then she spread her new dress over his bloody legs.

Vladimir

Vladimir Putin was drunk. Alone in his library, he sent his palace guards away for the evening. Vladimir was upset. More to the point, he was confused and angry. He wanted to be alone to think, but with no dinner and half a bottle of hundred-year-old vodka consumed, he found himself mired in the quicksand of self-pity. Not often prone to such emotions, he felt paranoid and a little bit afraid.

He was the sole master of Russia—Eastern Europe if he chose to unleash his new panzers—so why was he engaged in a pissing contest with Donald Trump? The Orange Man! That's what his enemies called him. Vladimir could conjure worse descriptions. The bastard had bested him, and for that Vladimir sought revenge. But how? Trump held the high ground when it came to weapons. He had access to funding all over the world. Russia was a poor country by comparison. They had weapons too, nuclear weapons, but in an exchange he knew the Kremlin and Moscow would be obliterated. How could he hit that son of a bitch and survive?

Trump had boarded his ships and kept them, supplies and all. Then he shipped his sailors back to Russia without a word of explanation. Trump kept everything. Schiff and Nadler were pissing in their pants. Worst of all, the army in Georgia had no fuel, none at all. That idiot Snow White had fucked it all up! And now Trump had operational B-52s. The Marxists stood no chance against that. They'll be blown off the map. Then he remembered a conversation from three months ago.

A smile broke across his face. He stifled a giggle. Then be burst out laughing.

"I have it!" he cackled in drunken glee. "I will show them! Tomorrow, I will change the world!"

He poured himself another half glass of the excellent vintage. Quaffed it down in three gulps. And fell asleep on the library couch for the remainder of the evening.

Goodbye to Some

Cauterizing the wound had stopped the bleeding, but Frenchie was as weak as a sick cat. Professor and Hattie spent their days feeding him and escorting him outside for brief walks to build up his stamina. This went on for three days until the morning of the fourth day when they discovered him out on the sidewalk enjoying the sunshine by himself. Hattie and Professor were elated.

"You finally got sum color in them cheeks, Mister Frenchie."

"Yes, indeed. You're out of the woods now, my boy."

"Something I can't remember. How did you two get me here?"

"When you passed out I went to get the Colonel to find us a ride. When I got back, Hattie had taken off her dress and was lying on your back. She probably saved your life. When I took your pulse you were cold as a cucumber. The Colonel arrived with a truck and we brought you here. Then I heated a kitchen spoon and we cauterized the wound. After that we took turns looking after you."

"What about my men? What about Henry and Johnson?"

"Honey, Johnson got kilt in the hospital fire. Henry saved Nancy an' Rocky. He killed one uh them awful men 'bout to shoot Nancy. They're fine now, but little Nancy misses her friend Captain."

"I can't believe Johnson is dead. He was my best friend. Him an' Henry."

"Mister Peabody won't leave Nancy's side. I think he knows she almost died."

"I would like to see the Colonel as soon as he gets free."

"I'll see to it. Sit on the porch swing and get some more sun. Vitamin D will do you good."

Washington State

A B-52 bomber was approaching the target at fifty thousand feet. Down below the world was a patchwork quilt of a hundred different hues and colors. The Pacific Ocean was deep blue. Tiny sparkles from the noon-day sun appeared like diamonds on the waves.

Descending to thirty-five thousand feet, the navigator began reading off his instruments. There wasn't any wind current below, so targeting the enemy base was going to be a milk run.

"Easy peasy, dudes," the pilot said. "Open bomb bay doors."

"Aye, Captain. Bomb bay doors open."

The navigator called out, "Come left on your heading one degree. Now back right just a hair. Hold it right there."

The giant bomber could not be seen from the ground nor could it be heard. It appeared only a speck in a pale blue sky. Her payload consisted of eighty-four, five hundred-pound, high-explosive fragmentation bombs. The enemy military base lay outside the city of Raymond, Washington.

"One minute to target, Captain."

"Bombs away."

Electronic Warfare Officer: "Captain! We got a missile on our tail!"

"Steady 'til all those bombs run!"

"Commander, seven miles and closing."

The last five-hundred pounder fell from the bomb rack.

"Close bomb bay doors! Hold tight. Let's hope the old girl holds together. Dump some flares!"

Commander McMaster dropped his right wing, applying hard right rudder. The ship fell like a stone. At twenty thousand feet he flipped her over on her left side to compensate for stress factors. The flares were having little effect. At ten thousand feet he leveled out full throttle.

"Captain! That damn thing is still coming.

He put the B-52 into a steep dive hauling back on the controls at twenty-five hundred feet. The ground came rushing up at a terrifying rate. With his right foot braced against the instrument panel, he pulled the controls back as far as they would go. The pilot initiated half flaps to slow their descent.

The radioman stood frozen in the doorway. The trees were growing larger by the second.

"Oh, God Jesus."

The navigator closed his eyes, praying to a god unknown.

At three hundred feet the huge bomber leveled off. McMaster eased her down to a hundred feet, snapping off the tops of tall trees. Her eight engines were blowing up all manner of limbs and debris from the forest floor

"Captain, that son of a bitch hit the trees. We're saved. We made it."

McMaster pulled back on the yoke, taking them back up to five thousand feet.

"Radio base. Those bastards have SAMs. Note the location. Our boys can examine the pieces and tell where it came from."

A general and three colonels came to the debriefing room. The bomb run was a success, but they wanted to hear about their escape from a surface-to-air missile.

"Son, where did you learn to fly like that?"

"Sir, I never flew like that before. I just made it up."

"So, you never tried it before?"

"No, sir. I never faced a SAM before, either."

"Well, I'll certainly admit it's an unusual maneuver, but you pulled it off. Explain how you did that."

"We had that thing on our tail. The flares weren't doing any good. I kept her nose down. My greatest fear was the wings might come off. But she held together. All those limbs and crap thrown up by our engines caused the missile to fly into a tree.

You saved a B-52 and your crew. You'll get a medal for this, Commander. I'll see to it myself."

"Sir, my crew asked to volunteer for the next mission."

"That reminds me of a group of volunteers in China during the war. Clare Chennault and his Flying Tigers. His P-40s were no match for dogfighting with Jap Zeros. So, he trained his pilots to get above the enemy, then come down firing their guns and keep on agoin'. They shot down around five hundred enemy aircraft with a loss of eight of their own. He acquired seventeen medals in his career, but they never gave Chennault the Medal of Honor which he deserved."

"I'm no Claire Chennault, General. But my crew believes in me. That's my badge of honor."

Ambassador Poe

Johnny Poe flew to America. He was met at the Ronald Reagan Airport by the Secret Service and driven straight to the Pentagon. The largest man he'd ever seen escorted him to the second floor. Greetings were exchanged and he stepped into an elegant room where four men were sitting around a red mahogany table.

"Johnny Poe, welcome to America. We've been expecting you."

"Good afternoon, Mister President. I hope I'm not interrupting anything."

"Not at all. We're here to learn more about your Field Marshal Chang Feng."

He sends you a gift, Mister President. A samurai sword from the Ming Dynasty. It's dated 1512 underneath the wooden handle. It was owned by a war lord. I also have a framed photograph of Marshal Feng and myself taken last year. These are his gifts of friendship."

"And I have a gift for Marshal Feng. It's a pearl handle six shooter owned by Wild Bill Hickok. It still shoots too. My offering of peace to a great man. I read his profile last week."

"He will be pleased, Mister President. He collects ancient firearms. But most of them no longer shoot. This will make him very happy."

"On my right is General Black, Marine Corps. On his right is Colonel King, Special Forces. These men are my trusted advisors. Feel free to talk in front of them. And this gentleman on my left is David

Israel with Intelligence. He speaks fluent Russian, Chinese, and some English."

Johnny laughed.

Many questions were asked about China and Johnny Poe's background. Finally, he reached inside his jacket and removed his cell phone.

"I have a message from the Field Marshal on my cell phone. May I set it up on your table?"

"Go right ahead."

"Greetings, Mister President from Chongqing, China. My sincere apology for New York City. Xi Jinping was an arrogant fool, but he and his warmonger elites are no longer with us. What matters now are our combined futures together. There are countries in this world who wish to destroy America. I have many eyes watching and many ears listening. I will keep you informed through my trusted ambassador to you only, Johnny Poe. He is a brave and intelligent lad. Please protect him. He is like a son to me.

"Rogue elements in China who were shipping arms and supplies to your Marxists have been found and arrested. Nine were hanged. There is something going on right now in Russia, but I have yet to uncover the facts. I will inform Johnny as soon as I have something solid.

"Beware the Ayatollah Khamenei. A radical cleric of the Quran. He is training assassins to kill you. I should know more about this in a few days. Another man to watch out for is Venezuelan Nicholas Maduro. He is a drug lord and ruthless to the bone. This man murders at the snap of a finger. He wants you dead.

"If something happens to me, my younger brother by eleven years will take my place. He is a patriot with access to all of my assets. General Hu is completely trustworthy. He and Johnny are friends.

"Goodbye for now. I will speak with you again soon.

"Chang Feng."

"I have a room prepared for you two doors down. You will be safe there."

"Does anyone have a question before I turn in for the evening?"

Colonel King spoke up. "How did the Field Marshal survive Mao's Red Guards after he turned against Mao?"

"Excellent question, Colonel King. Marshal Feng lived in a northern province in those days. It was back in the mountains and you had to go through a steep gorge to get there. He mined the top of the gorge with dynamite. When the Guards filled the gorge down below he set off the dynamite. About four hundred Red Guards were buried alive. After that the people protected him until the danger passed."

"Was General Hu with his brother when they fought the Americans in Korea?" General Black asked.

"Yes, he was just a child then but he was with his brother. The little boy was nearly killed by a shell. Sergeant Feng scooped him up and got him to an aid station which saved the boy's life. Part of his face is scarred but his mind is always ahead of the game. The Field Marshal depends on him quite a bit now since he's gotten older."

"What is your personal perception of the Field Marshal?"

"I'm the one he sent to ferret out the rebels sending supply ships to your Marxist rebels. I discovered the source, but they caught me. I called my friend and told him who they were, but I had been discovered. He came with a battleship and terrorized the commander of the port who was going to cut off my head. He saved me. I call him 'Father' because I love him. He is truly a man of the people."

"Is he a communist?"

"No, he's not a communist. I'm not sure what he is, but he hated Mao for killing so many of our countrymen. I guess you might call him an independent."

"Johnny Poe, you have relieved our concerns with your professional manner and your straightforward answers. Is there anything you want before you retire to your room?"

"Yes, please. May I have a bowl of egg drop soup with green onions sent to my quarters?"

2025

The year 2025 changed the world forever. Red China attempted to enslave the United States by seeding her upper atmosphere with nuclear explosions. That knocked out the American power grid coast to coast. All means of transportation ended. With no cars or trucks to search for food, millions starved to death. New York City was destroyed by an atomic bomb. Then Peking and Shanghai suffered the same fate. Sensing vulnerability in Washington, the American Marxists attempted a power grab which resulted in civil war.

Capitalist and Marxist armies clashed over control of their republic. Thousands perished on both sides and thousands more suffered injury. The fighting was reminiscent of the 1864 American Revolution.

The tide began to turn when Donald Trump got part of his B-52 force back online, but Russia had smuggled missile batteries into the country for the Marxist Democrats. The second bombing raid almost resulted in the loss of the bomber and her crew.

Johnny Poe was sent to Washington by Field Marshal Feng as his personal representative to the president. Communist Party leaders were killed when Donald Trump retaliated against Peking. Marshal Feng and his brother General Hu sought to free China from the grip of communism. But many communists remained in power throughout China. And they hated the brothers. Donald Trump had come to trust the Chinese Field Marshal and his protégé, Johnny Poe. The die was cast. The world would live in freedom or beneath the jackboot of a communist United Nations.

The year 2026 had arrived.

Free Will

Nancy and her dolls were discussing Captain and Mister Johnson.

Missy: "I don't care, Mama. It's not fair."

Moxie: "I wish I could bring them back. I don't understand it either."

Matilda: "There's nothing to understand. Captain said it's man's will."

Missy: "Well then man needs his legs switched."

Matilda: "God created man, Missy. God gave man free will."

Missy: "Maybe God needs his legs switched too."

Moxie: "Missy, don't say such awful things."

Missy: "If God gave man free will, it's his fault. He needs a good switchin'."

Matilda: "You two are incorrigible."

Moxie: "What's that mean?"

Matilda: "I don't know. Mister Johnson said it about Henry."

Nancy: "Henry saved us. A bad man was about to shoot me an' Rocky."

Missy: "Were you scared?"

Nancy: "I wet my paints. But Henry said it was okay. He got me a clean pair."

Matilda: "I like Henry. He's always nice to us."

Nancy: "I saw Henry crying at the funeral."

Missy: "I guess he misses his friend just like we miss Captain."

Moxie: "I miss Mister Johnson too."

Missy: "Do you think they're in Heaven with the little rabbit?"

Henry had come to pay Rocky a visit. They were sitting on the back porch drinking lemonade and watching Nancy playing with her dolls.

"Yer noggin okay now?"

"Yeah, I got five stitches. But my headache's gone."

"I wisht life was as easy as Nancy's out yonder."

"It was a long time ago, Henry."

"Why ain't it like that no more?"

"Politicians. They can't leave well enough alone. They always change things which just makes things worse."

"Johnson tole me 'bout them last 'uns."

"You mean Biden an' his useful idiots? They caught a bunch of 'em, ya know. Hanged part uh the sorry litter!"

"I reckon there'll be more hangin' when this is all done, Henry."

"I reckon so. The Colonel told me the country was a happy place to live back in the 1950s after the war."

"Ain't worth diddly-squat now, is she?"

"It's pretty messed up, all right, but it's gettin' better. Colonel said we got bombers now. That'll help out a lot."

"I wisht I could fly me one uh them bombers. I'd make 'em squeal like little piggies."

"I wish you could too, Henry. I'd go with ya."

"Say, why don't me make sum 'mater saniches outta them fresh 'maters I brung over?"

Surface-to-Air Missiles

0243 hours.

Johnny Poe was knocking on Donald Trump's private door in the Pentagon. He knocked a second time.

"Yes, who is it?"

"Johnny Poe, Mister President."

The door opened. The president was standing there in his house robe and slippers.

"What is it, Johnny?"

"The Field Marshal just called, advising me to wake you right away. It's important, sir."

"Come in. Follow me to the kitchen. I'll make some coffee. What's this about?"

"Missile batteries, sir."

The president pushed a button on his cell phone. "Blackie? Wake up, Blackie. Come to my quarters at once. How do you like your coffee, Johnny?"

"Do you have honey, Mister President?"

"Yes, Johnny. Was the soup to your liking last night?"

"It was delicious, sir. The best."

The president busies himself with the coffee maker. A knock comes at the door.

"Come in, General Black. Our young friend here has important news. How many subs do we have in the Atlantic?"

"Five, Mister President."

"Weapon systems?"

"Trident II D5s and Tomahawks."

Coffee was served.

"All right, let's get to it. Go ahead, Johnny."

"I took notes so I wouldn't forget something. I'll read from my notes."

General Black switched on a recorder.

"An Iranian ship bearing Norwegian identification loaded sixteen missile platforms at Archangel. These were offloaded in Ottawa and shipped by rail to the marshaling yards in Chicago where they were disbursed probably west. Russia was behind the transaction. Iran made the delivery. Someone in the Trudeau Administration cleared the Canadian railway system through to the United States."

He took a short break when another call came in from his brother.

"A lot of money changed hands from Mister Putin. This same Iranian ship is scheduled for another pickup of missile batteries at Archangel in two weeks. His port of call will be somewhere in South Carolina. A man was shot after gathering this information. He gave it to General Hu as he lay dying. It was delivered to me by cell phone from the Field Marshal thirty minutes ago."

"I'm blown away by the intelligence network of those two brothers,"

General Black said. "And the sacrifice of that man who gave his life. This information is pure gold. It will save lives, maybe thousands. It could help win the war. Is it safe for the Field Marshal if we contact him?"

"He instructed me never to call unless it was an emergency. There is much unrest in China these days. It started when those rebels were arrested. Others have taken their place. There's also a price on my head but that doesn't concern me. I'm safe here."

"Should I bring the brothers here for their safety?" President Trump asked.

"We discussed that possibility. Father told me they would be of no use here. All of their contacts are in China and around that part of the world."

"I'll have breakfast brought up. None of us will be sleeping after this. Blackie, call Admiral Wingate. Have him meet us at 0700. Johnny, is that the cell phone the Field Marshal calls you on?"

"Yes, Mister President."

"Is it fully charged?"

"It reads forty-four percent. I better go get my charger cord."

Breakfast was served. The dishes were cleared away then Admiral Shear appeared in the doorway.

"Admiral, how capable are our submarines at locating a false flag cargo vessel?" the president asked. "I can tell you it's Iranian flying Norwegian colors."

"There aren't that many ships at sea these days, sir. We'll find her using radar."

"I want to know what's going on and who's responsible."

0945 hours the next morning, the nuclear submarine *Starfish* reported in. "Mystery ship located 180 miles south of Archangel. Sixteen knots heading south. Eleven thousand tons. Low in the water. She's loaded. Will follow at five miles with decks awash."

1500 hours. "Mystery ship has rendezvoused with a Russian oiler."

"Captain Peters, this is President Trump. I want you to board both vessels and take prisoners. Identify the cargo then sink both ships. Do you copy?"

"Take prisoners. Identify cargo. Sink ships. Approaching targets now, Mister President."

One hour and seventeen minutes later.

"Mission accomplished, sir. Davy Jones's locker has two more ships in his keep. Iranians chose to fight. One dead, two in sick bay. Nine more in lockup. Russians gave us no trouble. They seem happy to be away from Mister Putin. I have twelve crazy Ivans singing in the galley. These men may have valuable information. Cargo hold was full of equipment, and missiles in long wooden crates. Request instructions."

"Well done, Captain Peters. Release those Iranians at Casablanca or any nearby port. They can find their way home. Then return to base. Keep those Russian sailors happy. They probably do have information we can use."

Iran

Seyed Ali Hosseini Khamenei was enjoying a lunch of *khoresht e gheimeh* with herbal tea and honey on his palatial veranda overlooking a courtyard and the downtown streets of Tehran. Interrupted by a telephone call, the eighty-four-year-old Supreme Leader of Iran had just lost his appetite. Vladimir Putin of Russia was on the other end of the line. An Iranian interpreter was assisting the Supreme Leader. President Putin was assisted likewise in Moscow.

"You mean both ships?" Khamenei lay down his spoon and stared away into the distance. "My men in Casablanca! Your men taken prisoner!"

"It's true, Excellency. An American submarine attacked our ships and sank them both. And with them went those anti-aircraft platforms

I promised our friends in America. I have arranged passage for your brave sailors. They will return home tomorrow."

Khamenei recalled 1979 when the Shah was overthrown and Ayatollah Khomeini assumed command. Those were days of glory until Saddam Hussein attacked in 1980. Eight years of war and bloodshed ended in stalemate in 1988. Troubles with Lebanon and Syria. And always the Little Satan. Now the Great Satan has shown his hand once again.

"Blasphemy! A curse upon their offspring! Once we ruled half the world. Now this outrage! The infidels deserve to burn in the furnaces of Allah."

"Indeed they do, Excellency. And I would like to help you put them there."

"What do you have in mind, Comrade President?"

"You mentioned you have a crack commando team. Are they still available?"

"They're away training in the desert."

"Would you send them to America?"

"That would be foolish. Forty-three soldiers of Allah sent to their martyrdom. And to what end?"

"To kill Donald Trump."

The Supreme Leader sat thinking silently for several moments. Finally, he spoke. "How would you get them there? How would you get them near that capitalist pig? And how would you get them back?"

"I have spies, dozens of them, across Canada and the U.S. I can get your soldiers across the Atlantic Ocean in one of my submarines. My American spy network will have the aid of the American Marxists in getting your soldiers to the Pentagon. From there it will be in the hands of Allah. This will cost millions of rubles.

"Your only risk will be your men. Most of them will be killed. If they kill Trump, survivors will receive one million dollars each. If they fail, fifty thousand dollars for survivors. Families of those killed, I will pay twenty thousand dollars."

"An interesting proposal, Comrade President. But you haven't mentioned your friend in Persia."

"What does my Persian associate consider a fair exchange, Excellency?"

"Iranian rial, Russian rubles, American dollars, these trifles do not interest your neighbor in Persia. A more fitting reward is something you have that I do not possess."

"Anything you desire, Great One, within my sphere of influence."

"Iran shall be forever grateful to you, Comrade Putin, when you deliver this coveted prize."

"What is it you desire, Excellency?"

"An atomic warhead for one of my Simorgh rockets."

Putin viewed the old man as a valuable but strange asset. Both of them hated America and both of them ruled by force. But Vladimir had never fathomed the attraction of a hereafter with seventy-two virgins. What a nightmare. He had his hands full with just two women. But if Islam could take out the American President that could be a game changer.

"What size warhead does your Excellency require of me?"

"Anything capable of destroying Tel Aviv."

Israel

Benjamin Netanyahu was on the telephone with Donald Trump. They had been talking for over an hour. Both men were concerned over recent events around the globe. The situation in North Africa was going from bad to worse. Thousands of innocent villagers were being slaughtered by ISIS. India and Pakistan were engaged in artillery duels over a contested border. Iran was building up her military at an alarming rate. Russia had just sunk an Australian spy ship off her northern coast. And

North Korea was test firing ballistic missiles across the Sea of Japan. Meanwhile, Cambodia and Thailand were in a heated dispute over fishing rights. With America and China out of the picture, the Fifth Horseman was waiting at the gate.

"I know, Bibi. We've been aware of that ever since Beirut and Arafat. But what can you do with a nation led by lunatics who believe in killing everyone who doesn't conform to their religion? That's not a religion. That's a blueprint for murder and conquest."

"President Truman recognized the State of Israel in 1947. Then the United Nations partitioned off a strip of desert from the State of Palestine. The Palestinians claim the land was stolen, which led to the 1948 Arab-Israeli War. They still refuse to make peace, which in an odd way I do understand. David Ben-Gurion said as much about the war. Maybe you can reason with them. Iran hates us because we're Jews."

"I've studied this Khamenei character a little. He was big friends with the Ayatollah Khomeini. He was also involved in our hostage negotiations before Ronald Reagan yanked their chain. He's a hardline conservative. He hates the West and he favors a large military. There's unrest in Iran over those Sharia laws, particularly regarding women. He's eighty-five, but I don't know his state of health. What comes next could be worse."

"Intelligence tells us there's infighting on the sidelines over who will take over. It appears the hard-liners are in the driver's seat. That could change. I hope so, for all our sake."

"Putin is another matter. I just sank an Iranian cargo ship loaded with SAM missiles from Russia. We also intercepted a Russian oiler servicing the Iranian vessel, so we sank them both. I imagine the lights will be on late tonight in the Kremlin."

"Putin has become a loose cannon and that Ayatollah Khamenei is just as crazy. With the troubles you're dealing with in your country and with Iran in the picture, we better watch our backs because there's no telling what those two might try. With enemies like these, we can't afford any mistakes."

"Can your Iron Dome stop an incoming ICBM, Bibi?"

"I don't honestly know, Mister President. It does well against conventional missiles, but an ICBM would be traveling at a much greater speed. And even if it did stop one, Tel Aviv might be destroyed if the thing went off. My greatest fear is Iran developing a nuclear weapon."

"Do you need anything from me?"

"Just your prayers. Tel Aviv is surrounded with a hundred missile batteries. I can't think of anything else we might do to protect the city. Can you?"

"We have supersonic weapons I can send over. They're designed to engage ICBMs in the upper atmosphere. How many do you think you need?"

"A dozen if you can spare that many."

"I'll get this underway by the end of the week. It'll take a day or two to get them to a seaport. Our big cargo planes are still undergoing maintenance."

"The people of Israel thank you, Mister President."

"We're old friends, Bibi. Please call me Donald."

"How's your fight going against the Marxists?"

"I got some of our B-52s back online. Intelligence tells me we can render those SAM sites inoperable with electronic jamming installed in our F-15s. They should be ready to go in another week."

"It's hard to believe so many people in your country tried to overthrow your government."

"Washington had become hopelessly corrupt. Biden and at least a hundred congressmen were in bed with China, Russia, and half a dozen other no-goods. Capitol Hill resembled a damn yard sale. Hundreds of bureaucrats were guilty of disloyalty and treason and so was the media."

"We have fools in our Knesset just as you did. I believe they would vote for Hitler if he ran on a liberal ticket. Those people can't get it through their thick skulls that socialism is national suicide."

"Lately, I caught up on my reading about our military involvements. With the exception of World War Two, there's been a risk-aversion malady, ever since 1950, throughout the military and our government. We never finish the job. Truman refused to cross the Yalu River and go after those MiG-15 bases in China, so Korea became a draw. Johnson dragged us into Vietnam. But Johnson and McNamara were afraid of China too. We whipped Saddam Hussein then Washington stepped in and the Iraqi soldiers turned against us. Afghanistan was more politics and more Military-Industrial Complex. Then Biden cut and ran like a damned pussy. And for what? What did we gain?"

"Looks like you have a lot of dead lads and lassies."

"All because of politics. The majority of politicians don't have the foresight God gave a mule. If we fail, Bibi, if we go down that road of appeasement one more time, letting the bad guys off the hook, sooner or later the world will fall into the abyss of George Orwell's *1984*. We were almost there last year. I'm not going to let that happen to the American people. I know you won't either. We must destroy the evil sons a bitches for the sake of our children."

"Donald, Israel is with you no matter the cost in blood and treasure. England is with us, and Australia, Japan, Italy, France, Germany and eight or nine others. The rest will betray you. I harken back to the words of Martin Luther King Jr, 'In the end, we will remember not the words of our enemies, but the silence of our friends.'"

"How terribly true. There's one more name I want to add to our list, Bibi. A grand old gentleman in China by the name of Field Marshal Chang Feng."

Elmer Jones

Tom was out in the front yard, sitting in an easy chair and gazing down at the produce stand. It had been two weeks since he'd been shot, and he had regained most of his strength. Maw and Elmer just drove by in the pickup with a load of melons. The Gypsies had discovered the seeds at Lowes for growing mini-melons. The little melons were delicious and everybody wanted one. Tom decided to walk down and see how they were getting along. It was a warm summer day and all the birds were singing.

Maw, Esmeralda, and Anastasia were busy sacking orders. Elmer had resumed his station at the pass-through, taking orders and making change. A line of vehicles sat on the shoulder of the highway.

"Tom, take over fer uh few minutes, will ya? I gotta go take uh leak."

The lady standing at the window wore a threadbare dress and had holes in the toes of her slippers. "What kin I git fer forty cent?"

"Forty cent. Let me think … uh-huh … forty cent. That'll buy one bag uh corn, one bag uh potatoes, an' one bag uh green beans, and one, no two, melons for your little girls there."

Maw, Esmeralda, and Anastasia stood in the background with their mouths open and tears in their eyes.

"Lord, Mister Tom. I heard you was uh Christian man, but I didn't 'spect no handout."

"This ain't no handout, ma'am. It's an investment in you. What do you do for a livin'?"

"I was uh seamstress before the war, took in laundry, done all right. But the war come along an' ruint things fer everbody."

"Could you take in laundry again?"

"I surely could, Mister Tom, sir. I got a big ole boilin' pot all rarin' ta go."

"My field hands need clean clothes. Can you come back tomorrow around noon?"

"I'll be here tomorrie in mah ole pickup truck."

The women sacked her order and carried it out to the truck.

The next person in the window was a tall gentleman wearing thick glasses with a cracked right lens. He was about forty with a handlebar mustache and a bald head. "Mister Tom, that there was the kindest thing I ever did see."

"Thanks, Freddie. Some folks needs a helpin' hand now and then. You want a melon?"

"Gimme two. Here's you ten dollars."

"They ain't but fifty cents apiece."

"Never mind that. You folks earned it and then some."

A gorgeous young woman with red hair and sparkling brown eyes appeared at the window. "You got any cherries or strawberries?"

"I got a whole shelf uh strawberries. They come in these little baskets here."

"I'd like twenty, please."

"That'll be ten bucks. Say, don't I know you?"

"Maybe you seen my picture in the paper. I was high school prom queen three years ago. Me and mama makes preserves and jellies an' sells 'em in the neighborhood. It ain't big money but we get by."

"Here's a melon for you and one for your mama. Tell her I said she raised a beautiful daughter."

Tom stood at the window another twenty minutes. Then he experienced a dizzy spell. "Paw, could you take over, please. I gotta go lie down."

Maw spoke up. "Anastasia, you go with Tom an' fix 'im a glass uh sweet tea. Get 'im on the sofa then come on back. We got uh mess uh cars waitin' out front."

With her husband situated on the living room couch, Anastasia turned out the light and went back to work. Tom fell asleep and dreamed.

Boss and Tom were driving up the highway to Franklin … up ahead was the Esso station … two men were inside … him and Boss were down in a trench under attack from an artillery barrage … he was holding his dead friend's hand and crying … Tom said goodbye to Captain and Colonel Mosrie … a young woman was crying in an old barn … she gave him a bouquet of daisies …

Tom opened his eyes. There was movement in the room. Someone was there. Tom slid his hand down in the crevice between the cushions and the back of the sofa, pulling out a long barrel .38 revolver. "Who goes there?"

"Don't shoot, Mister Tom. Don't shoot. It's me, Clyde Butler. Elmer done fell dead at the stand. He jus turn around an' fell over dead. They want you down there."

Maw was down on the floor holding Elmer. Anastasia and Esmeralda were crying. All the customers were gathered around. Then the Gypsies began arriving. Tom knelt down beside Maw and Paw.

"He broke his spectacles, Tommy. He can't see without his spectacles."

"Elmer don't need his spectacles no more, Maw. He's with Jesus now.

"You think so, Tommy? I don't want my husband trippin' an' gettin' hurt."

When Tom picked up the slender little man, Maw regained her senses. Tom carried him up to the house and placed Elmer on the kitchen table. Maw removed his work clothes and threw them in the trash. Then she bathed Elmer and dressed him in his Sunday attire with his new jacket and new shoes. Tom remained in the kitchen with her. The others waited outside.

"Put 'im in the bed, Tommy. I want to spend our last night together.

Tom got up in the middle of night for a drink of orange juice.

From the kitchen he could hear Christine talking to Elmer in their bedroom. She was talking about their honeymoon at Niagara Falls. They stayed on the Canadian side and rode in the Maid of the Mist. The cascading waters frightened Christine. Tom became embarrassed.

This was too personal. He drank his glass of juice and went back to bed beside his pregnant bride.

Next morning, after breakfast, Maw and Tom wrapped Elmer in a white bed sheet then a quilt. Tom carried Elmer outside. The Gypsies had dug a grave during the night. Tom placed his friend very gently in the bottom then scooped in dirt with his hands around the body. Tom climbed out and the Gypsies filled it in. Valdez brought pretty river rocks in his wheelbarrow. They placed them around Elmer's resting place.

Esmeralda stood at the head of the grave and gave the eulogy. "Mister Jesus, a special man come your way yesterday. Elmer Jones. Elmer took me an' my people in off the road an' give us a home. He taught us how to grow things and he cared for us like family. Then he made us part owners of his farm. They ain't no better man no place on earth. He was country as cornbread with a heart as big as Texas. Find him a nice place in Heaven with a good hearth an' green grass an' plenty uh sunshine. We love our Elmer, and we surely do miss him. Amen, Lord."

Goodbye to Some

President Trump was just sitting down to an Italian dinner when a loud pounding came at his door. "Johnny Poe! What in the world?"

"The Field Marshal just called. You have about fifteen minutes to evacuate the building."

"Johnny, get in here. Melania, get ready to leave. Barron, bring the radio. Luigi, you're coming with us."

Trump dashed into his office and dialed a central number. Seconds later an alarm sounded followed by a verbal warning over the intercom to evacuate the building. The President gathered up his Top Secret documents then hurried back to the dining room. Melania was just coming out of the bedroom carrying her case. Barron wore a backpack.

Luigi had replaced his Italian getup with a smart sport jacket and his brown derby hat.

"It's the steel door down at the end of the hallway. Let's go, everyone."

An enclosed stairwell led down to the first level where the main exit was located for the right side of the building. This led to a parking area outside. A Marine Master Sergeant was standing in the doorway.

"Hold on a minute, folks. We got bandits up on the service road. Your chopper can't land 'til we secure the area."

"Do you know who's responsible, sergeant?"

"Not yet, Mister President. We're still getting a handle on the situation.'"

"Can your Marines hold them?"

"Don't worry, sir. There's over three hundred of us. I'm guessing there's maybe fifty uh them. We'll nail their asses."

"Did the evacuation go off as planned?"

"Yes, Mister President. Those practice drills worked like a charm. Everyone went through the tunnel to the underground Metro. All the office staff and military personnel are safe and sound."

Bullets began striking the side of the building, so the sergeant stepped back inside. A barrage of gunfire erupted outside. More gunfire and explosions were heard coming from the front of the Pentagon.

When the gunfire slacked off, the master sergeant stepped back outside. He was gone five minutes.

"You can come out now. Your helicopter just landed."

"Did you find out who they are, sergeant?"

"One of my men speaks the language. He recognized the tattoos on one of the dead ones. They're Iranian."

"I'll be at the White House when this is over. Come see me. Bring all the information you can gather."

"It will be my pleasure, sir. I'll bring my interpreter with me."

"Be careful out there, sergeant. That's a hell of a racket around front."

"Yeah, sounds like my boys could use a hand."

"Stay safe, my friend."

"*Semper Fi*, Mister President."

The Pentagon

Master Sergeant John Lamson had just rounded the corner of the building with his seven squad members when an armored truck sitting at the right front entrance to the Pentagon exploded. The blast was so powerful it hurled the truck motor through the building. Shattered glass and splintered framing was all that remained of the entranceway. And all around, for dozens of yards, tiny bits of a pale yellow substance and yellow dust floated down.

Sergeant Latham had attended classes on dirty bombs. "Get out of there! Fall back! Fall back! It's radioactive. Get the hell outta there! It's radioactive!"

The Marines scattered, dragging their wounded with them, away from the smoking crater and the falling bits of deadly material. Dead men lay everywhere, Marines and Iranians. Putin and Khamenei had conspired to kill the American president. Their plot had failed. Instead, the Pentagon was declared uninhabitable from a dirty bomb. Twenty-two Marines were dead and forty Iranian soldiers. Once again the sleeping giant had been awakened.

China

"That's right, Mister President. The plan was to crash a truck through the front entrance then set off a thousand-pound bomb surrounded by canisters of yellowcake. They almost got inside but we shot out their engine. They weren't aware of that underground tunnel leading to the Metro. "

"How many Marines are dead?"

"Twenty-two dead. Eleven wounded. One lady Marine breathed the dust. She'll be gone in two weeks."

"I'm sorry about your brave soldiers. How did you find out they had a thousand-pound bomb?"

"We took three prisoners. Very uncooperative individuals. So, Bill Stanley, my interpreter here, told them to talk or he would shoot them and bury their bodies with pig guts."

"Pig guts?"

Bill spoke up. "Their religion views swine as filthy animals. They believe if they're buried with pig remains their souls will get dirty. They can't enter Paradise with a dirty soul."

"That's the craziest thing I ever heard."

"Mister President, those people are ignorant as a box uh hammers. They're still living with Muhammad back in the seventh century. Iranian women have no rights. They treat their womenfolk like livestock. And they kill anybody who doesn't worship Allah. They've been cutting off heads for fifteen hundred years."

"Sounds like your typical Progressive."

John and Bill laughed.

"Where are your wounded being cared for?"

"They're at the base hospital, sir."

"I'd like to pay them a visit."

"I'll arrange for your escort, Mister President. We can't be too careful these days."

"Thank you. Set it up for Wednesday or Thursday after breakfast. I don't want to interfere with the hospital schedules."

"We'll be in touch. Goodbye, sir."

Trump summoned Johnny Poe to the oval office from the Lincoln bedroom. "How do you like your new quarters, Johnny?"

"Oh, sir, it's such a great honor. I can almost sense his presence in the room."

"I want you to sit in on my staff meeting. If you think of something we overlooked, speak up. Those men are aware that you and the Field Marshal saved a number of us and our families from a horrible death. That thousand-pound bomb blew those radioactive particles into the ductwork which circulated throughout the building."

"Mister President, your confidence humbles me. The Field Marshal will be very pleased. "

"Next time the Field Marshal calls, patch him through to me. I want to thank him for his warning and to discuss a few matters. I know I can't call him for security reasons."

Five days come and go. The President stays occupied making plans and preparations for the B-52 bombers. Maintenance is nearing completion with the jamming equipment in the jet fighters. Meanwhile, two more battle cruisers have come online. The Navy has regained a complement of two hundred and sixty surface vessels, not counting submarines and flattops.

President Trump's cell phone rings. "Field Marshal, it's a pleasure to hear your voice again."

"And yours, my friend. There has been much trouble here. Revolution has broken out. Rebel factions have killed a number of my friends. I only escaped when my guards rescued me by fishing boat. It was touch and go until their ring leader was captured. He is now dead. That is why I was late warning you about the attempt on your life. I was one step ahead of my enemies until my brother overran their headquarters. Two thousand Maoists were killed and over fourteen hundred taken prisoner."

"My God, Chang, do you want me to bring you and your brother over here? I can dispatch one of our submarines to pick you up. You would be much safer here with my Marines protecting you."

"Thank you, but no. I must remain here. China is trying to break free from Mao's years of dictatorship. General Hu, myself, and a host of others are helping with this. We may yet fail, but we support those brave men and women engaged in the struggle. Young people in China are no different from your own young Americans. They want to be free from all the lies and corruption. I want China to be a safe place for Johnny to come home to someday."

"The tide is about to turn here. What can I do to help you?"

"Thousands of Maoists struck unexpectedly. They were very well organized. They captured our main naval base at Zhanjiang, and the Hainan Island where all of our submarines are based. They overran our Pengshan Airbase and captured all of its aircraft. Our freedom fighters have planes and tanks too, but the rebels have much more, plus five battle cruisers they're using to attack our forces from the sea. Can you send a submarine to sink those ships?"

"Admiral Wingate is over in Pearl Harbor inspecting our fleet. I'll ask him to set this up. Do those cruisers carry nuclear weapons?"

"Yes, Mister President. They are also equipped with our latest anti-submarine technology."

"I'll inform Admiral Wingate. He'll know what to do. We're heading into a storm, my friend. Biden and his Marxist Democrats opened that door with Afghanistan. Now these tin pots are making their move. A lot of innocent people are going to die because of liberal stupidity. It's up to us to stop this insanity. We'll have to wage total war, possibly with nuclear weapons."

"Putin and Khamenei conspired to kill you and your Pentagon personnel. My informants tell me that Mister Putin is shipping nuclear weapons to Iran. That can only lead to war with Israel and Western Europe."

"We can't stand by and allow that to happen. We have to intervene."

"My brother and I trust your judgment, Mister President. If we go down to defeat, you must shoulder the burden alone. Trust no one in my country who comes to you speaking of détente. That will be the rebels seeking more time to marshal their forces. Like Hitler or the Khmer Rouge or Boko Haram, when you let down your guard they will attack."

"I'm concerned about you and General Hu. Are you in a safe place? Is there anything else I can do to assist your troops against the communists?"

"Are your spy satellites still operational? Ours are not."

"Yes, most of them. Once we identify the Maoists, Intelligence can feed their locations and troop movements to your people. We did that in the Ukraine against Putin's armies."

"General Hu can put his tanks and artillery to their best use with such information. We are outnumbered, but this could place fear in the hearts of our enemies. Sun Tzu often employed fear tactics in his campaigns against stronger forces."

"Your fleet is bottled up by those Maoist rebels. If you want our navy to assist you, I will ask Wingate to send aircraft carriers and escort ships to help you and your brother defeat those communist has-beens."

"That would be wonderful, Mister President. We can certainly use your able assistance. It is unfortunate that you and I must fight and kill our own countrymen. But that is a task we cannot avoid, else the whole world will be plunged into a new dark age."

"The Marxists here are finished, they just don't know it yet. I have two B-52 squadrons ready to go. With our F-15s jamming the SAM batteries, the bombers will have smooth sailing. If our flattops can't get the job done, I'll send over the bombers. Together with England and a few others, we're going to build a new world, my friend. It will be the polar opposite of 1984."

Memories

Esmeralda had the day off. She was up on the ridge admiring the green valley that stretched for miles across the highway. The leaves were beginning to turn. The little shelter was her getaway when she wanted to be alone or just relax. It was enclosed in the back and on both sides with cedar boards and 4 x 4s; the roof was made up of hickory planks covered over with a tarpaulin. Her furnishings consisted of a small table, a linen tablecloth, complemented by a crystal candle holder, two canvas chairs, and an aging recliner. Out front was a bed of pretty flowers she had planted and cultivated.

Today she was recalling her past, and why Charity had to die. Why did Boss have to die? Why was the country at war with itself? And why were so many governments ruled by foolish and incompetent men? *If there is a god, where was he or she when all of this stuff was taking place?*

Boss was a Christian. He always looked on the bright side, encouraging others to have faith that everything would work out. And oftentimes it did. Like their encounter with Elmer, sitting on the side of the highway with his injured foot. Elmer took them in and treated them like family. What were the odds of that happening to a traveling band of Gypsies? And why did Elmer have to die?

Charity had been a Christian. Her mother and father were killed in a house fire, so she went to live with an uncle who abused her until she ran away when she was sixteen. Boss found her living under a bridge. He never asked questions. He fed her and gave her a home. In time, she and Esmeralda became the best of friends. Esmeralda was twenty-two years older, so Charity looked upon her as a mother figure. She loved Charity and Charity loved her. Thinking about her getting killed still brought tears to her eyes.

Maw? How would one describe a woman who has weathered so many storms and remained pure of heart? Elmer was a sweetheart, but it was Maw who made them heirs to the farm. She toiled everyday cooking for them, quite a chore in itself. And whenever one of the field hands came in hurt, it was Maw who made him lie down on the sofa so she could tend to his injury. Then she would give him lemonade or buttermilk or a glass of moonshine. She treated them all like her sons

and daughters. Elmer's death hurt Maw deeply, but the next day she
was back in the kitchen cooking for her family.

She liked Anastasia, but there was something about that woman
she couldn't put her finger on. She knew she came from society because
of her mannerisms and speech, but Anastasia never talked about her
past like young women do. There was an air of mystery about her. But
no matter, she was pregnant and Esmeralda had helped deliver five babies. She would assist Anastasia with her delivery.

Long Tom was another mystery. He walked into camp one day,
spoke with Boss, then settled in, keeping to himself most of the time.
Whenever there was a disturbance inside or outside the camp, Long
Tom could always be found standing close to Boss. He was there to
protect him. She suspected he had seen action in the military, but that
was never discussed. People just felt better whenever Tom was around.
Then when he got shot, she saw another side of him that surprised her.
Tom was just as vulnerable as anyone else when he was hurt. Anastasia
led him by the hand those first few days until his balance returned. She
fed him and dressed him. Maw helped too because he was such a big
fella.

Orlando had asked for her hand a week earlier. She was fifty and
well past the childbearing years. Could she still get pregnant? Some
older women do. Orlando was a good-looking man and a hard worker,
but she didn't love him. Still, it might be nice to have someone around
the house to talk to and plan things together. *Jesus, what a decision to
make at my age.*

Charity told her that man is God's children. If that's so, why does
God allow them to rob and rape and start wars? Charity said it's because God gave man free will. If God is a good parent, maybe they
need their bottoms spanked.

She thought about the father she never knew who was killed in
Vietnam in 1974 when she was one year old. At age eighteen she began
studying the war. Ho Chi Minh should have become president, but the

CIA overturned the elections, giving South Vietnam to Diem and his evil brother. Vietnam was a civil war but President Johnson turned it into an American crusade. Over one million Vietnamese were killed and fifty-eight thousand plus Americans. What a waste, she thought. All because of foolish men and their politics.

She recalled when President Trump made America energy independent. Then President Biden came along and ran a booming economy into the ground with his silly New Green Energy nonsense. Esmeralda knew the sun was responsible for climate variations, not man. Gypsies know these things about the earth and the moon.

If God created man, if there is a God, the product appears to be flawed. Man keeps doing stupid things that hurt others. So, if God created man, does that make God liable for man's misdeeds? Is there a cosmic court that would hear the case?

Esmeralda decided she was thinking too much about things she had no control over, so she went outside to weed her flower beds. She was pulling out a string of pesky crabgrass from the base of her rose bush when Tom came up the hill.

"Maw fell and hurt herself. Can you come take a look? She asked for you."

Down at the house, Maw was resting on the sofa where she had treated so many before her. Esmeralda lifted her dress to observe the damage.

"You got a nasty bone bruise, Maw, an' a patch uh skin's been raked off. How'd you do that?"

"I fell over one uh them dang crates out in the kitchen."

"I'll mix up a poultice to kill infection an' take down the swellin'. I'll tie it on with uh clean hand towel. You'll have to stay put for a few hours for the poultice to work. If you gotta pee, go do it now."

"No, honey, I went an hour ago."

"You want something to nibble on or a drink, maybe?"

"I'd like me a glass uh that ho-made white whiskey."

End of the Line

0905, three F-15s flew over at ten thousand feet, employing barrage jamming, which overrode the two Russian SAM sites, making it impossible to pick up the echoes from the incoming bombers. The enemy camp was located four miles below O'Hare International Airport on both sides of Highway 294. The F-15s continued their jamming as they circled the perimeter.

0910, Three B-52 bombers flew over at twenty-five thousand feet with two hundred and ten bombs. Two bombers carried eighty-four, five-hundred pound bombs for each side of Highway 294. A third B-52 was carrying forty-two, seven hundred and fifty-pound bombs scheduled for the O'Hare runways.

With an air raid siren wailing its mournful cry, gun crews ran to their Bofors 40 mm guns which had a range of six and a quarter miles. But it was too little, too late. The bombers were already on the outskirts of the city. There was too little time to load, aim, and fire. The five-hundred-pounders were beginning to fall from the bomb racks toward the barracks and the fuel depot.

"Lake Michigan sure is beautiful with the sun shining down on the water. I can see five fishing boats."

"How's our bomb run doing?"

"I'll know in a few seconds, as soon as the first ones hit the deck."

"Oh my God! There went the fuel dump. You dropped 'em right down the ole pickle barrel, Jonesy. They're plowing through that place like a damn tornado. "

Down on the ground, men, buildings, and machines were being blown to kingdom come. Timbers, arms and legs, and pieces of equipment were raining from the sky. The shattered fuel depot was billowing flames two hundred feet into the air. The bombers circled out over Lake Michigan and headed for base.

Meanwhile, seven hundred and five miles south, two additional F-15s flew over Possum Trot then across the Army Reserve Center heading toward the Anniston Army Depot. There was only one Russian SAM battery located there. Two B-52s were five minutes behind the F-15s. They were after the Abram tanks and those Anniston repair facilities.

When Snow White heard the air raid siren he ran to the window to see what was happening. He saw the first explosions in the distance. They were coming his way at a terrific pace. He turned to run for the door and the air raid shelter. But a five-hundred pounder crashed through the ceiling, blasting Snow White through the roof with the remainder of the building. Tanks were blown apart and flipped upside down. The Anniston Army Depot was out of the war.

United States Navy

Donald Trump was sitting behind his desk in the oval office with his team of advisers. Johnny Poe was with them. They were celebrating the success of the bombing raids the previous morning. The B-52s were a welcome relief from all the blood and treasure sacrificed over the past eighteen months.

"Jamming went off without a hitch. Anniston was a total wipeout. O'Hare's main runways were cratered. We got the storage tanks and ammunition bunkers. But we missed about twenty of their barracks. They have no fuel and their ammo bunkers are history, so I believe we can write off Chicago."

"San Diego is our next objective. What about that herd of monkeys down in Charleston? They've been stealing food and gasoline from the locals at gunpoint."

"That's a medium-size base. I'll send out two extra bombers with the San Diego raid. Gentlemen, once we pull this off, we will have eliminated fifty percent of their capabilities. One more of these raids and they'll have to surrender or face annihilation. Now, let's decide on China. Colonel King?"

"My team has studied the satellite photos and all the information sent over by Field Marshal Feng. This is quite an undertaking. The Maoists number upwards of three million. Marshal Feng's forces, about a million and a half. China is a large country. We believe the most humane course of action, and this is up for grabs, would be to eliminate the leaders of their armies. That might induce the rank and file to sue for peace."

"How big is their main army?"

"About six hundred thousand."

"How would you go about killing those men in charge?"

"Good question. We don't know yet."

"Is that army all in one location or spread out all over?"

"Their base of operations is in and around a giant cave called Zhijin in the Guizhou province. That's a mountainous region. Marshal Feng and his brother have the launch codes. So, there's no risk of a nuclear response. I don't want us to resort to nuclear weapons unless our country is threatened. We all know about the aftermath of Hiroshima and Nagasaki."

"It seems impossible to take out so few men surrounded by so many."

"David Israel suggested creating a diversion of some kind to draw out their leaders onto a single killing ground. But what bait could we use?"

"What if you used me as bait?" Johnny Poe said. "They would be curious to see who exposed Wufong and his followers."

President Trump was the first to respond. "Johnny, Mao was a ruthless dictator, worse than Hitler or Stalin. We'll find another way to deal with those Maoists. You are China's future. China can't afford to lose you."

General Black spoke up. "I respect saving lives but those men leading the rebel forces are communists, our sworn enemies. They will give no quarter to Marshal Feng, much less to any of us. They have seven army groups located in central and southern China which, to put it bluntly, is a shit-load."

"Bomb all seven headquarters in a synchronized attack. Then knock out the marshaling yards and bridges between the Maoist armies and the Field Marshal. Hit their main battle group. Bomb the bejesus outta their communist asses with B-52s."

Discussions went on for another hour.

Finally, Admiral Wingate revealed his plan. "We estimated nine carrier groups will get the job done. Our flattops will have over seven hundred fighter planes. Those rebel pilots won't stand a chance against our boys. We have enough missiles onboard over a hundred escort ships to defeat any situation that may arise."

"Our Navy sounds like our best alternative," President Trump said. "I believe we should go with Admiral Wingate. Any objections? Does anyone have a better alternative?"

The men remained silent. They liked the idea of aircraft carriers.

"Start assembling our ships. San Diego is scheduled in three days. That's their largest military base, including those docking facilities. Four bombers are going on this mission, and two to Charleston. Any questions?"

David Israel raised his hand. "Yes, Mister President. Would you object to my going on the Charleston raid? I would like to see our results from the air. And to tell my grandkids I flew on one of the planes that won the war."

Iran

Yazd, Iran, dates back to the fifth century and is the second most historic city in the world, after Venice, Italy. It was located on the Spice and Silk Roads, trade routes from dozens of locations in China, Indonesia, and Japan. Trade crossed over the deserts of the Middle East, then the Mediterranean Sea, to dozens of Western European cities, including

Athens, Constantinople, Rome, and Barcelona. Marco Polo visited Yazd. In 2025, it is known for its industrial textile centers, and its silk and quality carpets. Other industries of note were ceramics and construction materials. With a population of five hundred and eighty-five thousand, it is surrounded by the Bafgh Desert.

An eleven-year-old boy is on the roof of his two-story apartment building, feeding his pigeons. Young Aries has built a roost, using scrap plywood and old 2 x 4s, for them to sleep in at night. He loves his pigeons, who gather around his bare feet when he feeds them grain and bits of bread. His father works in one of the textile mills, helping maintain the machinery. His mother is a housewife who cares for him and his five brothers and sisters.

Tomahawk

Tomahawk is a surface-to-surface missile powered by a turbo jet engine with a range of one thousand and five hundred miles. Subsonic speed is approximately five hundred and sixty miles per hour. The missile weighs two thousand nine hundred pounds, with a one thousand-pound warhead. It is satellite-assisted and guided by TERCOM radar. It has an accuracy within five meters and travels thirty to fifty meters above the surface of the earth. It has hardened electrical circuits, so it's difficult to divert or bring down.

Aries was cleaning out the feathers and bird droppings from the pigeon roost when a flash of sunlight on metal caught his eye across the desert. He didn't know a Tomahawk missile was en route, using Yazd as a reference point.

He watched in awe as a tiny speck grew in size by the second, coming straight toward him. Aries dropped to his hands and knees when the Tomahawk swept past, heading north. It had been fired from an American submarine thirty miles out in the Gulf of Oman. Once past

Yazd, its point of destination was forty minutes away. The missile rose and fell as it passed over hills and valleys.

Tehran is the capital of Iran. Its 2025 population was approximately nine million. Ninety percent practice the Shia religion. Iran is a totally male-dominated society. Women are forced to wear the burka when outside the home, a black tent like affair which covers everything but their eyes. Women are treated as second-class citizens. They are not allowed to leave the house without a male escort. Thought police patrol the streets. Clerics and ayatollahs preach the seventh-century visions passed down by Muhammad's scribes. Citizens are stoned to death and sometimes beheaded for infractions of the strict religious code. Poverty level is eighteen percent. Seventy percent of Iranians own their homes.

Ayatollah Khomeini was having tea on his balcony overlooking the city. It had been a trying morning. He was faced with the dilemma of declaring martial law again because of all the protests in the streets. He didn't want another Chinese Tiananmen Square where the People's Liberation Army brought in nearly a hundred tanks and killed over a thousand people. So, he went ahead and signed the decree beginning next Saturday.

Why are those young men so ungrateful? he wondered. *They have jobs and food on the table. The women are kept in their place, as they should be. What is this nonsense about free speech and democracy? The Quran forbids such Western behavior.*

His attempt on Donald Trump's life had failed, but it taught the infidels a lesson. They were vulnerable. He would consult with Comrade Putin about transportation for another commando team. Those nuclear warheads from Russia were a dream come true. Soon the filthy Jews would burn in Allah's furnace. And perhaps the Great Satan, if his scientists could produce a rocket capable of reaching the United States.

The tea was exceptionally good this morning. The cook must be using that new blend from Poland. A spark of light caught his attention across the desert. It grew in size … and appeared—it was coming straight at him!

He knocked over the table in his effort to reach the chamber door. As he reached for the handle, an 18 foot, 4 inch package of whoop-ass burst through the outer wall. He never heard the explosion. He was blown into a thousand pieces with tons of stone and mortar crashing down into the courtyard below.

An ensign onboard the nuclear submarine *Tilapia* was monitoring traffic coming from the castle compound. Suddenly, the radio transmissions went ballistic. He alerted his captain. The submarine captain relayed a message to President Trump at the White House:

"Ayatollah Rocknrolla."

Donald Trump was settling an old score with the arch enemy of Israel and Uncle Sam. He wondered where Barack Obama was hiding? The George Soros blue plate special. It was discovered in 2022 that he was born in Mombasa, Kenya, and not Hawaii as claimed. His brother and a grandmother confirmed the report. Obama was responsible for starting the war against the police and fossil fuels, and resurrecting the specter of racism. President Trump had a special cell picked out in Leavenworth for the Manchurian Candidate.

On a Wing and a Prayer

San Diego had American SAMS, as well as two missile platforms from Russia. American SAMs had been stored there ever since the Gulf War in 1991. They also had an array of anti-aircraft batteries. The Air Force was aware of this, so the bombing mission was scheduled for forty-seven thousand feet which was three thousand five hundred feet above the effective range of the 90 mm AA guns. Radar would pick them up miles before they reached the target, but with F-15s running interference, the

SAMs would not be able to lock on. Fourteen F-14 Tomcats had been stationed there before the civil war. Sixteen F-15 Eagles would accompany the four B-52 bombers.

The lead bomber was carrying thirty one-thousand-pound bombs for the docking facilities. The remaining three bombers were loaded with five hundred-pound bombs. At forty-seven thousand feet, the falling bombs would scatter over a broad area due to the shifting air currents.

"Commander, check out your ten o'clock."

"I see 'em."

"We're hung out like grandma's laundry with seven, no eight, bogies six miles and closing."

"There go the Eagles."

"Hey, they got one!"

"They got one of ours too. Look at your four o'clock. There go the parachutes."

"There's a contrail coming our way. Jettison those flares."

"Here comes another one."

"More flares, Mistro."

Commander Lloyd Miller and his four crewmen maneuver into formation beside the other three B-52s. The lead radar navigator gives his go-ahead and the bomb bay doors open.

"Two minutes to target."

All around them dogfights begin taking place between the enemy F-14s and the American Eagles.

"One minute to target."

They didn't suspect death was waiting in the clouds one thousand four hundred feet above them.

"Bombs gone!"

A Tomcat dove out of the clouds firing his 20 mm rotary cannon. Miller and the pilot watch in horror as the tracers walk the starboard wing of the lead bomber into her fuel tanks. The tanks explode and the wing begins to collapse. Down she goes toward the sea.

"Jesus God! Here it comes!"

The enemy Tomcat sweeps around and fires his last Stinger. It strikes the starboard outboard engine pod of Miller's aircraft. The Tomcat then fires a 20 mm burst into their inboard engine pod. A missile from an F-15 Eagle soars up his tailpipe. The Tomcat explodes.

Three parachutes appear from the falling bomber. The pilot and his navigator won't be going home for Christmas.

"He got some of our cables. I'm having trouble keeping her nose up."

"Arizona border is four hundred miles. Can we make it that far, Captain?"

"I gotta burn boo koo fuel portside, but I believe the ole girl will get us there. Anything loose in back throw out the bomb bay door. We're losin' air pressure. Put on your oxygen masks."

With three engines out, the bomber was down to three hundred and eighty knots. It would be an hour before they reached the Arizona border and safety. With so much drag from the damaged starboard wing, the aircraft was slowly losing altitude. Base was alerted of their situation. They were informed the remaining two bombers made it out safely.

"Satellite report came in. Base estimates seventy percent destroyed. We done good back there in spite of our losses. We got all their Tomcats but they took down five of our Eagles. That's fifteen brave men, counting the bomber."

"Vibration is getting worse. We're down to eighteen thousand feet."

"I can see the Colorado River. Interstate 8 will be off to your right heading east out of Yuma. We can land on the highway."

"There it is. Fuel tanks are running low. I'm setting the ole girl down. Hang on."

They came down at a hundred and fifty-seven knots, hit the

pavement, and bounced. Ninety-one tons was too much for the asphalt. It broke and the great bomber slid off the highway, down an embankment, through a grove of pine trees, and a split rail fence, shattering a barn before crushing a toolshed. Directly in their path sat a farmhouse with smoke curling out the chimney.

"Oh please, God. Please. Not the house."

Closer and closer the heavy bomber slid, grinding a birdbath in its path.

With four feet to spare the nose stopped right beside the front porch.

A man stepped out on the porch with a double-barrel shotgun. Right behind him came a gray-haired lady carrying a second double-barrel. She was dressed in a pink housecoat and pink house slippers. He wore faded blue jeans, a red, white, and blue long-sleeve shirt, and a cowboy hat. Her hair was down to her shoulders. The mister's hair was iron gray.

"You them damn communist bastards from out yonder in California? Come in here wreckin' my place! Speak up er I'll blow yer ass ta hell!"

"No, sir. We ain't communists. We just bombed San Diego."

"Well, what the hell you doin' in my front yard?"

"We got shot up, sir. This is as far as we could make it. The United States Air Force will pay for any damages."

"Well, by God! Ya hear that, Sarah? They're Americans!"

"Ask 'em in, Horace. I'll put the coffee on. We got apple pie an' cherry pie. From the looks uh that airplane they could use a bite."

Inside the farmhouse the five airmen were humbled by what they saw on the oak mantelpiece above a stone fireplace. A folded American flag. A picture of a young man in his Army dress uniform. And a glass case with his medals and his buck sergeant stripes inside.

Sarah explained. "Jonathan was killed in the fighting in Africa. They sent our son home in a metal coffin. We buried him up on the hill beside the church. We got an official letter sayin' he'd given his life for his country an' all the usual gobbledygook. We don't see how dyin' in Africa solved nothin'. Bureaucrats an' bullshit. That's all Washington was before the war come along."

Horace wiped tears from his eyes with his handkerchief. "Me an' Sarah are pleased to meet y'all. Your bombin' them cockroaches out in California made our day. They needed killin' from what we been hearin' 'bout how they been goin' around robbin', an' sometimes worse."

"There was four of us bombers and sixteen fighter planes. We lost one bomber and five fighters, but we blew the hell outta that dang base. I hope that makes up a little bit for your son. We're proud to meet you all too. You and a passel of other folks are what we're fighting' for."

"Horace, I'm thinkin' these fellas might like a taste uh shine."

"Yes, ma'am! We surely would."

Horace laughed and went out to the kitchen. He returned with seven glasses on a Coca-Cola tray and a cold jug of white lightning from the freezer. An hour later none of them were feeling any pain. Sarah was laughing and having an enjoyable evening for the first time since the death of her son two years ago.

It wasn't long before a helicopter landed in the backyard to take them back to their base in Houston.

"They'll send flatbeds and a crane to get that mess outta your yard. And they'll pay for us wreckin' the place. I'm sure glad we got to meet you all. It gives us inspiration to do our jobs. And to know men like Jonathan went on before us. Take care and be sure to write. We'll stop back by some day."

Horace shook their hands. Sarah handed them a cardboard box with ham sandwiches and a cherry pie inside. Then they were on their way.

Three-quarters of the Marxist bases in America lay in ruins.

China

China is the second oldest country in the world, preceded only by Japan. Russia is nearly twice the size of China, followed by Canada, then China. China consists of three million, seven hundred and five square miles with a shoreline of nine thousand and ten linear miles. There are twenty-three provinces, five autonomous regions, and four municipalities. China invented gunpowder, paper, the compass, and printing.

Emperors and warlords ruled China for centuries. Civil war broke out between the Communists and the Nationalists during the 1920s and lasted two decades. Mao Zedong was finally victorious, so Chiang Kai-shek and his followers fled to Taiwan. China was proclaimed the People's Republic of China in 1949. Richard Nixon formally recognized China in 1972. Mao was responsible for the deaths of tens of millions. Mao Zedong died in 1976.

China was governed by a one-party, Marxist-Leninist dictatorship after Mao took control. The population in 2022 was 1.4 billion. Following the Peking attack against the United States in 2024, Donald Trump destroyed Peking and Shanghai. Shanghai was the financial nerve center for China. With Shanghai gone and the communist central government destroyed, the country fell into chaos, followed by starvation. By 2026 the population had dwindled to just over one billion. Civil war broke out again between the Mao Loyalists and the followers of Field Marshal Feng who sought freedom for the Chinese people.

The American fleet was deployed just south of Taiwan in the South China Sea. Admiral Wingate was waiting for reports from his nuclear submarines patrolling the China coast and inside the Taiwan Strait. His nine flattops were vulnerable to missile attack, so the admiral was being cautious. His was a grave responsibility for the one hundred and fifteen ships of the U.S. Navy under his command.

"Admiral, this is Kincaide on the *Sunfish*. We've covered about sixty miles and I ain't seen nothin' that looks unfriendly. But they could have an army back in those trees. We did spot a couple of patrol planes but nothing that posed a threat."

"Same here, Admiral. This is Kelly on the *Angelfish*. We've seen junks and one patrol boat, but nothing resembling trouble. It's like Kincaide said, we can't see beyond the shoreline and all those shanties."

"Sir, Captain Fletcher here. We have in our periscope one of those 055 warships. She's a long mother, about eleven thousand tons. Request permission to engage."

"This is Admiral Wingate to all submarine commanders. Keep your eyes peeled for those 055 ships. Captain Fletcher, you are cleared to engage."

USS *Yellow Tang* opened an outer door at three thousand yards. She fired a 1.75-ton Mark 48 torpedo with a 655-pound warhead. At 28 knots it would take 3.18 minutes to reach the target. Modern torpedoes are designed to detonate beneath a ship. The concept is to break the keel.

"Time check."

"One minute and seventeen seconds, Captain."

"She hasn't changed course."

"No, those people are not regular seamen. They should have detected us by now on sonar."

"Thirty-four seconds, captain."

Watching through his periscope, Captain Fletcher sees sudden activity on the deck of the enemy warship. The 055 begins a sharp turn but it's too late. Suddenly, she buckles amidships. A huge geyser of water shoots a hundred feet above her mast. As the water cascades back into the sea, he can see the ship has broken in half. Survivors can be seen in the water.

"Surface. Surface. Proceed at quarter speed to the wreck."

When they were within twenty yards of the men in the water,

Captain Fletcher ordered a dozen inflatable rubber dinghies tossed overboard. *Yellow Tang* reversed her propellers and backed away.

"That was outstanding, captain. Why did you do that?"

"My grandfather was in World War Two. He had a cruiser shot out from under him at Guadalcanal. He told me about the sharks. Those men can make it to shore in those rubber dinghies. War is a filthy business, Chief Mate Perry. They deserve better than being eaten alive by sharks."

Forty-six minutes.

Four submarine captains have reported in except for the *Stingray*. The Admiral's radio crackles onboard the aircraft carrier *Abraham Lincoln*.

"Admiral, are you there?"

"I'm here, Captain Floyd. Go ahead."

"About nine nautical miles from me are two rebel warships. They have air cover. I count eight aircraft. I've kept my distance so they can't spot my shadow in the water. This looks like a job for the flyboys, sir."

"Good thinking, Captain. Send your position and I'll get our people on this immediately. Keep them in periscope contact."

Six F-35C stealth fighters approach the enemy formation at thirty thousand feet. Following ten miles behind are two torpedo bombers carrying Quicksink bombs. Quicksinks are two thousand-pound JDAMs with a guidance kit attached. A Quicksink drops down beside a ship never actually touching the hull. The explosion creates a pressure wave which snaps the keel in half.

"Jimmy Durante to Mrs. Calabash. They don't know we're here. You are cleared to plow the field."

Five Sidewinders spiral down into the communist formation. Alarm systems sound followed by five explosions. Five burning aircraft plummet toward the sea.

"Outstanding! Pour on the coal, boys."

Two additional aircraft are shot down as the last J-11B streaks for home. The stealth fighter jets strafe the decks of the warships keeping the heads of their gunners down as the torpedo bombers line up their attack. Tremendous geysers shoot skyward from the explosions. Both ships break apart and sink in minutes.

"Both ships sunk, sir. There are dozens of men in the water, Admiral."

"Go in there and give them some life rafts then get the hell out. They may come back with reinforcements. I don't want to come fishing you out of the drink. Patrol that east shore for a while longer."

Two hours later.

"Admiral, this is Captain Floyd on the *Stingray*. We got bogies coming from the northeast. They're hugging the waves so you can't see them behind Taiwan. I estimate well over a hundred, maybe two hundred. They're not interested in us, sir. They're coming for you."

"We're going to battle stations. Stay where you are, *Stingray*. You're the eyes and ears now for the fleet. There may be others on the way."

The Admiral managed to get over ninety fighters aloft before the enemy formation began arriving. The American pilots held their position at thirty-nine thousand feet. The ships opened fire. Hundreds of missiles fill the sky. Enemy aircraft begin going down in flames. One ship after another is hit. An ammunition frigate explodes, sending a towering mushroom cloud high above the fleet. A Kh-59 missile cuts a destroyer in half. Dozens of burning aircraft tumble into the sea. An oiler explodes, spreading burning fuel oil across the waves. Columns of thick black smoke from burning ships rise above the South China Sea as far as the eye can see. Hundreds of sailors and airmen cling to floating debris in the water.

American pilots engage.

".... Billie, you got one on your tail. Break right! Break right! .... throw me a life jacket. I can't swim .... here they come again .... more ammo, John. More .... God Damn! They got Jerry .... I'm hit! I'm hit! .... it's stuck. Oh God! We're going down .... wake up, Rocco .... Medic!

Medic! …. we need some help over here …. kill the sons a bitches ….
Watch out! We're running over them …. Do not be afraid, my son.
You're going to a better place …. Flank speed, helmsman …. bail out,
man. Get outta there …. I shall fear no evil for thou art …. bend the
fucker back so they can get out …. tell my husband …. Jamie Boy, I got
ya, Jamie Boy …. concentrate on that lead sumbitch …. fuck this! My
engine quit! …. Look out, look out…. we got men in the water …. I'll
see you fellas on the other side …. send one up his commie ass …. here
one for yo badass mama an all yo nasty-ass cousins too …."

The battle raged for twenty-five minutes. Running low on fuel, the
enemy disengaged. Planes of the fleet pursued, shooting down two
more. The final tally was a grim statistic. The American fleet had lost
four destroyers sunk, with two more sailing for Pearl. Three aircraft
carriers were hit, the *Abraham Lincoln* twice. One oiler sunk and one
damaged. One ammunition ship blown up. Two guided-missile cruisers heavily damaged. One anti-aircraft warship sunk. A hospital ship
took two hits but remained on station. More than nine hundred killed
and thirteen hundred injured.

Battle Damage

"Yes, Mister President. Their pilots were better than we anticipated.
Some of them were Russians. We got our asses kicked. They lost nine-
ty-six aircraft. We have no idea what they have in reserve planes. Our
losses were thirty-one aircraft. We lost seven ships, none above ten
thousand tons. We have thirty-four ships damaged. The fleet account-
ed for most of the enemy shot down."

"How did our planes stack up against theirs?"

"We have better planes and better pilots, but there were close to
three hundred enemy aircraft, so everyone had their hands full. We
had lookouts posted a hundred miles out but they came in so low we
didn't pick them up soon enough. I managed to get ninety-four fighters

aloft. I should have had twice that many airborne, engaging them miles before they reached the fleet. Our losses are my fault, sir."

"Sounds like you managed something resembling a draw. Coming in behind the island was a smart move on their part. Once you're past Taiwan they won't have the island advantage anymore. Contact the Field Marshal. He needs your help right now."

Desperate Hours

"Field Marshal, this is Admiral Wingate. We're here to assist you. I have your position on the east side of the Xinjiang River above the city of Yingtan. Is that correct?"

"Yes, Admiral, that is correct. You couldn't have come at a better time. We have our backs to the Xinjiang and we're taking heavy artillery fire."

"My staff advises that you mark the tops of your tanks and trucks with paint, and any buildings you occupy. It's hard to distinguish friend from foe from the air."

"Give me a few minutes. I will call you back."

Ten minutes elapse. "We found orange paint. They're doing as you requested. How soon before your airplanes arrive?"

Wingate could hear explosions in the background, men shouting, and the rumble of tanks.

"I'm launching as we speak. What locations require immediate attention?"

"Sushan Mountain is southeast of the city. They have artillery there, and all along Highway 320 which runs northeast of Yingtan. If you can silence those big guns that will be a great help. They are cutting my soldiers to pieces."

Nine flattops had turned into the wind and were launching aircraft. With thirty-six fighters airborne, Wingate sends them on ahead. Others continue to arm and form up above the fleet. F-15s, F-22s, and

F-35s race toward the Sushan Mountain. As the mountain comes into view, the pilots are amazed at the vast array of artillery on the mountain and down on the highway.

Atop the mountain and for two miles along Highway 320, confidence of victory is swept aside as horror and high explosives plows through the crowded ranks of the artillery crews. More and more planes arrive, delivering bombs, rockets, and 20 mm cannon fire. Plane after plane attacks the mountain and Highway 320, employing their Vulcan Gatling guns. The asphalt flows bright crimson with blood.

Then it became the turn of the Maoist soldiers facing Field Marshal Feng and General Hu. Earth, trees, and men are blasted skyward as hundreds of bombs and rockets rain down. The Gatling guns are relentless. The carnage goes on for an hour. Suddenly, the warplanes are gone.

A shattered army was all that remained in the smoldering wreckage. The Maoist commander radios Field Marshal Feng requesting help. His dead are unknown. He has thousands of wounded and dying. The Nationalist troops lay down their weapons and go over to the aid of their hurt and dying countrymen. A first victory has just been achieved for the Nationalist Army.

A Question of Tactics

"I don't know, Mister President. It makes no sense that their air force didn't come to defend their troops on the ground. The Field Marshal was backed up against a river, so he was in a tight spot. I'm just thankful we got there when we did. I take nothing away from Marshal Feng. He and General Hu have been in the thick of it for months now. They did well with what they had to work with. Those Mao soldiers have more of everything."

"You defeated their best and biggest army. My staff thinks you did more damage to their air force than originally thought in your sea battle. A number of those enemy aircraft that made it back to base had to be damaged. They may be licking their wounds and preparing for another attack. So, keep your eyes and ears open. Do you need anything?"

"No, sir, but the Marshal requested two shiploads of plasma and medical supplies. The Nationalists have gone over to help those thousands of Maoist troops we just blew away. That man is something. To be as old as he is and out there in the midst of all this killing speaks volumes about the man's character. I hope China has more men like him."

"They do, Admiral. One of them is sitting right here in the office with me, Johnny Poe."

A Blessed Event

Anastasia was sunning herself on a lounge out in the front yard overlooking the highway and the produce building. She was thirty-six weeks pregnant and a little fearful of what lay ahead. She had heard stories about childbirth. It sounded dreadful.

She was almost asleep when she had her first contraction. That wasn't so bad, she thought. Then she had another one. It dawned on her she was going into labor.

"Maw. Esmeralda. It's my time. I need you, please."

Then her water broke. The next contraction hurt.

"MAW! ESMERALDA! COME HELP ME!"

Esmeralda was up at her retreat on the ridge when she heard Anastasia. Down the hill she came running. Maw stuck her head out the kitchen door. She tossed her apron on the countertop and hurried out to where Anastasia lay.

Esmeralda unbuttoned Anastasia's skirt, took it off, then slipped off her soaked panties. "Maw, get some towels and a bucket uh hot water."

"Oh God! I didn't think it would be like this."

"Take deep breaths, honey. Then let it all out."

"Ohhhh shit! This is awful."

Maw returned with the towels and water. Esmeralda slid a towel under Anastasia's bottom. Then she rolled one up and placed it behind Anastasia's neck. Forty-five painful minutes pass. Contractions are coming one minute apart.

"Push, Anastasia. Push!"

"*Auughhhh.*"

"Keep those knees up. We're getting there. Push!"

"*Awww* JESUS!"

"Deep breath. Push!"

"You fuckers are killing me. OOOOH GOD!"

Maw chuckled. "No, honey, jus' 'bout halfway will do."

Thirty-five minutes later, amid Anastasia's cursing and Maw's country humor, a little boy is born. Esmeralda ties off the umbilical cord, sponges off mother and child, then unbuttons Anastasia's blouse and places the infant between Anastasia's breasts. The little fellow takes hold of a nipple with his tiny hand and falls asleep.

"Ain't that just like a man?"

Esmeralda cackles. "That was a quick childbirth. You're lucky."

"It didn't feel very lucky, but golly am I glad that's over. He's beautiful, isn't he? And he has hair."

"What are you going to name him?"

"I don't know. I'll ask Tommy to help me."

Just then Long Tom came driving up the driveway in the pickup truck.

"Cover me up. I don't want Tommy to see me all naked. Thank you, Esmeralda. Thank you, Maw. Thank you for helping with my little boy."

"Hey, Tommy. Come over here a minute."

When he saw the child he rushed over and knelt down beside his wife. "What a day this has been. I just bought the farm next door, and here you are with a baby. I'm the luckiest man alive. Are you alright? Is the baby alright? Is there anything I need to do?"

"Yes, dear, help me to the bedroom. I'll be more comfortable there."

Maw pins a towel around Anastasia's waist and Tommy assists her with the baby up to the house. Once Anastasia is dressed in pajamas and tucked in bed, Maw brings out a bottle of muscadine brandy.

"That lady what makes them preserves an' jellies brung this over. She said don't open it 'til the baby comes. Well, the little rascals here. I reckon we can celebrate a mite, can't we?"

"I reckon we can."

Esmeralda heads out to the kitchen for four glasses. They pull up chairs around the bed and share their brandy, toasting the child, the mother, the father, and the new farm. The addition of the farm next door added another two hundred and twenty acres. The old man living there was going to go live with his daughter in Corpus Christi. The newborn would soon witness produce being delivered by van and pickup truck to grocery stores and restaurants up and down Highway 10. Miss Liberty was regaining her footing on the world stage.

German U-boat

Meanwhile, on the other side of the world, deep beneath the frozen tundra of Central Siberia in a steel reinforced concrete bunker, a man small in stature was discussing the possibility of World War Three with two Cossack generals.

"If we fired all our missiles at one time, could we beat them?"

"No, they have fourteen sea-based nuclear subs. They have other submarines, but those fourteen are always on station. One might beat us in a war. Two could destroy Mother Russia."

"What if we concentrate one big bomb on Washington?"

"Same result. It would take longer, but someone down the chain of command would order a strike."

"Could one of our subs go up the Potomac River?"

"Only where it empties out into the Atlantic. The rest of the river is too shallow."

"Wait a minute. Remember those Type Vll German U-boats we confiscated after the war?"

"Of course, what about them?"

"There's a channel twenty-four feet deep running one hundred and eight miles up the Potomac River. If we could attach that American H-bomb we fished out of the sea off the coast of Spain to a Type Vll and sail it in close to Washington …."

"… and blow those capitalist swine straight to hell. They would never know it was us!"

"Right! It would have to be a moonless night. Type VIIs draft fifteen feet. At two hundred and twelve feet in length it would run aground if submerged."

"Paint the superstructure black."

"How could we get the thing over there? An old U-boat might break down in the middle of the Atlantic."

"We have that new submarine that's six hundred and three feet long, the *Belgorod*. We could piggyback a Type Vll behind her tower then detach the U-boat off the American coast and sail it up the Potomac in the dead of night."

"By Jupiter, that could work."

"There would have to be a team onboard the German sub to operate the ballast and manage the ship. Our naval engineers will have to figure out how to attach and release a German submarine from our *Belgorod*."

"That type of bomb will incinerate everything within three square miles. Massive damage and fires will occur beyond the blast zone. The shock wave would damage buildings miles inland. Radiation would kill far beyond ground zero. Washington would be destroyed."

Putin rubs his hands together gleefully and smiles. "That is exactly what I want, comrades. Get your people started on this right away.

I'm going back to Moscow tonight. I will meet you here again in three weeks."

Womanhood

Nancy was twelve years old. The day after her twelfth birthday, she boxed up her baby dolls and put them away. She didn't fancy herself a little girl anymore. Her breasts were developing and she even had hair down below. She didn't much care for the hair, but she was very proud of her perky little breasts. So, she went to Colonel Mosrie and asked if she should wear a bra. The colonel told her he didn't know, so he took her to a women's clothing store in Franklin. Department stores hadn't made a comeback yet, so people bought and sold used clothing.

The lady clerk found an A cup that fit perfectly. The sales person matched Nancy with two pairs of silk panties, a white nylon slip, a smart business suit previously worn by a real estate agent, plus an extra skirt and two pretty blouses. The colonel paid the woman and they drove back to the base.

Colonel Mosrie had recently organized a school for all the kids in the compound. It was deemed safe now, since Anniston had been put out of business. There were four classrooms, two for ages twelve to seventeen and two more for youngsters six through eleven.

Nancy noticed an attractive fifteen-year-old boy in her class, but he was so full of himself that she lost interest. One day he came up to Nancy and asked her name. She responded that she didn't make friends with egotistical boys. The next day he brought Nancy an orange with a ribbon around it as a peace offering. Nancy refused his gift. So, he tried again the following day with a shiny red apple.

Two weeks later they were walking to school together and enjoying hikes in the forest. Skylar Smith was smitten with Nancy Jones. And the feeling was mutual. One afternoon at their secret place in the woods, Skylar kissed Nancy. It made her feel funny and it disturbed

Skyler because it made his penis erect. They vowed to never do that again. Less than a week later he kissed her again.

Nancy experienced a strange sensation she'd never felt before. So did Skylar. Nancy pushed him away, saying they must wait until they were older. Henry had purchased birth control pills, telling Nancy to use them when the right man came along. She started taking her pills, just to be on the safe side.

A week went by when Nancy became the aggressor. She kissed Skylar several times then lay down on their blanket and slipped off her blue jeans and her white panties. Skylar didn't need any further encouragement. They coupled. It was wonderful, delightful beyond anything they ever imagined. Skylar said it was magic. They liked it so much they did it a second time. This became a pattern. Oftentimes after school, they slipped away to their hideaway in the forest and made love.

Nancy was in love. Skylar was attentive to her every need. They went to the movies, he carried her books after school, they hitched rides to the library in Franklin, and oftentimes they ate in the canteen together. Nancy was maturing into a woman. And Skylar Smith was contemplating a future with Miss Nancy Jones.

Battle Stations

General Hu was advancing a Nationalist division of twenty-five thousand troops against a similar Maoist stronghold a few miles northeast of the North Vietnam border. The communists were dug in on the outskirts of Nanning and holed up inside the city's ancient fort overlooking White Dragon Lake. Nanning was home to some seven million, five hundred thousand Chinese. Field Marshal Feng was concerned over the safety of so many civilians.

General Hu halted their advance when they were within sight of the enemy positions. He brought his tanks forward, placing his troops behind them. Field Marshal Feng telephoned Admiral Wingate for the second time that morning.

"It looks like a trap. My brother thinks they're underground. I can see what looks like pillboxes, but they're so grown over you can't see them from the air. General Hu says he can mark the targets with smoke shells."

"Any sign of enemy air cover?"

"Not one aircraft, but that doesn't mean they aren't nearby. My brother thinks that too is a deception. They may have changed tactics following the beating they took at Yingtan."

"Hold off on your attack. Wait until I get some bombs in there to soften things up."

"Very well, Admiral. We are standing down."

Admiral Wingate ordered fifty of his fighter jets armed with half ton, high explosive bombs. He called for another fifty fighters to be armed with a pair of seven hundred and fifty-pound bombs. One hundred F-15s, F-22s, and F-35s were to escort the attacking bomber aircraft. An additional one hundred and seventy fighters were to remain on station above the fleet. Wingate was being frugal with his bombs. He knew more fighting lay ahead. The fleet was prepared for action in case enemy aircraft appeared.

"Marshal Feng, our planes will be there in about fifteen minutes. When you hear them, start marking the targets."

"Admiral, this is Captain Floyd with the *Stingray*. My radar screen just went crazy. You got hundreds of bogies coming your way."

"Thank you, Captain Floyd. We're ready for them this time. Stay safe out there and keep me posted."

Nine carriers turned into the wind and began launching their remaining aircraft. Expecting trouble, Wingate and his flattop commanders had armed all of their serviceable fighter planes in the early morning hours. It took thirty-six minutes to get the remaining one hundred and nineteen aircraft airborne.

Two hundred and eighty-nine American fighters flew east for a date with destiny. Another one hundred planes attacked the ground forces at Nanning. As soon as they released their bombs, they flew east with their one hundred escorts to join their brothers and sisters in harm's way.

The communist pilots felt confident of victory. After all, they had ninety more aircraft than their previous encounter, plus they had twenty-two of the new Chengdu J-20 Mighty Dragon jet fighters. To their astonishment, over two hundred Americans attacked them while they were still a hundred and twenty miles from the fleet. An F-22 Raptor went down then a J-20 exploded. The Maoist pilots put up a fierce resistance, but the American pilots were better trained and more kept arriving. In less than fifteen minutes, forty communist aircraft were shot out of the sky. And it was still seventy miles to the target. Sixty-one additional Chinese fighters were shot down before the fleet came into view.

The American pilots disengaged and the fleet opened fire. Nevertheless, the communists broke through and the aircraft carrier *Abraham Lincoln* was struck again and again. So were other ships of the line. *Abraham Lincoln* began to list and one of her fuel bunkers caught fire. Admiral Wingate was on the telephone when a missile struck the bridge, slamming him against a bulkhead and killing everyone else inside the room. When he came to, he was being carried to a chairlift between the stricken carrier and the missile cruiser *USS Nashville*.

"The ship ... Is she going to sink?"

"It's touch and go, Admiral. One fuel bunker is burning out of control. And we've got a thirty-foot hole below the waterline. If we leave now we might make Pearl if we don't encounter rough seas. Our port side looks like Swiss cheese."

"Go, Captain. Go now. Save the ship."

"Good luck, sir. It was a pleasure serving with you."

"Goodbye, my friend. God bless you and your brave seamen."

The crippled carrier did make it across the Atlantic Ocean to Pearl Harbor. She was riding so low in the water when she came into Oahu that she scraped the bottom. Then began the grim task of pumping out the sea water and bringing out the dead.

Admiral Wingate was recovering onboard a hospital ship with broken ribs and a severe concussion. A message was handed to him from the man who found him on the *Abraham Lincoln's* bridge.

> "Admiral, we made it! I'm told it will take eight or nine months to make repairs.
>
> "If you remember your military history, you will recall the Great Marianas Turkey Shoot in the Marianas Islands in 1944. Our Hellcats shot down over three hundred Jap planes at a cost of twenty-nine Hellcats. And our submarines sank two Japanese carriers.
>
> "We shot down three hundred and seventy-one communist aircraft with a loss of thirty-three of our own. We lost two more ships. None were capital class. Here in the islands you're being celebrated with the South China Sea Turkey Shoot.
>
> "Will return as soon as I can catch a ride."
>
> Captain Turner

PART III

A SMALL GROUP OF POLITICIANS, Marxist Democrats, were hiding underground in the subway system of Chicago, Illinois. The trains have stopped running. They dare not go topside for they are being hunted by the Trump people and by street gangs. A bounty of $2,000 each has been placed on their heads. Four days ago they ran out of food. A vagrant was bribed to go up and find something to eat. He almost succeeded, but was attacked, beaten, and robbed while returning with black market supplies. Angry at having his nose broken and receiving only two hundred dollars for his troubles, he retaliates by tormenting the group's weakest member. He'd been needling the poor woman for an hour.

"Ya ain't so high and mighty now, are ye?"

"Shut up! I'm sick of listening to your ignorant drivel, you filthy little man."

"Want to know what they'll do when they catch ya? Fingers and toes, *snip snip snip.*"

"Shut up! Shut up! Shut up! You disgusting old wretch."

"*Snip Snip Snip.*"

"Stop it, I say. Stop it or I'll make you sorry!"

"*Snip Snip Snip.*"

Gretchen was at the end of her tether. Dirty and starving, she fancies herself something special, above the common herd. The old man with his broken nose and foul breath was far beneath her station in life. *He is not fit to be in the same room with me, and he smells bad*, she tells herself

"Please stop. I can't stand you anymore."

"*Snip Snip Snip.*"

Gretchen pulls a .32 caliber revolver from her handbag and shoots the vagrant in the head.

"Good Lord! Put that thing away. They'll hear us upstairs."

The smell of blood attracts an army of rats. The group moves on down the tunnel to get away from the crunching sounds of the rats feeding. They behave as if the dead man never existed. In the world of woke, one cares only for woke.

A group of street thugs come down the stairs to investigate the sound of a gunshot.

"Be quiet. Don't move. Don't make a sound."

They linger for ten minutes, staring into the darkness. These are the ones who robbed the old man. Finally, they depart back up the stairs.

Fat Jerry steps up. He's lost so much weight that his pants are falling down. Desperate for food, he offers to go topside. They take up a collection and he leaves with $2,000. But luck was not with him that day. The street gang was loitering at the top of the stairs. Their leader, a six foot youth of eighteen with pimples and bad teeth, knocks Jerry down and stomps his legs and stomach. They take the money and run down the street for more drugs and candy bars. Jerry's ribs are broken, so are both of his ankles. He will lie there in shock on the dirty concrete and die in the early hours of morning.

But the gang is not content with the $2,000. They purchase a flashlight and come back. There has to be more money where that $2,000 came from. Back down on the station platform they shine the light up and down the tunnel. The group is spotted and held in the bright beam.

"Please go away. We don't want any trouble."

"You got some more money, honey?"

"No, we have no money. Please, leave us alone. Please."

"You're not such a bad lookin' heifer under all that dirt an' makeup. Don't let 'er get away, boys. I'm gonna get me some woolly bugger."

The men in the group are cowardly and afraid. Not one of them has ever been in a fistfight. They cower against the concrete wall as the hoodlum approaches Gretchen. Gretchen is at her breaking point, with tears streaming down her cheeks.

"Come on, bitch. Get them drawers down."

She howls in agony, yanking out her revolver and firing two rounds point-blank into her assailant's chest. He looks at her with a stunned expression on his face and falls dead between the steel rails. His gang runs for the platform steps in terror.

The rats will get their little tummies full this September evening.

Pencil Neck is beside himself. He is so hungry he is drifting in and out of swooning. He wet himself when Gretchen fired her revolver. They take up another collection and off he goes. He finds Jerry dead at the top of the stairs. He asks an old lady across the street where he can find food. She directs him down the street to a black man standing on the corner. Pencil Neck asks if he has food. The black man asks to see his money.

A heavy wooden door is unlocked and he is shown inside. The room is full of canned goods, potatoes, onions, cabbages, oranges, and fish and meat inside an ancient floor freezer. Pencil Neck is told he can have all he can carry for the $2,000. He loads up two large shopping bags and staggers down the street to his friends in the tunnel.

There are abandoned buildings along the street, so they move into a three-story structure with a dozen apartments inside. The subway had become too cold. They find mattresses and blankets, and they barter with the black man for food. There is no electricity or water in any of the abandoned buildings. After cleaning one out, they utilize a city trash receptacle for collecting rainwater.

The gang whose leader Gretchen killed has abandoned the block. The Marxists are a miserable lot because they were accustomed to the limelight, limousines, and being waited on hand and foot. Fear of capture never leaves their thoughts.

Living like hunted animals has made them afraid of strangers and sounds in the night. When the snows came they were frightened by the creaking and popping of the snow shifting on the rooftops. One night when a slab of snow slid off into the street, Lori was reduced to a screaming fit. It took half an hour to get the terrified woman calmed down and back under her blankets. It was freezing.

Pencil Neck has conjured a plan for his deliverance.

Georgia

"Frenchie, can you hear me?"

"Professor, is that you?"

"Yes, I can use my cell phone now. The danger has passed."

"What happened?"

"The soldiers used to comb these woods searching for Capitalists, an' me too, I guess. But ever since Trump blew Anniston away, the worm has turned. Those soldiers that weren't killed in the bombing attack are afraid to come in here now. These people aren't afraid to fight back after Anniston.

"The last incident we had was about a month ago. Seven of those commie bastards come up here nosing around, an' five of our fellas I call the Hootin' Holler Express ambushed 'em and killed all seven. We ain't been bothered since."

"That's great news. I'll pass it on to the Colonel. How is Hattie getting along?"

"Hattie has become my right arm. She's an excellent nurse. And something else, folks are bringing us all kinds of food since the danger passed. I don't have to eat my own cooking anymore."

"Sounds like those hill folks are glad to have you back."

"They came over and fixed up my extra bedroom for Hattie. Brought a ham we dined on while they were here. They repaired my old barn which was about to fall down. And they fixed a leak in my tin roof. I don't have to set a bucket out in the kitchen now when it rains."

"I'm happy for you both. I have good news. Trump bombed the last two enemy strongholds of Marxists and wiped them out. There are no more communist strongholds in our United States. But there are Marxist individuals roaming around the countryside, so keep your hogleg handy."

"I'm glad you warned me about that."

"Something else. We're helping a Chinese Field Marshal and his brother fight the communists over there to help free the Chinese people. We've lost some ships and several airplanes and a bunch of sailors, but we're winning the war. We've destroyed the commie air force, and now we're pounding their ground forces with our planes from the aircraft carriers."

"Could that start a nuclear war?"

"The Field Marshal has the codes so that ain't gonna happen."

"Do we have people on the ground?"

"No, just our naval forces."

"This is unbelievable. If you need me and Hattie, sing out."

"The Colonel is having a big celebration here next month over the defeat of our communist armies. We can send a chopper for you and Hattie. Will you come?"

"Sure, keep me posted. It sounds right up Hattie's alley."

A Toast for Mister Johnson

Nancy was sitting on a park bench with Skylar in the military compound. It was forty-seven degrees so they had on their winter coats. They were feeding the pigeons and talking about their future together.

"Look at that one. He's such a pig."

"He's the biggest so he must be the top dog in the pecking order."

"I don't know. That little white one keeps pecking him."

"I bet she's a female."

"You stop. She's just trying to get her share."

"Like me, I guess. We haven't done it in five days."

"If we go five more days, I may become a virgin again."

"Nancy, I'm serious. We need to find a place."

"What about when you go away to college? You won't be able to enjoy me then."

"Nancy, what are we going to do?"

"You're going to get your degree in psychology. Then we'll get married, and I'll work while you get your doctorate. Then I'll have our babies, and you'll be the breadwinner of our family."

"I love you so much it makes me goofy sometimes."

"Captain said I'm gifted. I don't feel gifted."

"You're different, Nancy. I don't know how or why, you just are. I wish we were married now."

"I just thought of something. Captain's place is empty. Nobody lives there and I know where the key is."

"Do you think it's safe?"

"I guess so. Have you decided on a college?"

"I wanted to go to Vanderbilt so I'd be here, but it's too expensive. I guess it'll be UT. Knoxville is a hundred and eighty miles. We can see each other on weekends."

"You know something, Skylar? We're letting sex cloud our thinking. Captain always said put the most important things first. That means your education then us getting married. Sex is a byproduct of a loving relationship. We love one another so our course is charted in the stars. Time will take care of all the rest."

Skylar was often amazed at how easily Nancy broke down complex situations to their component parts. She made their separation over school sound simple. To him it was a big deal.

"Come on, Skylar. Let's walk over to Captain's place."

This went on for a little over a week. Then, one afternoon when Nancy opened the front door, Rocky was sitting on the living room couch. The blood drained from Skylar's face, but Nancy remained calm.

"You and I need to have a talk, Nancy."

"I know, Rocky. I owe you an apology. I should have told you about Skylar."

"Tell me about Skylar now."

"Skylar and I love one another. He's going away to UT next fall to get his degree in psychology. That will take about three years if he goes to summer school. Then we plan to get married and I'll work while he studies for his doctorate degree. After he secures employment, we want to have children. The legal age for marriage in Tennessee is sixteen so I'll be old enough. I love you, Rocky. I hope I haven't disappointed you or hurt your feelings."

Rocky wasn't hurt or angry, but he was overly concerned because Nancy was only twelve years old. He didn't want her to get pregnant or end up in a bad relationship.

"Skylar, what have you got to say about all this?"

"I ... uh ... well, sir... what Nancy said is true. I plan to get my degree then I want us to get married. I love your daughter very much, sir. I want us to have children. I'll make a good father. And I want to make you proud of me as your son-in-law."

Rocky was amazed at their maturity and he told them so. Then he asked Nancy to place her sexual relationship on hold until he had a chance to sort things out. Nancy agreed and hugged Rocky. Skylar shook Rocky's hand and they left the building. Nancy handed Rocky the key.

Next day in the Colonel's office, Rocky laid out the whole nine yards. He was confused and wanted to hear what the Colonel had to say about Nancy having sex at such a tender age.

Colonel Mosrie hemmed and hawed for a couple of minutes, finally admitting he didn't have a clue. The Colonel was a sixty-year-old bachelor who had never married or raised a child. His life experience had been the United States Army.

"I don't have the answer, Rock. But I know someone who might."

He took up his cell phone and dialed a number. "Can you hear me, Professor?"

"Yeah, sure, what's up, Colonel?"

Colonel Mosrie explained the situation.

"Hold on a minute. Hattie's out back feedin' the chickens. I'll go get 'er."

"This is Hattie. What can I do fer ye?"

Colonel Mosrie explained the situation a second time.

"She ain't bein' loose with men, is she?"

"No, she claims she loves this Skylar character an' they plan to get married. She's a straight arrow, Hattie. He is too."

"Land sakes, Colonel! Give that little gal 'er head so's she can sew 'er wild oats while she's still a filly."

"So you approve, then?"

"Colonel, the world we live in is dangerous as uh cocked pistol. Think about all them dead friends you thought would still be with us today. They ain't no promise 'bout tomorrow, just uh little place we live in today."

"Thank you, Hattie. You've taken a load off our minds. You're comin' to our party, ain't cha?"

"Professor tole me. You comin' ta git us?"

"Thursday week about ten o'clock."

"We're bringin' uh keg uh ho'made beer fer yew an' Frenchie an' Henry. I wisht Johnson was still here. We oughta drink uh toast to 'im."

"Yes, Hattie. A toast for Mister Johnson."

Deliverance

The scent of pine needles hung on the night air like a lingering perfume. Hills and valleys were bathed in moonlight. Trees on the broad plain below appeared to be made of silver. A shooting star pierced the night sky. Every now and then a pair of barn owls called to one another in the distance. One could hear the voices of the wolves over on the mountain. Down below, thousands of campfires glittered in the darkness. It was a perfect autumn evening, except for a squad of young soldiers on a ridge overlooking the valley with night binoculars. They were the scouting party for a communist general and his army two miles back.

The trap was complex. Moscow had been called in. The American satellite for that region had been blinded by an experimental laser cannon in Russia. Local radio stations broadcast false information about how peaceful and quiet the valley had become. Field Marshal Feng and his brother were enjoying a welcome respite from all the fighting and killing. Their exhausted army needed a rest. No one suspected death was watching from the crown of a tree-lined ridge.

At 0230, Maoist sappers crept down the hillside, silencing Marshal Feng's unsuspecting sentries.

At 0300, five hundred communist loyalists slipped down the hillside and into the sleeping camp with leaden clubs and razor-sharp machetes. Hundreds of Nationalists were bludgeoned or hacked to death before the alarm went out.

Captain Lee burst into Marshal Feng's empty headquarters as he was ending a conversation with the commander of the U.S. Fleet. The Marshal's staff was engaged outside in the desperate fighting.

"Broken Arrow! We are being overrun. Broken Arrow!"

"Hold on, commander. We're coming. Estimated time of arrival is fifteen minutes. Make smoke on your perimeter. Keep this line open."

"Come on, sir. There's no time. They're right behind me."

They exited the rear door just as the front door was blown open.

"Hurry, sir. Down that path on your left. Run!"

The Field Marshal was ninety-three years old. He jogged for a hundred yards then stopped. "Let me get … my breath … don't let them … take me alive."

"We're almost there, sir. Take deep breaths. Let's go!"

The Field Marshal labored on with Captain Lee pulling him by the arm. Feng stumbled and fell. Captain Lee dragged him to his feet, driving the old man relentlessly along the moonlit path. They stumbled around a bend in the trail. He fell again.

"I can't … go on … I can't …you go … shoot me … save yourself."

"No need for that … Great One … we made it."

Nationalist soldiers rushed from their camouflaged foxholes. They carried the exhausted Field Marshal to a pickup truck they had waiting behind their front lines.

"I'll take him to the farmhouse. You must hold this position at all costs. The Field Marshal must be saved. The planes will be here any minute. May the gods be with you, brave comrades."

Gunfire erupted as they drove away.

At the farmhouse overlooking the valley, Captain Lee received an unexpected call on his cell phone. "Is this Captain Lee?"

"Who's calling, please?"

"This is Donald Trump. Do you have the Field Marshal with you?"

"Yes, Mister President. I just put him to bed. He's sleeping."

"Marshal Feng has become the national symbol for your Free China Campaign. Flyers of him are being distributed everywhere. Citizens are rising up against the communists. You must keep him safe. He must not be captured. Do you understand the significance of this man?"

"I understand, sir. We just escaped by the skin of our teeth. But we're safe now for the time being. I can hear the planes. I'm going outside and take a look."

Down below, naval aircraft were wreaking havoc on the totalitarian forces. The attack was beginning to stall.

Captain Lee informed the president that their early warning system had failed and they were caught sleeping. "I don't understand what went wrong. It always worked before."

"Our spy satellite for your region was put out of commission two days ago. We think the Russians did it. That's what caused the breakdown. I didn't find out until two hours ago or I would have warned the Field Marshal."

Cluster bombs and white phosphorus were taking a grisly toll.

"It looks like they have their tails between their legs, sir."

"I'm sending a helicopter to bring you and the Field Marshal out to one of our aircraft carriers. It's too dangerous for him to be involved in any more fighting. China can't afford to lose this larger-than-life symbol of freedom. They'll be there in half an hour."

"I'll let him sleep until they get here. Thank you, Mister President. Thank you for helping my country."

"Thank you, Captain Lee. Thank you for saving the architect for a free China."

Hard Decision

Three days later President Trump had Admiral Wingate and the Field Marshal on a three-way telephone hookup. The Admiral was in recovery onboard the hospital ship *USNS Mercy*, and the Field Marshal was regaining his strength onboard the aircraft carrier *CVN Nimitz*.

"It will save lives, but it may create hard feelings around the globe, sir."

"That's what bugs my staff. They're afraid of a political backlash."

"You'd get backlash if you were giving away free ice cream, Mister President."

"That's usually the case. Politicians are a feckless lot. Many of them would follow a Judas goat like Sanders or Rice straight into a briar patch. "

Field Marshal Feng joined in. "I believe we can save upwards of two million lives if you do limited ground bursts, Mister Trump."

"I wish there were some way to put a positive spin on this."

"So many people hate our government because of Barack Obama and that idiot Joe Biden," Admiral Wingate said.

"I could go on television and radio. Tell my people I did it to gain freedom for China."

"By golly, Marshal Feng. That might work. But it could bring hard feelings down on you."

"Some bad, yes. But the majority will remember what living under a dictator like Mao was like. They will understand. I can refer to those young lives already lost on both sides. Many of the communist soldiers aren't bad, they've simply been brainwashed since they were children. I will tell them what Mao was really like. A monster, like Hitler and Stalin."

"That will certainly raise a few eyebrows."

"Indeed it would, Mister President. Truth among politicians is as rare as hen's teeth."

"Ah, but some politicians are good," Field Marshal Feng observed. "Take your John Kennedy. He made mistakes, but he grew with the office. And for his plans to pull your troops out of Vietnam, he was murdered. He knew he was taking a chance going to Dallas that morning, but he went anyway. John was a brave man. So was Abraham Lincoln. He held your country together while the Southern Democrats were tearing it apart. He freed the slaves and for that they murdered him."

"Let's hope they don't murder you, my good friend."

"Or you, Mister President."

"Well, it looks like we're all on the same page. Admiral, the ball is in your court."

"And I wish you good luck, Admiral."

Trident II

The U.S. Naval Fleet cruising off the coast of China was accompanied by three "Boomers" sailing beneath the rolling swells of the South China Sea. These were nuclear-powered submarines carrying nuclear-tipped ballistic missiles. Ohio Class subs have twenty launch tubes which carry the Trident II missiles. Range is four thousand miles. Blast equivalent is eight times the destructive power of the Hiroshima bomb, Little Boy.

Little Boy exploded with a force of fifteen thousand tons of TNT at a height of one thousand five hundred feet. Six Trident warheads had been modified to a projected force of two thousand tons of TNT, eighteen thousand tons less than the Nagasaki bomb, Fat Man.

The Boomers were cruising on standby alert.

A Call to Arms

Colonel Mosrie, Henry, and Frenchie were enjoying their Thanksgiving dinner. All three had gone back through the mess hall line for a second helping and more cranberry sauce. Dusk was settling on Franklin, Tennessee. The world of Middle America was finally at peace.

"Scuttlebutt has it we've lost uh slew uh people over there."

"Yeah, and one of our aircraft carriers got shot all to hell. They're sayin' it was so low in the water it drug the bottom coming into port. And it had big-ass holes in one side."

"You think we'll get sent over there?"

"Not likely, they probably took Marines with 'em."

"What about all them leftovers from our bombing campaigns? One or two show up ever day at our front gate. Some are hurt. They're all half starved."

"I been uh studin' on thet. Our hospital is burnt up but the foundation is solid concrete. Burn the rest uh them boards an' whatnot then build us uh new hospital. We got plumbers an' 'lectricians. I bet sum uh them refugees is too."

"We also have fifty-eight acres we ain't usin' for anything but parkin'. Find out what we can grow in winter an' plant it. When spring rolls around we can plant all manner of good things to eat. That will keep folks busy and give 'em a sense of accomplishment. When we get the hospital raised up we can start on the rest uh the place."

But building a new hospital and growing spuds and onions was to be a short-lived project. Destiny was about to take a hand. The three friends eating their Thanksgiving dinners would soon find themselves in the crosshairs of history.

The Fifth Horseman

Conversation between Admiral Wingate and Captain Floyd had been underway for two minutes.

"Captain, are your men familiar with what you have in three of your silos?"

"I schooled 'em on that coming over, sir. They know."

"Do they understand those weapons are meant to save lives?"

"Some of the men hold church services on Sundays. We held an open discussion on nuclear weapons two weekends ago. One of the men quoted a bible verse, 'Renounce war and proclaim peace.' I read my bible every night in bed, so I was familiar with the quote. I responded, 'The Lord also said that we are sometimes justified in defending our families, nations, and freedoms against destruction, tyranny, and oppression.'"

"That's quite good, Captain Floyd."

"Thank you, Admiral. I told 'em a little about China, about Mao and Xi Jinping, and how the Chinese people have lived under a dictatorship ever since 1946. I also explained the difference between a ground burst versus an air burst, and how two kilotons is one seventh the power of the Hiroshima bomb. These men are patriots, sir."

"You have the targets and the timetable. Engage your silos at 0200. Good luck, Captain Floyd. And God bless the Chinese people."

0219, General Zhu Long was walking along a footpath to the latrine when night became day, a thousand times over. Zhu Long and everything within four hundred yards was incinerated instantly. Temperature reached 3,700 degrees Fahrenheit. Everything alive inside a half mile diameter ceased to exist. Men died in their beds, never knowing what killed them. An airburst would have spread over two miles. Many lives would be saved with the ending of hostilities.

Eight seconds later and twenty-two seconds, respectively, two more Trident missiles detonated at treetop level, wiping out the last two communist command centers. Steel melts around 2,400 degrees. Tents and buildings burst into flame, quickly becoming residue. People burst into flame, reducing to gray ash. Sap inside trees turned into steam, bursting the wood then burning to cinders.

Fireballs were seen twenty miles away. Shock waves were felt at sixty miles. Thousands of soldiers suffered severe burns. Many were blinded. Others received broken bones. Marshal Feng and Donald Trump had anticipated such chaos. A convoy of food and medical supplies were on the way across the Atlantic Ocean. Word went out around the globe, asking for doctors and nurses, and more medical supplies. Taiwan and the American fleet responded immediately.

Trump and Feng were surprised at the number of nations offering assistance. Hundreds of doctors and nurses were making the journey onboard shiploads of food and medical equipment. China was no longer a world pariah. Civil war in the United States and Red China had brought much of the world to its senses. The use of nuclear weapons had not proven a stumbling block to world peace.

But Vladimir Putin allowed no Russian involvement. Neither did

North Korea or any of those other Marxist regimes. In the meantime, more problems were beginning to show their ugly faces in China.

Sea Voyage

Colonel Mosrie was on his cell phone talking to the Professor in Georgia.

"We've been chosen to go over to China to act as military policemen. Some of those old gangs are still active and causing trouble. I'm taking a battalion with me and leaving the rest here. They also need doctors and nurses. Can you and Hattie get away for a few weeks?"

"Of course we can. When do we leave?"

"Next Wednesday, the day after that party I promised. Get your things together and I'll send a chopper down Monday afternoon. Are you still bringing that homemade beer?"

"We got it coolin' in the creek."

"Henry and Frenchie are looking forward to that. Wear your top hat. The Chinese will think you're some kind of ambassador or something."

"I got one for Hattie. She'll be wearing hers too."

The Burn Ward

Hattie was standing in the hallway of a Chinese hospital in Macau, with tears in her eyes and gripping the Professor's arm. Professor had just walked Hattie through one of the burn wards, showing her the patients they would be working with.

"Oh God, Professor. I ain't never seen nothin' like that. I don't think I kin stand it."

"Now you listen to me. I want you to place yourself in their shoes, in your mind. Think about the pain they're suffering. Then they see you coming to take away that pain. You'll be an angel in their eyes,

Hattie. And you'll be doing God's work, caring for those who can't care for themselves no more."

Hattie began to cry, big muffled sobs against the Professor's dinner jacket. Hattie didn't want the injured soldiers to hear. Then she wiped her tears away and looked up into his smiling face.

"It's plum awful, ain't it?"

"As bad as it gets. That's why they need a white angel to give them the morphine. Some will ask for a second dose. Give it to them so they can journey on to be with their ancestors. Now straighten your hat."

"Them poor ole souls. I reckon I'm ready now."

By the time Hattie pushed her hospital trolley down to her eleventh customer, she had become an old hand at giving shots and changing bloody bandages. Number eleven, however, would live on in her memory for the rest of her life. The man's fingers were burned to the bone, and the left side of his face was charred. He reached out a skeletal claw, taking her hand in his while giving her the V sign with his free hand. She didn't flinch or pull away. Instead, she administered his first shot then a second shot while singing him a lullaby she had learned as a little girl. As the morphine took hold she watched his face change from that dark world he was trapped in to his cherry blossom journey home.

Number twenty-one was worse. His face was charred black and he was blind, but he was alert and coherent. He gave Hattie the V sign and she administered his first shot. The morphine took away his pain. Hattie sat on the side of the bed and held his hand while softly singing "The Old Rugged Cross." Then she gave him his second shot and sat there while he slipped away into eternity.

This would become her routine in the weeks to come.

Freedom Sword

Trouble was afoot in the city of Fuyong on the eastern shores of the Pearl River. This was in the Guangdong Province of China. A gang of opium smugglers were terrorizing the local community. Women were being raped, and their husbands beaten and robbed. Two policemen had gone missing. They were found dead. The policemen had been tortured and murdered. The citizens were afraid to leave their homes, and the local police were heavily outgunned. Five had been wounded three days earlier in a riverfront shootout.

Colonel Mosrie and his troops arrived in Taiwan on the first day of December. They were billeted in Taipei in the same barracks Chiang Kai-shek had occupied eighty years earlier. Word had already been received in Taipei, requesting help. The Colonel assigned Frenchie and seventy troopers to handle the situation. The men drew weapons and ammo then flew across the Taiwan Strait to the Shenzhen Airport where they were greeted by a Chinese police captain who spoke broken English.

"Smuggler men velly bad. You be careful, yes?"

"How many varmints ya reckon they are?"

"Forty maybe … fifty maybe … velly bad."

"We need uh truck with uh trailer hitch, an' rides for seventy soldiers."

The police captain radioed headquarters. Half an hour later an old Ford pickup pulled onto the concrete apron beside the cargo planes, followed by three school buses. An odd-looking contraption was attached to the trailer hitch then the caravan headed for the waterfront in town.

The smugglers' warehouse backed up to the Pearl River with a wharf running out into the water with a crane anchored at the far end. The building itself resembled a fortress. Fifty-five gallon drums filled with sand sat upright across the front of the structure. The sides and roof were reinforced with thick slabs of marine plywood and galvanized sheet metal. Two dozen cars and pickup trucks sat out in the parking lot.

Two men were seated with shotguns on the front loading dock, listening to a shortwave radio station broadcasting a Chinese soap opera.

Frenchie was busy getting his men situated in safe firing positions above the warehouse when a shot rang out, striking the man standing beside him in the leg.

"Son of a bitch! Open fire! Open fire!"

The man on the roof and the two out front ran inside. A hail of gunfire did little damage to the sheet metal and marine plywood. Return fire began pouring out the doors and barred windows. Another trooper was hit.

"I need six men to turn this thing around. Roll it up against that tree root then crank it down, pointing at the warehouse. Two of you will feed the guns. Ammo is in the truck bed. It's the same as any fifty, only more of 'em. Carlos, you qualified on one uh these. Climb on-board an' make that sucker sing."

A quad fifty is four synchronized .50 caliber machine guns mounted on a single chassis. The four guns fire at a combined rate of twenty-two hundred rounds a minute. Nicknamed the Meat Grinder, it is a terrifying weapon when used against enemy soldiers.

Carlos sighted in on the warehouse then engaged the weapon. Electronics allowed the guns to move right and left and up and down. Corrugated metal, chunks of marine plywood, and siding boards flew every which way, exposing the interior. Carlos traversed the weapon slowly across the concrete floor. Ricochets cut the men inside to ribbons. A few managed to make it out the front door. Carlos caught them in the parking lot, blasting them and their vehicles into a dry creek bed.

Opium distribution from the city of Fuyong had finally come to a close.

When they got back to the Shenzhen Airport, they were surprised to find a group of people waiting for them. The Fuyong mayor was there, the chief of police, heads of the city's agencies, and several hundred citizens. A young Chinese lady stepped forward, addressing Frenchie.

"My name is Su Ling. I have been chosen as your interpreter. My people want to thank you for saving our humble city. And they have a special gift they wish to give to you."

The mayor and the police chief spoke briefly, praising the Americans for what they had accomplished. Su Ling then motioned for a lone individual to come forward. A crippled little man with a white goatee and long white hair hobbled before Frenchie, holding a sword with precious stones embedded in the scabbard.

"This is Sung Donghai. His father fought with Chiang Kai-shek in the revolution. The father was friends with Bill Donovan of your OSS and General Chennault with your Flying Tigers. He was a major general and very popular. Mao had him assassinated because he was jealous. Then Mao's thugs broke the son's arms and legs so he could never become a great warrior like his father. The sword was given his father by Chiang. It is an imperial beheading sword many centuries old. Sung Donghai and our people want you to have this as a token of our friendship and appreciation. You brave Americans are our heroes."

"Tell Mister Donghai that I accept his gift in the name of the United States of America. President Trump thanks him and so does our Chinese ally, Field Marshal Feng.

At the mention of the Field Marshal's name the old gentleman's eyes lit up and he spoke so rapidly Su Ling could barely keep up.

"He says he was hesitant to give the sword to a stranger but his heart told him to do so. Now he knows that was the right decision. He and the Field Marshal have been friends for over fifty years."

"Ask him what I should name the sword. The sword should have a name to go on a bronze plaque telling its history."

The old fellow thought for several moments then he smiled and spoke, facing Frenchie.

"He says Freedom Sword. It will be our national symbol for a free China."

Lo Wu

Back on Taiwan, Colonel Mosrie was examining the artifact.

"This thing is a work of art. The sword itself is valuable. The story behind it makes it priceless. I think we should send it out to the *Nimitz* and leave it with the Field Marshal for safekeeping. It could get stolen around here."

"I agree. Losing that sword would make us look like idiots."

"I'll do that in the morning. We have another assignment. It's in a place called Lo Wu, about fifteen miles north of the Hong Kong airport. A dirtbag they call Chop Sticks is dealing in the slave markets. That's the politically correct term for sex trade. He sells women and children. There's a railroad trestle across the Indus River to a marshaling yard right below his stronghold on top of a mountain. Those trains deliver his victims there. These assholes are killers, so we'll take flak jackets again this go-round."

"Is there some way we can get on one uh them trains?"

"The Field Marshal is working on that. I should have an answer in a day or so."

The following afternoon Colonel Mosrie had his company commanders and Frenchie in his office for a briefing on their upcoming assignment.

"The Field Marshal came through big time. Chop Sticks owns a steam locomotive making trips around China. He also has two helicopters he keeps inside his compound. One for delivery of his auctioned prisoners, and one for escape in case of trouble. There's an old watering station about twenty miles back up the line for steam engines to replenish their water. That's where we'll ambush his guards and ride Mister Choo Choo right through this asshole's front gate. Any questions?"

"Chop Sticks will have guards. What about them?"

"The Navy is going to bomb the mountainside before we start. They can't bomb the compound because the Field Marshal thinks there may be captives inside. Getting inside that place is our job."

"When do we go?"

"Tomorrow morning. The train will be at that watering station around 1200 hours. Be ready to leave here at 0800 hours. Draw your weapons tonight. And get to bed early."

Three guards were shot and killed at the watering station. They made the mistake of pulling their pistols. Commandeering the locomotive was a piece of cake. Colonel Mosrie shoved a .45 in the engineer's crotch and ordered him to proceed or he'd make him a girl. Inside a boxcar they found five beautiful women bound together. The women were freed and rode with them. After they crossed the railroad trestle over the Indus River, they encountered a second checkpoint. Three guards there were overpowered and tied up. Then Mosrie called for the navy to commence with their bombing attack.

Gazing up at the front of the building through field binoculars, Frenchie called to his Colonel. "Sir, those gray things look like pillboxes. Here, take a look."

"Sure does look that way. I'll call our flyboys. Groundhog to Raven. Groundhog to Raven. Do you copy?"

"Loud and clear, Mister Hog. What can we do you for today?"

"Those gray structures below the perimeter wall look like pillboxes. What do they look like up there?"

"Let me drop down a little. Yeah. Looks like it. I'll crack one open and see what comes out."

A missile blew the concrete top off, killing the men inside and setting off the ammunition. White contrails from tracer rounds flew in a hundred directions.

"They're bunkers, all right. I'll instruct the flight to nail their behinds."

"Thanks, Raven. We'll stand by 'til you guys get finished."

The underbrush caught fire from all the bombs and white phosphorus. Flames were spreading up the mountainside, burning away the camouflage for the concealed gun emplacements. The heat drove the enemy out in the open in front of the fire. The planes dove, strafing the enemy. Finally, those still alive threw up their hands and surrendered. There remained only the mountain compound to secure.

Surrounded by their men, Colonel and Frenchie were standing in a parking area at the top of the ridge, discussing their next move. Thus far, no one had been hurt which seemed a miracle. The mountain was no longer a threat. But the compound remained to be breached—and its ten-foot security wall.

"It's too high and we brought no satchel charges. I better call Raven."

"Ask if he can blow them steel doors. That's our best way in."

"Groundhog to Raven. Groundhog to Raven. Come in, please."

"Raven returned to his carrier. His plane got shot up from ground fire. This is Blue Bird at your service, sir."

"Hello, Mister Blue Bird. Those front doors need an adjustment so we can get inside."

"Stand clear. I'll open it up for ya."

The heavy steel doors were blown into the courtyard. Colonel Mosrie and his platoon rushed through the opening. Two machine guns opened fire. Four soldiers fell wounded. Everyone else scrambled for cover. The machine guns continued raking their positions.

"Blue Bird, get that sumbitch inside the entrance. He's got our asses pinned down."

A thousand-pound JDAM sailed through the front gate. The ground quaked from the heavy detonation. Wooden 2 x 4s and roofing shingles came raining down. Gunfire continued from next door. Another trooper was struck.

"Son of a bitch! Blue Bird, knock out that second building. We're still taking fire."

The building went up in a fiery blast and the shooting stopped. Things became eerily quiet except for the planes overhead and the crackling of the burning building in the background.

"Sir, you're bleeding."

"Let's see if we can get inside. I'll make it okay. Take a few men and check it out."

The front door was unlocked. Frenchie found five employees standing in a line facing the door with their hands in the air. No sign of Chop Sticks. They were taken away then he went back out and brought the Colonel inside.

"Go find Leroy Jones."

"You astin' fo' me, massuh."

"Yes, Leroy. I need some doctorin'."

"You white peoples always needin' sumthin'. Lemme see now. I gots uppers, downers, red debils, west coast turn-arounds, wha'chu want?"

"I want a shot uh morphine."

"Oh, you wants da juice. Lemme take a look atcha … Damn, Colonel, you been shot in the ass!"

"Yes, Leroy. And it hurts."

Leroy discarded his accent. "Frenchie, help me get his boots off. Them bloody clothes gotta go. Go see if you can find some pajamas and maybe a pair uh house slippers."

Morphine was administered.

"Sir, I'm gonna clean you up then I'm gonna put alcohol on them holes in yer butt. Put this leather piece in your mouth and bite down when I do the alcohol. It's gonna burn some."

"That thing has teeth marks in it."

"It's clean, Colonel. I always sterilize after usin'."

"Here goes. Bite down on that suckah."

"AHHHHH!"

"All done, sir. Them germ critters done gone belly up. Now I'll do your bandages."

"What rank are you now, Leroy?"

"Corporal."

"When we get back to Franklin, I'm makin' you a sergeant."

"That'll make mama happy. I send all my paychecks home."

"Why do you do that? It leaves you no spendin' money."

"The guys buy me drinks. Mama has cancer."

"Is she bad?"

"Pretty bad. She takes pain medicine. We can't afford no operation."

"Is her address the same one you have registered at the base?"

"Yes, sir."

"There's a cancer clinic over in Knoxville. I'll send your mother over there an' the Army will foot the bill. Does anybody live with your mother?"

"My sister an' one ole blue tick hound."

"Do they have a cell phone?"

"No, I always call our neighbor next door."

"Call the neighbor and tell your mama an' sister to get their things together. I'll send a chopper an' pick 'em up. And bring the dog. After her treatment in Knoxville, your family can come live on the base. What's your dog's name?"

"Mama calls 'im Elmer Gantry 'cause he has his way with so many lady dogs."

"I gotta meet this Elmer Gantry. Does your mother or sister work?"

"Ruby works in a dry cleanin' place. Mama does odd jobs now an' then. She was a rounder back in the day. Had me when she was sixteen. Ruby come along when she turn twenty."

"Your mother must be something special to have raised a son like you."

"You white peoples sho' is good to us dark peoples."

Going Home

"You look uptown in them white PJs, colonel."

Here, feel 'em. They're silk."

"They's two walk-in closets plumb full out back."

"We'll take that stuff with us. Share it with the men. What about Chop Sticks? He put up much of a fight?"

"He ain't the fightin' kind. He's soft like a girl. We found 'im hidin' under a bed."

"The Field Marshal said he was the biggest slave trader in China. I sent him and our wounded on out to the *Nimitz*. The women and most of the men will be leaving in a couple uh hours. How many packets of hundred dollar bills did you find?"

"Last time I checked they'd counted out six thousand bundles. That's sixty million. That bastard musta sold a hell of a lot uh people. Did the Field Marshal say anything about them journals we sent out?"

"He told me he read the first few pages and quit. Said it was disgusting. Some very prominent people are in those journals. Politicians, royalty, billionaires. I had no idea the world was like that."

"With those names some uh them women an' kids can be traced. Mossad, MI5, and the Field Marshal can help. The US is too beat up right now to go it alone."

"The president called while you were outside. We're going home. About half of Field Marshal Feng's army is still intact. They can manage things from now on. He plans to rebuild China along the lines of our Constitution and our Bill of Rights. I told him about the money you found. He said take what we need. He'll use the rest caring for the Chinese soldiers on both sides that got hurt."

"What about Hattie and Professor?"

"General Hu is flying them here in the morning. Thank God Hu made it out alive. He told his brother he an' his staff hid in a sewer when their position was overrun. Then our planes came over an' blew the place away. Anyway, we're going home on the *Nimitz* with the Field

Marshal. The rest will be flying home day after tomorrow. I kept one platoon back to look after this place 'til we leave. I'm responsible for that money."

"You can go on to sick bay if you want. I'll keep an eye on this place."

"I'm responsible, so I'm staying. Leroy can give me a shot whenever I need one. He said the bullet went in and out so I don't have the slug in me. It's not that big a deal."

"Leroy reminds me a little bit of Johnson. Johnson was always telling jokes and goofin' on me an' Henry. I never felt like I much belonged anywhere 'til I met those two. They became my brothers. Some men have a special quality, an instinct or karma. You know they'll always have your six. Leroy is like that. You know he'll be there no matter what."

"I felt that way about Captain. When you're responsible for an army, making mistakes costs lives. Going off to Chicago without double-checking Anniston was a mistake. Snow White was another mistake. It got Johnson killed and a bunch more. Now you know why I have to stay."

"I don't believe it would have made much difference either way. Anniston just snuck up an' bit us in the ass. Least ways we got a heads-up from Boss an' that big guy. Snow White flew in under the radar. He was a competent soldier."

"The Field Marshal is going back with us then on to the White House to study the way our government was run before the Marxists and the RINOs ruined everything. I want you and a few of our older veterans to go with the Field Marshal. Take Henry an' Leroy with you."

Grim Reality

Onboard the aircraft carrier *Nimitz* the Colonel, Frenchie, Professor, Hattie, Captain Lee, and Field Marshal Feng were having dinner together. The conversation had moved on from events in China to the hostages Chop Sticks had sold into slavery.

"I read some more of those journals last night. Did you know that members of your Congress were aware of this? Your Intelligence agencies knew about it and kept it secret from the public. The *New York Times* and other news organizations also knew. Some were involved."

"Before the war, Capitol Hill had become a political cesspool. Everything was for sale. Biden was just the tip of the iceberg. Soros owned the Swamp. Only a handful of Republicans an' Democrats kept sounding the alarm. They were labeled racists and Nazis. The real racists an' Nazis were the ones calling them names."

"The republic was on the verge of going under. After Trump destroyed Peking and Shanghai, I knew we were still in the game. But until he got those bombers in the air it was still a close thing."

"Back in them hills I never knowed much about nothin' 'til Frenchie an' his friends showed up in mah front yard. That's when I called fer our Professor here ta come doctor 'em."

Professor laughed and so did the Colonel.

"Hattie talks with a southern way, Marshal Feng, but behind those blue eyes is the sharp mind of an American patriot and a very kind individual. She was a big help in your Macau Hospital. Those patients loved Hattie."

"I am honored to know each one of you, and to have the friendship of your President Trump. Without American military assistance General Hu and I would have been defeated. There in the Fuzhou Valley I remember running until I collapsed. It was like a dream. Then I remember being on this ship on oxygen. I owe my life to Captain Lee and these wonderful physicians."

"I would like to share with you the Great One's heroic escape. Our destiny must have been written by Tyche because we ran until I was out of breath, and I'm fifty years younger than Marshal Feng. We made it okay until those last dozen yards. That's when the Field Marshal fell down, exhausted. He asked me to shoot him and save myself. How could I shoot our national hero? He was so brave. I got him back on his feet and we stumbled on around a bend in the trail, and there they were, right in front of us. Our men came running and we were saved."

The Colonel rose to his feet, clapping his hands. So did the others including Captain Lee. They were honoring the Field Marshal and his long difficult journey for a free China.

"You will find President Trump to be a businessman. He's not a politician. He doesn't like politicians. He blames them for the war. He has great respect for you, Mister Field Marshal."

"I'm an old man now. But the gods smiled down on this humble soul long years ago. China is free now and will soon have a free government. Johnny Poe is waiting for me at your White House. President Trump is going to help with our studies. He will have copies made of important documents for Johnny and me to take back to China. Your president has been a great friend to my country, much like we were in the 1940s. I regret that it has taken China eighty-five years to renew that friendship. Let us go forward together arm in arm into a bright and promising future for the benefit of all mankind."

Professor stood with a glass in his hand. "I propose a toast to the man they call 'Great One.' To Field Marshal Feng."

Everyone took a drink of Chinese *baijiu*.

Then Hattie posed a question. "What kin be done 'bout thet Putin devil?"

"Hattie hits the nail on the head ever time," the Professor said. "What can we do about this tyrant with a nuclear arsenal? He's a threat to both our countries. And he shows the symptoms of being a psychopath."

"Xi Jinping did business with Vladimir Putin. The two of them were united against the West until Peking was destroyed. Russia still sells gas and oil to NATO and a number of other countries. But the

Russian economy has been weakened ever since China stopped trading with Russia."

"We might try and persuade those countries trading with Russia to
stop doing business with its dictator. If we could get England and one
or two others to stop buying oil and gas, that could cripple the Russian
economy. But then we might have a cornered animal on our hands."

"I suggest we adjourn for the evening. It's almost ten and the Field
Marshal is not fully recovered from his narrow escape. He needs his
sleep."

"Thank you all for a memorable evening. I am a little tired. Let's
have breakfast in the morning."

Esmeralda

Esmeralda was minding the eight-month-old child at her getaway on
top of the hill overlooking the highway. Little Elmer Jr had taken his
first steps at five months. Now he was into everything. He had just
pulled up one of her iris plants but she didn't scold him. She loved the
little boy the same way Maw loved him. Anastasia and Maw were down
at the produce building helping Tom. Business was good. Word had
spread and people were coming from all over to buy fresh fruits and
vegetables.

That morning she was reminiscing about those hard times Boss
had pulled them through before they joined up with Maw and Elmer.
She marveled at his approach to reality. Oftentimes, strangers didn't
want anything to do with Gypsies. Boss just shrugged off their insults
and kept them moving until they found acceptance.

She thought about the three men she killed with a shotgun. Rotten
bastards deserved killing. She missed her friend Charity. She missed
Charity a great deal. And that time three weeks ago when a man on a
motorcycle asked for some green onions and a sack of potatoes. When
Tom turned his back for the little ties of green onions, the man pulled

a pistol. She picked up a .38 they kept in back of the building and shot the son of a bitch six times. They took the body down to the swamp where the alligators live. She wondered if there was some cosmic connection between her and Tommy. Boss always said some Gypsies have powers. She wondered if she was some kind of avenging spirit in the form of a woman.

Tom was coming up the hill, carrying a thermos bottle. She admired Tom for his business savvy and the kind way he had with people. Mister Tom had become a local celebrity. The child squealed when he saw his father.

"Maw made you and Elmer some lemonade."

"Come in and sit a spell. The little fella's been having a big time in my flower bed."

"He's pulled up a couple. I better bring him in."

"Leave him be. He's just learnin' about things."

"I sold the motorcycle for $450.00. Here's the money. I want you to have it."

"I been studyin' about our future, Tom. What do you think might uh happened if that motorcycle ape had killed you, an' maybe me too?"

"I ain't studied on it none. I'm just glad you blew his ass away."

"You're the glue that holds this place together. I come in a distant second but I'm not a leader like you are. If we're dead an' buried, Maw an' Anastasia would be facing them highway punks alone. The field hands are good workers but they don't have the skills to manage a five hundred-acre farm. I think you oughta teach 'em about banking, insurance, crop rotation, an' all the rest that makes this place turn a profit. What about a foreman?"

"Would you like the job?"

"I could do it for ya on a temporary basis, but I want one of our men to be the ramrod. Once you incorporate, you're going to need a foreman to keep up with demand."

"Esmeralda, you shoulda been a lawyer. You be the foreman for a few months until I can train one or two uh the fellas to take your place. Will you do it?"

"Sure I will. An' I'll be packin' that .32-20 just in case. I don't want us losin' you, Tommy."

The child wandered in, smiling up at Tom.

Three days later, Esmeralda was weeding Elmer's grave when she noticed a motorcycle parked beside the produce building. Something about the motorcycle made her uneasy. So, she walked down the driveway. Crawling on her hands and knees she crept up beside the front of the building. Esmeralda peeked around the corner.

"I don't know what you're talking about, Mister."

"I seen Jack's motorcycle in town. But somebody else was ridin' it. So, I asked him where he got such a nice machine. He said Mister Tom out at the produce place. I know you killed Jack because he told me he was comin' out here ta kill you. You're the one that shot our friends from Anniston."

"You mean that commie shithole down in Alabama?"

"That's right. I was stationed there until Snow White got blown away."

"Who the hell is Snow White?"

"Never mind that. I come here to kill you, Mister Tom."

Esmeralda cocked the hammer then slid the barrel of the revolver around the corner, aimed, and squeezed the trigger. The bullet struck the biker in his right side. He staggered sideways, dropping his weapon. Esmeralda swept around the corner and shot him twice in the chest.

"Looks like you got another motorcycle to sell, Tommy."

"Esmeralda, I think you'd make a better bodyguard than a foreman. That's the third time you saved my bacon."

"Them alligators will get fat if this keeps up. You didn't see 'im comin'?"

"I did, but it never dawned on me he was here to shoot my ass. You're like my guardian angel. I'd a-been dead last summer if it hadn't been for you. Help me with Maw. She fainted an' fell in the potatoes. You in there, Maw?"

"Oh God, Tommy. I thought … are you all right?"

I'm fine, Maw. Esmeralda saved us both. Looks like you scraped your arm. We better put somethin' on that. Esmeralda, take Maw up to the house for doctorin' an' ask Anastasia to come back so she can help out. An' ask the field hands to come haul this dirtbag off to the swamp. I'll pull him and his motorcycle around behind the building."

Ten days later the farm was incorporated, with everyone's signature notarized and recorded. Elmer's Gypsy Produce would soon be selling throughout the State of Georgia.

Sea Voyage

Six battle groups and their escort ships had left the South China Sea and were two hundred miles into the Philippine Sea sailing toward Palau Islands. From there they would cross above Australia into the Indian Ocean. Two carrier groups were left behind as backup for General Hu's army.

Sailors had set out deck chairs for Hattie, Professor, Colonel, and the Field Marshal on the platform off the bridge overlooking the sea opposite the flight deck. Above them was primary flight control. Down below was the flag bridge.

"We won't see another sight like this in our lifetime," The Field Marshal said.

"I 'spect not. It shore is purty. All them ships is a sight too."

"Hattie, tell me what it was like in the burn wards. The attitudes of the doctors and nurses, and how the patients felt about the nuclear weapons. I'd like to visit when I go back. But I want to know if they hate us for our use of those weapons."

"Well, like Professor would say, hit's complicated. A lot uh them patients was conscripts took off farms an' forced to join up with them

Mao people. They didn't like the Maos an' they didn't like gettin' burnt up neither. Most of 'em just wanted ta go home, but uh course they couldn't. I felt sorry for 'em. They was like lost souls with no home no more."

"What percentage would you say chose to die?"

"Maybe twenty percent, the blind ones 'specially. An' them hurt so bad they'd never git rite. An' them burnt ladies. I don't blame 'em none. I wouldn't wanna be like that.

"Do you think I should visit or leave well enough alone?"

"I ain't sure, Mister Field Marshal. Some of 'em might be glad ta see ya. Uh few of 'em might try an' kill ya."

"I wouldn't blame them if they did. What were the doctors and nurses like?"

"Some figured it was all right. Others said it was awful. They was all happy the war was over. Most of 'em was from other countries. I guess they was glad the fightin' didn't include them."

"Colonel, do you think I should visit the burn wards?"

"Let me think about that one awhile. If it's dangerous, no! A free China might be in jeopardy if you got killed. A visit would look good in the media, but that's superficial. The real question is, would it raise morale or just make things worse?"

"Professor, you haven't said a word."

"I been a-cogitatin'. They're your people. You are partially responsible for them bein' in them hospitals. If it was me, I'd go. I would explain why it was done. I wouldn't expect 'em to forgive me. But you can grease the skids a little by promising to look after their families. The worst ones will die anyway. That would make their passing a little easier."

"Hattie, would you go?"

"I think so, but take a gun with ya. An' no press. Folks would git the wrong notion. Tell 'em without them bombs an' airplanes them Maos woulda whooped ya. Tell 'em their sacrifice set China free."

"Hattie, that is good. My heart tells me yours is the righteous path to wisdom."

"Professor, are you familiar with any of the sea battles of World War Two?"

"Afraid not, Colonel. My reading is confined to medical journals and psychology books."

"Part of it took place in these waters between the Americans and the Imperial Japanese Navy. A lot of brave men are down below in Davy Jones's locker. Thousands of ships were sunk during that terrible war. It's a tragedy that we're still fighting and killing one another. My hope is for President Trump and Field Marshal Feng to find a way to bring peace to our troubled world."

"We're certainly going to try, Colonel. With people like you and Hattie and Professor on our team, I believe we'll cross that finish line. Is it time for lunch? I'm hungry."

DEFCON TWO

"No, Mister President. They don't know what to make of it. But according to my source in Moscow and another one in Stockholm, something out of the ordinary is taking place. They cite coded messages between Moscow and Siberia and night operations in the Baltic Sea."

"Is there anything new in Siberia we should be concerned about?"

"Just the usual missile silos and Siberian brown bears."

"Did your source in Stockholm describe what he witnessed?"

"He said there was an unusual number of Russian ships in Baltic waters. No capital ships, just frigates and numerous supply vessels. He said it makes no sense because the Russian economy is weak and doesn't warrant such an expenditure of fuel oil."

"Commander, what is your opinion?"

"I may be wrong, but I view Mister Putin as an unstable man. He keeps doing things that are irrational. Poisoning people, threatening nuclear war, the Ukraine conflict, and so on. Those are not the actions of a rational person. He dislikes the West and he hates you. Whatever it is probably involves the United States."

"I agree. Killing his friend the Ayatollah may have pushed him near the edge. That and wiping out that Iranian team he brought over here to kill me. Subtlety is not his long suit. His emotions betray him. He has an inflated view of himself and the ability of his military. That makes him dangerous."

"Mister President, are you on a war footing at present?"

"Yes, we've been at DEFCON ONE ever since we began intercepting Putin's ships. I wouldn't put it past the crazy bastard to try and nail me again. I think it prudent to place our Armed Forces at DEFCON TWO. I'm concerned about the American people."

"My sources inform me that Mister Putin also has it in for me and my brother. I warned the general. We did experience a food riot in one of our northern provinces but that had nothing to do with Russia. An overzealous magistrate refused to open the doors of a warehouse where rice was stored for emergencies. General Hu rescued the magistrate from being lynched, and opened up the warehouse. That ended the food crisis."

"Sounds like the same bureaucratic stupidity we experienced under Obama and Biden. President Bush is another example. His political appointee bungled our victory in Iraq. He failed to stop the Democrats from forcing the banking industry into subprime mortgage lending which caused the 2008 housing crash. And his Homeland Security was a repetitious waste of taxpayer dollars."

"It is sad that some take themselves so seriously that they do harm to others. The communists who ruled over China with an iron fist cared nothing about anyone but themselves. They were evil men and they deserved their undoing."

"Do you remember that senator I mentioned who lied every time he opened his mouth?"

"You mean the one called Pencil Neck?"

"Yes, it's amusing if you view this in a certain light. His name is Adam Schiff. He and some fellow Democrats had been hiding in the subway system and abandoned buildings of Chicago. He offered to turn in his friends to the authorities if they would grant him immunity. Our people agreed, arrested his friends then arrested Schiff. His associates were given a choice. Leavenworth or leave the country. They left. Pencil Neck was given a life sentence. He will spend the rest of his days in a 9 x 12 prison cell in Kansas."

"The same thing should happen to Kim Jong-un. His regime cannot survive without Chinese support. There's already been one assassination attempt. I'm told Maduro of Venezuela is in hiding. All those tin pots will get what's coming to them."

"Keep me posted on this Baltic Sea business. I have six battle groups crossing the Indian Ocean into the Atlantic. They should reach the east coast in about four days. I'll station them along the coast until we know what we're dealing with."

Belgorod

Two days later in the mid-Atlantic Ocean, Field Marshal Feng was conversing with Admiral Wingate. Additional information had been received from Feng's clandestine source in Moscow. The White House had been alerted.

"Moscow's call sign is Brooklyn. Brooklyn picked up a number. Nothing more was deciphered. It was all Russian code except for those three digits. Number 329 makes no sense until you combine that with the unusual activity in the Baltic Sea three weeks ago. That number, 329, may be the *Belgorod*."

"I heard that term once before in a war games class. Isn't that some kind of Russian submarine?"

"K-329 is the largest, fastest, most lethal nuclear submarine in the world."

"What's the big deal? We have nuclear submarines."

"President Trump informed me that American submarines have a maximum surface speed of thirty-two knots. The *Belgorod* is capable of fifty-four knots which equals sixty-two miles an hour. She carries nuclear powered torpedoes eighty feet long with unlimited range. Those torpedoes can be armed with warheads up to one hundred megatons. *Belgorod* was commissioned in 2022. She can outrun surface ships while submerged."

"That sounds like Mary Shelley's Frankenstein, or Adolf Hitler's giant railroad gun. It's something only a madman would dream up."

The following morning a report came in from Brighton of a disturbance in the English Channel. A fisherman told of a dark shape passing under his boat. He said it was larger than a submarine and it wasn't whales because no whales came up for air. He thought it was a UFO. Admiral Wingate took notice. He radioed the White House.

"That's right, sir. The fisherman thought it was a UFO, but it sounds like that Russian super sub the Field Marshal warned us about. If it was the *Belgorod*, the fleet may be in danger. One of those torpedoes can wipe out an entire battle squadron."

"What precautions are available?"

"The Navy has ASROC systems mounted on most warships. Those are vertically launched anti-submarine rockets with a range of twelve miles. It deploys a parachute, which is then discarded, before entering the water. But if the *Belgorod* is traveling faster than twenty-four knots an ASROC can't catch her. Aircraft can drop bombs, but if the sub goes deep that too will fail."

"Well then, what will stop this nautical nightmare?"

"Low yield nuclear rockets or torpedoes. We can install a nuke on an ASROC. Yields range from one to ten kilotons. Anything within eight or nine hundred feet should do the job."

"If you can catch the damn thing. What do you recommend, Admiral?"

"Two kilotons. Anything larger and we'll have radioactive material surfing on the wind. We'll have some anyway with a two thousand-ton burst but that can't be helped."

"Alert the fleet and arm part of your ASROCs with two-kiloton warheads. Spread out along our coast and begin your search. If the *Belgorod* is coming our way she must be stopped."

In Harm's Way

"Great One, I am so happy to hear your voice again. I was worried when they told me you were in sick bay."

"My marathon run in Fuzhou Valley certainly was an experience. I didn't know I could run that far with someone chasing me. Captain Lee saved us both. I'm afraid I gave out at the very end."

"You were magnificent. Is the Freedom Sword very beautiful?"

"That is a piece of our history that fascinates me. It is a master-piece. I tried to date it on one of the ship's computers, but I'm not sure how old it is. It might be from the Song Dynasty which lasted into the late-thirteenth century. The 1200s were the century Genghis Khan conquered China, so it could be a Mongol sword. We'll probably never know."

"When do you expect to get here?"

"Our schedule has changed. It will be a few more days. There's a Russian submarine I'm concerned about in the Atlantic Ocean. I warned President Trump earlier about this potential threat. The latest report from my agent in Moscow mentioned the word Potomac. I have no convincing evidence, but I believe the President is in grave danger. Warn him again, Master Poe."

After the initial scare, the six battle groups positioned themselves thirty miles off the eastern coast of the United States. Traffic between

Moscow and Siberia had died down to normal and no more unusual sightings were reported in the Baltic Sea. This lasted eight days. No one suspected the *Belgorod* was resting on the sandy bottom of the Atlantic Ocean seven miles out from the mouth of the Potomac River. Every night she came up to periscope depth so the U-boat could replenish her air supply. Evening nine saw the U-boat float free from the *Belgorod*. It was 0130 hours in the morning.

U-716 remained submerged until she entered the bay off Virginia Beach. There she surfaced proceeding north at three knots between Yorktown and Cape Charles. Her slow speed was in case she ran aground. Two crewmen stood on the bow watching for obstacles in the water. At the bridge above Morgantown they sat motionless in the Potomac waiting for a procession of trucks from Highway 278 to cross over the bridge into Newbury. Rounding the bend they had clear sailing all the way to Fairview Beach. Headlights passed over them at Wide Water Beach but they weren't noticed because of the black paint on the conning tower. Indian Head was another matter. She ran aground in the western shallows. Over the side went four frogmen to dig her free. That delay cost them ninety minutes. The skipper was growing edgy. Dawn would break in two and a quarter hours and they still had several miles yet to navigate.

Contact

To create a diversion, the *Belgorod* sailed north one hundred miles then turned out to sea at a nautical speed of forty knots. Five minutes later she was picked up on sonar.

"Sir, we've got a submarine submerged and hauling ass faster than anything I ever saw before."

"What is your location, Captain?"

"Sir, we're off the Delaware coast about a hundred miles above Washington, DC."

"Can you pursue the submarine?"

"That's a negative, sir. Our top speed is thirty-two knots. She's traveling around forty knots and that's submerged. This has to be that Russian sub we were warned about."

"Well done, Captain Dewitt. Remain on station. We'll take it from here."

Confusion

"That's right, Admiral. She surfaced then ran off and left us. We have a plane in the air following the *Belgorod*, but she hasn't broken any laws so what are we supposed to do?"

"Stay with her. I'll contact the White House for further instructions."

Twenty-Five Minutes

In the channel adjacent to Fort Washington, a police cruiser shined a spotlight on the U-716. One of the officers called out, asking for identification. He was answered by a blast from a Schmeisser submachine gun. His partner emptied her revolver at the muzzle flashes then helped her wounded partner back inside the cruiser, backed out of range, and called in.

"We have a submarine in our Potomac River heading north toward the Capitol. It looks like one of those things out of World War Two. They shot Johnny. I'm on my way to the hospital now. Call the White House and warn the president."

U-716 was hiding beneath the bridge at Alexandria. They were about four miles short from Capitol Hill but that would have to do. It would only be minutes before helicopter gunships came searching for them. The Russian skipper activated the bomb with a twenty-five minute delay. They abandoned the U-716 and set out for Alexandria in search of transportation back to the *Belgorod* which was waiting for them. They had walked a mile on foot when police cruisers surrounded them.

Headquarters patched the president through to the police chief at the scene.

"This is President Trump. Who am I speaking with?"

"Chief of Police O'Malley, Mister President."

"Listen up, chief! That submarine probably has a nuclear weapon onboard. Evacuate the neighborhood. Get your people out of there. The damn thing could go off any minute."

"What about all these armed men, sir?"

At that moment a firefight broke out.

Public Servants

Bomb Disposal was standing at the east end of the bridge. A mile ahead a gun battle was raging. The team leader asked for one volunteer. Sue Sarkis raised her hand.

"Thank you, Sue. The rest of you pull back about two miles. Alert any houses along the way to get the hell outta here. If this thing blows, please help Veronica with our kids. Come on, Sue. It's our turn in the barrel."

The stern of the submarine had drifted against the bank, so they had no trouble climbing onboard. When they cut open the metallic container housing the bomb, it was full of sea water. The bomb casing had leaked and the electrical circuits were shorted out. So, the primer encompassing the plutonium 239 failed to detonate. Washington was saved by a simple welding mistake.

Down the highway there were casualties on both sides. The Russian skipper was freaking out because the twenty-five minutes were almost up. He told his men to surrender and they obeyed. They were handcuffed and hauled away in police vans. O'Malley and several of his brave officers were busy evacuating the neighborhood. None of them expected to live to see the dawn.

A general evacuation of the metro area was halted when the bomb squad phoned in the good news. Trump radioed Wingate. He knew they were lucky as hell for the city to still be standing. General Black wondered out loud if maybe God had a hand in this. David Israel was pondering if the bomb had gone off would the Marxists have gained an upper hand. Johnny Poe was just glad to still be breathing.

"Admiral, that son of a bitch tried to blow up Washington. Putin is behind this. I'll deal with him later. Find that submarine and sink the fucking thing!"

The Die Is Cast

The *Belgorod* was well out to sea when word went out to sink her. A transmission from Moscow informed the crew that their mission had failed. Paris and London sent out planes to drop listening devices in the ocean. The American fleet was busy doing the same thing. Meanwhile, the *Belgorod* was sitting on the bottom of the Atlantic in six hundred fathoms of water.

Three days passed with no sign of the *Belgorod*. That evening after the sun went down, she surfaced. A discussion took place of whether or not to make a run for Murmansk and the safety of the Barents Sea. They had been informed that a gauntlet of warships were gathered in the Norwegian waters. So, they activated one of their forty-ton, eighty-foot Poseidon torpedoes. This nuclear device could sink a fleet of ships or render a large coastal region uninhabitable with radioactive tsunami waves.

The British Prime Minister was talking with Admiral Jack Donovan onboard the aircraft carrier *Queen Elizabeth*. The *Prince of Wales* was their other fleet carrier. Both ships were cruising in the North Atlantic four hundred miles west of Land's End.

"One of our ocean sensors picked up submarine screws. It only lasted a couple of minutes. I've got F-35s out searching that area now. If she's running deep, I doubt we'll find her. The French and the Germans have ships north of here. Maybe they'll have better luck."

"Be careful out there. That Russian sub is equipped with nuclear torpedoes eighty feet long. God only knows what kind of damage one of those monsters might cause. And Putin sounds daft enough to use one."

"Have you spoken with that Chinese gentleman, the Field Marshal?"

"Yes indeed, he's quite the character. We had a long conversation yesterday. The man has spies everywhere. He warned me again about Putin. Putin just tried to nuke Washington, but the bomb was a dud or he would have pulled it off. I'll be in touch with President Trump within the hour. America is extremely fortunate the plot failed."

"There's some excitement in the radio room. One of our planes may have found something. I'll call you back."

"What is it, Sparks?"

"It's a Swedish fishing trawler, sir. They were drifting with the current last night off Cape Farewell when a submarine appeared out of the fog and nearly ran them down. They don't believe the sub ever saw them."

"That sounds like the *Belgorod* all right. Notify our planes to shift their search farther north. Then contact Admiral Wingate and patch me in."

Great Britain

"Jolly good, Admiral. All of England followed your exploits in the South China Sea. I wish I could have been there with you. Field Marshal Feng is quite the rare breed. Our General Wingate was like that. So was Field Marshal Slim. We have a sighting I believe was the *Belgorod*. A fishing trawler was nearly run over in the fog last night off Cape Farewell. The trawler captain described it as a giant submarine. The description fits and so does the location."

"Two of my carrier groups are too far south. I'd like to send them your way if you have no objections."

"Indeed! Four flattops will present a formidable task force. We may need that, considering those torpedoes this submarine carries."

"It will take them a couple of days to reach you. I will instruct those commanders to follow your lead. You British are more familiar with Iceland and those Norwegian waters."

"Judging from the sighting last night, I believe the *Belgorod* will make a dash for the Barents Sea. If she makes it that far, we'll be facing the Russian Maritime Fleet. That could prove distasteful."

"I agree, Admiral. Putin has opened a can of worms that could lead to a war that only madmen can appreciate. He's tried to kill President Trump twice. God help us, if we make a miscalculation with nuclear weapons involved."

Moscow

"David, can our satellites track an individual on the ground?"

"Mister President, we can read a newspaper from a hundred miles out in space."

"I want you to track our friend Mister Putin. I want to know when he leaves the Kremlin and travels outside Moscow. I'm not interested in his residence near the Black Sea. I want to know when he's out in the boondocks."

"Might this lead to war, Mister President?"

"Not likely, I have an inside source."

"May I have the name?"

"No, David, and that is no reflection on you. I gave my word. If found out, the source and their family would be killed."

"I understand. I don't wish to be a party to such a delicate matter."

Contact

"Hello, Mother Hubbard. This is Captain Noah Peters. Patch me through to Admiral Donovan."

"Captain Peters. Do you have something for me?"

"Indeed I do, sir. I'm at thirty-seven thousand feet. The *Belgorod* is up ahead about ten miles. They don't know I'm here."

"Outstanding! What weapons are you carrying today?"

"Two Armaams and two one thousand-pound JDAM smart bombs."

"I should like to take these birds alive. She has twin screws and a top and bottom rudder. I doubt two Armaams would cripple her. Can you fly a thousand pounder up her peachy cheeks?"

"I don't see why not, sir. We've practiced with them often enough."

Captain Peters launched from twelve thousand feet. A Precision Laser Guidance Set was attached and assisted by GPS Insight to guide the thousand-pound bomb. It detonated on the starboard side of the top fin, blasting a nineteen-foot hole in the ship's titanium hull and jamming her top rudder at a seventy-degree angle.

"I got her, Admiral! I got her! She's hurt! She's coming about. She … Blimey! She fired one of those torpedoes!"

"Hit the bitch in her sonar dome where the tubes are located. Stay with her until help arrives. They'll be there in three minutes."

"I have to leg it now. Over and out!"

Decision to Launch

"Mister President, the Russian Premier just left Moscow in a small airplane. I have him on satellite."

"Get me Cheyenne Mountain."

"General Kellogg is on the line now, sir."

"General Kellogg, how's the wife and your little daughter?"

"Just fine, sir. Angie just entered first grade."

"How long does it take for one of our Minutemen to reach a target in Russia?"

There was a long pause on the line.

"Moscow, Leningrad, Stalingrad all take about thirty minutes, sir."

"How long does it take to launch?"

"Launch sequence takes less than five minutes."

"What payload do they carry?"

"All of them carry the W62 Mk-12 nuclear warhead. Each Mk has a yield of 170 kilotons. Some carry three, others carry two warheads. It all depends on the mission, Mister President."

"I may wish to launch a Minuteman with one warhead. I'll know fairly soon. Can I depend on you, General Kellogg?"

"Mister President, we were informed about the attempt on our capitol. And we know about the assault against you and the Pentagon. I will remain here as long as you need me. God be with you, Donald Trump."

Old Scratch

Queen Elizabeth and *Prince of Wales* were one hundred and sixty-four miles southwest from where the *Belgorod* launched her torpedo. Underwater speed was fifty-five knots. Range was unlimited. It would take two hours and seven minutes for the torpedo to reach their present position. Admiral Donovan reasoned that no matter where they went the thing would follow them.

A decision was made. Two destroyers, one oiler, an ammunition ship, and a cargo vessel would be left behind as decoys. The rest of the fleet would separate and sail south at flank speed. With luck they would be seventy miles away when the nuclear torpedo reached the decoys.

An hour and forty-five minutes passed. All the F-35 aircraft were safely back onboard. The *Belgorod* had been bombed and sunk. She and her crew lay in two thousand fathoms on the icy seafloor of the

Atlantic Ocean. The men on the bridges of the British warships kept gazing at their watches. They were aware their fate hung in the balance.

An hour and fifty-five minutes.

"I'd turn in me fanny rat license to be away from all this, snug in me bed at home."

"Righto! Or visitin' me favorite pub with a pint in me hand."

"Aye, mates, if them decoys turn out to be clangers, we'll all be poppin' our clogs, balls up."

"The bloody thing gives me the creepers. It's like havin' Old Scratch at yer backdoor."

Two hours and five minutes.

"It's due now. The bloody thing is due now."

"I wish it would hurry up. This waiting is murder."

"Have faith, lads. Maybe the thing ran aground."

"There's a sunny dimple charmer. You reckon maybe she mighta?"

Two hours and eleven minutes.

"Admiral, it appears our decoys have failed. I suggest …."

A blinding white flash filled the northern horizon. Minutes later a sinister crackling sound rolled across the waves. When they dared to look up, a boiling orange and black fireball a mile across was undulating into the heavens. Coming their way was a tsunami wave a hundred and ten feet high. Arrival time would be seven minutes.

White Room

"Sir, this looks like a secret location. That plane landed and he went inside alone. Then the plane took off again. This is Siberia so there's nothing there."

"Get me General Kellogg."

"Did you get those coordinates David Israel sent you?"

"Yes sir, they were loaded into the computer."

"Start your launch sequence."

"Yes, Mister President. The launch sequence is underway."

A heavily reinforced concrete slab sides back, revealing an open silo. Inside sits a 39.7-ton, 59 foot, 9-inch, three-stage Minuteman III ICBM. It will travel to a height of seven hundred miles and descend with an accuracy of a few meters. The guidance system is internal. Travel time to the target in Siberia will last thirty-three minutes. A column of smoke erupts from the silo as the Minuteman fires its rockets and lifts off, leaving a white vapor trail into the upper atmosphere.

Inside the Siberian bunker ninety-seven feet beneath ground level, Vladimir Putin is engaged in conversation with his two Cossack generals. The generals are loyal communists who admire Comrade Putin for his daring and determination to kill the American president.

"I don't see how the bomb failed, Excellency. Everything was done by the book. The bomb was alive when the *Belgorod* sailed."

"That's another bone of contention. The British sank the *Belgorod*. She got off one shot then her radio went dead. I'm told the Poseidon did extensive damage in coastal regions but the British got away without a scratch. What do you propose?"

"They know by now the U-boat was ours. We can't use nuclear weapons because they would destroy Mother Russia. Our submarines and naval forces are no match for the Americans. We're outgunned in every quarter, except one."

"What are you talking about?"

"Chemical weapons, sir. One of our scientists discovered a toxin so deadly it killed a roomful of laboratory technicians when one of them dropped a vial. It attacks the lungs and nervous system. Death comes in two to three minutes. The best thing about this agent, it dissipates in forty-eight to seventy-two hours."

"What can we use to saturate a wide area?"

"Submarine missiles can seed the upper atmosphere."

"Is it liquid or solid?"

"It's liquid but it can be refined down to a powder."

"How much would we need to seed the entire United States?"

"I thought you might ask that question. My guess is three to five tons. We could load each missile with three or four hundred pounds with an explosive charge to spread the powder. It will take every nuclear submarine we have, plus eight or ten conventional subs. Submarines can deliver their payloads in ten minutes when they're close in to shore. That way the Americans would be trying to understand what was happening to them but by then it would be too late."

"This is more than I had hoped for. At last we have something that can defeat those capitalist pigs. How long will it take to produce enough toxins?"

"Between four and six months."

"Wonderful, just wonderful, I am so pleased. I'm spending the night, so break out the spirits."

General Khmelnytsky was carrying a silver tray with ice cubes and three glasses across the room when he was knocked to the floor by a terrific jolt in the earth. Dust fell from the ceiling, pictures fell off the walls. There was a loud crash outside the bunker door where the elevator had fallen from above. Pieces of concrete and soil came down with the elevator. The top of the stairwell was sheared away. The concrete structure outside was completely gone.

The missile was a ground burst with a throw weight of one hundred and seventy thousand tons of TNT. The guidance system had malfunctioned in the last seconds. The Minuteman flew to earth four hundred and eighty yards from the bunker. A crater was blown in the permafrost one hundred and thirty feet deep and three hundred yards across. Things were burned to a cinder two miles in every direction. Vladimir and his generals were trapped. There was no way out and their communication equipment was useless. Water released from the permafrost ran down into the shaft of the elevator, making it impossible to open the bunker door. The blast had sprung the door and radioactive water was leaking into the underground chamber.

A battery-powered generator kept the lights on. It also heated the room, but the freezing water was becoming a serious problem. Already it had spread halfway across the carpeted floor. Putin was rattled and confused. The generals knew their fates were sealed.

"What can be done? How do we get out of here?"

"Dear comrade leader, there is no way out."

"But there has to be. What do you mean? I … I have responsibilities. I can't stay here. Do something. Call for help. I order you to call for help!"

"I am sorry, dear comrade. The phones are dead."

"You mean you can't call out?"

"Comrade Putin, if you are a religious man, now is the time for prayer. Our bunker is slowly filling with water. We are going to die here."

Vladimir collapsed into a leather chair, a look of desperation on his face. No way out! Two hours drag by. Slowly he comes to the realization that his situation is hopeless. A great sadness settles over Vladimir. And fear. Fear of drowning or death by hypothermia.

The two generals were drunk. They stood before Vladimir, telling him what a great man he is and how much they enjoyed working with him. Then they bade Vladimir farewell. Back at their table in the corner of the white room, they finished their bottle of vodka, embraced one another, and bowed their heads in prayer. Then they shot themselves in their temples.

Vladimir goes to his desk and puts his feet up to keep them out of the water. He recalls his childhood in Leningrad, his mother and father, and his sixteen years with the KGB. He enjoyed a few ladies along the way, but the Olympic athlete stole his heart away. Alina gave him four children. He will never see Alina again. Being the most powerful man in Russia is of no consequence now. He scoffs at the irony of the thought and where he is at the moment.

Vladimir pulls open the desk drawer and takes out a 1918 Crown

model German luger. It is a beautiful collector's piece. He charges a
9 mm round into the chamber, places the barrel in his mouth, bites
down on it, and squeezes the trigger.

It snowed that night and all the next day. The crater filled with
groundwater from the heat and froze over. A transport plane flew over
that morning, searching for the bunker. All they found was a pristine
blanket of white snow. A Geiger counter warned them not to land.

A state funeral was conducted with all the pomp and ceremo-
ny. Then Vladimir Putin was soon forgotten. Some members of the
Kremlin came to understand that communism was a dead-end utopia.
Always, it produced poverty and unhappiness. Changes began taking
place in Moscow and Russia. Consequently, the proletariat, the working class people, became happier and better adjusted. And waiting in
the wings with words of friendship, encouragement, and economic
assistance were the five architects of the new world: Donald Trump,
Abdrés Obrador, Prime Minister Rishi Sunak, Benjamin Netanyahu,
and Field Marshal Feng.

God bless us everyone!

— About the Author —

LARRY HENRY WAS BORN IN 1938. Unemployment was 19%. The Depression was once again gaining momentum. Hitler had marched into Austria while Imperial Japan was running amok in China. Then in 1941 Japan bombed Pearl Harbor and President Roosevelt declared war on Japan. Four days later Hitler declared war on the United States. WWII brought America out of the Great Depression.

The 1940s were glory years. But the best years America ever saw were the 1950s. They had Elvis and James Dean, Little Richard, Patsy Cline, Nat King Cole, and Humphrey Bogart. John Wayne was there, black and white TV, drive-in restaurants, nuclear power, and John Ford. There was Brando and Maureen O'Hara, Ole Blue Eyes, and Marilyn Monroe. God was in every public school and so was the pledge of allegiance. Jobs grew on trees. A crack had opened in the universe, and the cosmic images and events that came through can never be duplicated ever again. Henry and his friends didn't know it then but those images and events changed them forever. They were the children of the Greatest Generation, and in their own "rebel without a cause" way they too assumed greatness. No generation since has ever come close to those magical bygone days of yesteryear.

Larry Henry joined the Marine Reserves in 1957. Parris Island was a rude awakening for this young boy from South Knoxville, TN, but it opened his eyes to the mighty American Armed Forces and events to come in Vietnam and beyond. When a Democrat-controlled Congress refused to release the B52's in 1975, South Vietnam went down to defeat. Henry suspected something was not right so he began to read and study. All roads led back to Washington, DC.

At first he blamed the Democrats but there was plenty enough RINOs to go around. Korea had been a draw, Vietnam was a bloody mistake. This was not the American way. He didn't understand until he began following the money. Turns out a lot of corrupt politicians and business men and women were getting rich off those half-assed wars.

Washington has always been corrupt to a degree, but ever since the 21st Century the place has been going to hell in a handbag. Barack Obama was the Manchurian Candidate. Joe Biden is too loopy to find the door. So Larry Henry elected to write this book.

There's a lot of history in here. Larry loves his country and he asks for your help. He hopes *The Briar Patch* gives you a better understanding of just how far our United States has fallen since the 1950s. Lady Liberty and Uncle Sam can still be saved, but the hour waxeth late.

Write to the Author via the Publisher at:

Larry Henry
McAnally Flats Press
Alcoa, Tennessee
larryhenry4809@gmail.com

Printed in the USA
CPSIA information can be obtained
at www.ICGtesting.com
LVHW012334290723
753755LV00009B/1175